THE DARK
INTERCEPT

the dark
intercept

Julia
Keller

**TOR
TEEN**

A TOM DOHERTY ASSOCIATES BOOK

New York

THE DARK INTERCEPT

Copyright © 2017 by Julia Keller

A Tor Teen Book
Published by Tom Doherty Associates
175 Fifth Avenue
New York, NY 10010

www.tor-forge.com

Tor® is a registered trademark of Macmillan
Publishing Group, LLC.

The Library of Congress Cataloging-in-Publication Data
is available upon request.

ISBN 978-0-7653-8762-2 (hardcover)
ISBN 978-0-7653-8764-6 (ebook)

Our books may be purchased in bulk for promotional, educational, or business use. Please contact your local bookseller or the Macmillan Corporate and Premium Sales Department at 1-800-221-7945, extension 5442, or by email at MacmillanSpecialMarkets@macmillan.com.

First Edition: October 2017

Printed in the United States of America

0   9   8   7   6   5   4   3   2   1

To the memory of Professor

Marlene Longenecker,

who said to the silent girl:

"You have a voice. Use it."

THE DARK
INTERCEPT

PART ONE

TIME: 2294

Far away, but close enough.

The people of Earth are divided.

The Old Earth lies in ruins. Some people remain, scratching and digging in dead forests and in the smoldering gloom of cold, burnt-out cities.

Meanwhile, an elite population lives in a place called New Earth—a beautiful land of endless summer that spreads out high above the surface of the broken, desolate planet.

The only thing the two worlds have in common is a technology called the Intercept. It reaches inside your mind and pulls out your most intense emotions—love, hate, fear, joy—and uses them to control you.

Thus your feelings aren't just your feelings anymore.

They're weapons.

1

Moment No. 327

he watched.

It was her job to watch, but Violet would have watched anyway. She leaned over her keyboard, slinging her body so far forward that her nose almost bumped the screen. Her heart was jumping around in her chest. She could feel the sweat pooling in her palms.

The short, dirty person zipping across the picture on her monitor was named Tommy Tolliver. His nickname was Tin Man.

Violet knew those things because the data showed up in a small square box next to his face on the screen. The information only stayed for a flicker of an instant before it was updated, but that was long enough. In livid orange letters, the box told her that he was sixteen years old and really, *really* scared.

So scared that he was running as fast as he could through the twisted filigree of streets on Old Earth. So scared that his pulse rate was leaping up and up, and his thoughts were a crazy gray tangle.

The cop who was chasing him was named Danny Mayhew. Violet didn't need a box next to his face to tell her that. Which was a good thing, because there wasn't one. The Intercept didn't track cops. It only kicked in for the bad guys. Not the good guys.

Tin Man was fast. But Danny was also fast. In fact, Danny was a tick faster. Which meant he was catching up.

Violet sucked in a deep breath. She didn't let it out again right away. She was too focused on the action in that strange and distant place to remember to breathe. When she did remember, the breath came out as a frustrated sigh. She used her thumb to flick impatiently at a triangular slice of dark blond hair that had drifted onto her forehead.

Oh, Danny, she thought. *Not again. What are you* doing *down there, anyway?*

Tin Man swerved into a filthy alley. It was always raining on Old Earth. Or at least it seemed to be on those not-very-frequent occasions when Violet was required to look down there. The rain draped the place in a greasy sheen, slickening the bricks.

Tin Man's luck suddenly left him.

He slid. He slid hard, and he wasn't able to catch himself before he crashed into a row of four garbage cans. They were the ancient gray aluminum kind, flimsy and dented. The kind you never saw on New Earth.

Tin Man bounced, teetered, and fell on his narrow butt. The computer connection was excellent and so Violet heard the *whump* sound crisply and clearly. She winced, even though it was happening to him and not to her, and even though it was happening thousands of miles away on Old Earth. She knew what it felt like to trip and fall on your butt. Everybody did, right?

Somehow, despite the fall, Tin Man managed to hold on to the ragged cloth sack he was carrying. The sack was tied off at the top by a little drawstring that looked like a brown shoelace. Violet watched him jam it into his front pocket with frantic fingers. He tried to scramble to his feet again, but he was trapped in a sticky makeshift maze of upended cans and still-wobbling lids, plus assorted smelly shreds and rotting lumps and gooey rinds. His feet kept skidding out from under him. His butt bounced against the grimy ground over and over again.

Tin Man felt helpless. Violet knew how he felt because a rolling ribbon of flashing numbers at the bottom of her screen told her.

It wasn't that the Intercept could read his mind—or anyone's mind. It couldn't. It didn't have to.

By riffling through the archives of his past emotions and using the algorithm to apply those emotions to the present situation, the Intercept extrapolated the probabilities of his current feeling and, in less than a trillionth of a second, selected the most likely one and sent it via numeric code to Violet's computer. Tin Man knew he looked ludicrous—big tough gangster-boy, marooned in moist trash. That made him feel vulnerable and ridiculous, which in turn made him feel extremely pissed off.

And a pissed-off Tin Man was a dangerous Tin Man.

Violet leaned even closer to the screen.

Let him go, Danny, she thought. *Just let him go.*

And then she lectured herself: *Yeah, right. Like* that's *gonna happen. Get a clue, girl.* Danny never backed off from a fight or gave up on a chase. Never had, never would. She understood, because she was the same way—but that didn't make it any easier to watch.

Anxiety was skittering madly through Violet's body. What would Tin Man do? Her throat felt dry and tight. She couldn't remember the last time she had blinked. She was afraid to blink. Afraid she might miss whatever was going to happen next, because everything was happening so fast.

Tin Man groped in the waistband of his jeans, twisting and grunting and yanking. The slab gun had been digging into his skin while he ran, its louvered sides sharp as a shovel's edge, its muzzle pricking him like a hypodermic. Violet could almost feel the slab gun against her own skin, even though she'd never touched one, much less hidden one in her pants.

Tin Man's mind, according to the box that followed him on the screen, simmered with petty irritations as well as great fear, a fear that spread out over the rest of his thoughts like a black rainbow.

A holster would have made the gun easier to carry, but a holster would've been harder to hide, especially on a body as skinny as his. So Tin Man had carried it in his trousers, despite the very real risk that his body temperature would rise high enough to trigger the thing.

Violet had read about that. And she'd seen pictures, too—hideous, look-away-*now* pictures, filled with liquid and anguish. People sometimes forgot about the heat-sensitive firing filament, and in a terrible tenth of a second, the slab gun would blow a hole in their side so big that they could reach in and rearrange vital organs like cushions on a sofa.

Danny was coming up fast. Violet, right along with Tin Man, could hear the rapid and relentless *smacksplat smacksplat smacksplat* sounds of his boots as they struck the wet bricks.

Violet watched. She had to wait until the last possible second to intervene. Intervention had to be absolutely necessary. She couldn't be wrong.

Tin Man was tensed and ready. There was only a thin grazing of light left in the alley, and so the cop, he surmised, most likely wouldn't see the gray flank of the slab gun until its pulverizing ray had peeled back his skin and melted a portion of whatever it hit. Sometimes it happened so fast the victim didn't even bleed. The heat of the light-pulse instantly cauterized the wound at the same time it created it.

Violet saw the numbers jump and squirm at the bottom of her screen, recording a probabilistic shift in Tin Man's emotions. She interpreted the numbers instantly, reading his feelings as if he were writing them in a journal in real time:

Tin Man was confused. Why the hell had this cop shown up, anyway? Cops almost never came down to Old Earth anymore. For anything. New Earth didn't bother to monitor it regularly. New Earth had given it up for lost, and Tin Man approved.

Lost was how he liked it. Lost let the monsters loose. And that was how Tin Man saw himself: as a monster. Old Earth had made him that way. Old Earth—and the people he needed to protect from its many perils.

A quick visual of the previous three minutes of Tin Man's life popped up in the bottom corner of Violet's screen. The pictures came from the squad of drones that patrolled Old Earth. She followed the video avidly, so that she'd have full information before Intercept Deployment:

In the fragile, moody pallor of dusk on Old Earth, Tin Man had been selling the day's last bag of deckle. He hadn't even bothered to divide the bag into smaller parcels. He didn't need to. His customer was happy to snap up his entire supply of the pink powder, and to pay him well for it.

For the past several months, Tin Man had run a good, steady, efficient business in illegal drugs. He sold a lot of deckle. When the deckle ran out, he switched to tumult, and when tumult was hard to come by, he could always dig up a bit of trekinol. Trekinol was trash, but if nozzled directly into the heart, it could create a flutter. A baby buzz.

The transaction had been seconds away from completion. And then, from out of nowhere, the cop showed up.

Tin Man heard an official-sounding voice say, "What's going on?" The customer heard the voice, too, and it caused him to jerk in the middle as if somebody had pulled an invisible string knotted around his waist. The customer vanished, twitching through the mud-colored twilight of Old Earth.

Tin Man also took off.

And then the cop, to Tin Man's surprise, had followed him.

What the hell? was Tin Man's irritated thought while he slammed across the dark and dismal streets. Nobody interfered with drug deals down here anymore. Nobody. It. Just. Wasn't. Done. This cop, though, apparently had missed the memo.

Tin Man ran. The cop ran faster.

"Hey, wait!" the cop had yelled. "I just want to—"

Tin Man kept running.

The alley. The rain. The skid. The spill. And now, in a very short space of time, The End. For at least one of them.

But the question was: Which one?

Smacksplat. Stop. Danny hunched over Tin Man. He was panting, his black-booted feet spread wide, his body quivering, his hands grabbing the fabric that bunched at his knees. His blue tunic was flecked with mud. His dark hair was wet from rain and sweat. His face was pale.

Tin Man stared up at him, incredulous. All this trouble for a bag of deckle? New Earth didn't care about Old Earth crimes anymore. Old Earth could do as it pleased, even if that meant the people down here ripped one another to shreds, or poisoned themselves with drugs, or whatever. Nobody cared.

What was *wrong* with this guy?

Tin Man didn't wait for an answer. The cop had to die.

Tin Man wrenched the slab gun out of his trousers.

"Sector four," Violet said.

She'd seen enough. All the official criteria had been met:

Imminent bodily threat to a New Earth citizen.

Lack of plausible escape parameters.

Reasonable expectation of negative outcome.

So now she had a job to do.

"Seventy-eighth parallel," she added. "Old Earth zone sixteen."

She gave her partner a quick sideways glance to make sure he was listening to her. Their workstation was one of a thousand two-person modules arranged across the glass-walled Protocol Hall, the nerve center of New Earth.

"Why's he down there without authorization?" Rez said. "What the—"

"Sync up the parameters," Violet declared, interrupting him. Rez's screen was next to hers, but he'd been watching something else. Another sector. Or maybe playing a game. Whatever. "It's my call." Her voice was cold and steady. She'd gone through the checklist in her head. Twice, even. "And I'm calling it."

"Copy that." Reznik squinted, reading the swath of rich code that decorated the bottom of his screen, catching up with the information that Violet had been absorbing for the past few seconds. He laughed. "So—is that right? 'Tin Man'? How'd he get such a stupid nickname?"

"Don't know. It's the alias of record."

"What's Danny doing down there, anyway?"

"You already asked me that. It's irrelevant. Go on. Lock and load."

Reznik shrugged. He fist-bumped four buttons in rushed succession on the console in front of him. His screen shifted to another variety of code. He punched another button—last week he'd actually cracked the red cover-cap on one of his console triggers, so violently emphatic were his gestures when he was in the throes of his official duties—and the orange-tinted code shimmied and wiggled as the algorithm automatically recalibrated itself in response to incoming data.

Reznik's gaze followed the vapor trail of the code's gyrations like a man in love. Code was a thing of beauty, like a really great song. That's how he had described it once to Violet. He'd practically swooned when he said it. Sometimes, he would add, looking glassy-eyed and bewitched, he loathed the sluggishness of his brain when he beheld code. Compared to the cool sleekness of code, he told her, his brain was like a sweaty fat boy trying to climb a rope in gym class, all sagging butt and pitiful little grunts of doomed effort. Reznik didn't have happy memories of gym class.

Violet occasionally wondered how his love of code registered in his Intercept file. Code recording his obsession with code: It would be like taking your finger and writing the word *sand* in the sand. He was totally smitten with code. Sometimes it got a little weird.

But no matter how obnoxious he was, Violet had to admit that Rez was a good person to have as a workstation partner. He knew all the shortcuts in the Intercept. He knew all the tricky little backdoor maneuvers that helped them do their jobs—as well as a few that had nothing to do with their jobs.

"Okay," Rezink said. "Ready to rock 'n' roll." It was a funny-sounding phrase he'd picked up in Old Earth history class.

Violet did what she often did when she was nervous: She touched the small area in the crook of her left elbow. This was the spot where the Intercept chip had been inserted, slipped under the skin so swiftly and so delicately that she hadn't even felt it. No one did. There was no scar, just a slight area of discoloration in the shape of a tiny crescent moon. Violet's father, Ogden Crowley—Founding Father of New Earth—had insisted on that: Nobody should feel any pain during the installation. He'd ordered his staff to find a way. Because the Intercept wasn't there to hurt. It was there to help.

And as always, they'd done it. People wanted to please Ogden Crowley. Violet had noticed that from the time she was a little girl.

"Ready," Rez said. "Four. Seventy-eight. Sixteen. On my mark."

"Copy that."

"Mark."

"Protocol initiated." With two fingers, Violet depressed the black bar across the top of her keyboard. She felt a surge of relief. Everything was going to be okay.

Well—not for Tin Man. But that was his fault, not theirs.

She studied the screen. Tin Man tightened his grip on the handle of the slab gun. He aimed its ugly gray snout.

And then the Intercept pounced.

No sizzle, no crackle, no whoosh, no boom. No thunder. No lightning. Not even a click or a ding. For a second there was no outward sign that anything at all had happened.

But it had. Irrevocably.

Deep within the sprawling catacombs beneath their workstation, tucked snugly inside a computer system unfathomably vast, the Intercept was roused to invisible fury.

Tin Man was about to enter hell. But for Violet and Rez, it was just another day at work. Their job was essentially finished. There was nothing more for them to do. Except watch.

"Got any big plans for the weekend?" Rez said.

Violet shrugged. She had plenty of plans, but none to share with Reznik. He was always hinting around about wanting to hang out with her and Shura Lu, her best friend. *Not gonna happen,* Violet thought. Not meanly, just firmly. She wished he'd get a clue. Why was it that the guys you didn't really care about were crazy about you, while a guy you *did* care about—in fact, a guy that you thought about *a lot*—kept you guessing about whether or not he even noticed that you were . . .

No. *No.* She elbowed the thought out of her mind. She wasn't going to give the Intercept anything to work with. Nothing beyond her annoyance, at least. Nothing beyond her irritation that Danny had put himself in jeopardy. *Again.* What was going on with him?

Reznik didn't seem to mind that Violet had ignored his question. He was used to it; she ignored him on a regular basis. It couldn't dent his good mood. Their shift was almost over, and once it was, he could get back to doing what he loved to do, which was to use his computer savvy to explore the depths of the Intercept.

"Showtime," he said.

In the crook of Tin Man's left elbow they spotted a brief flash of blue. That meant the Intercept chip had just been activated. Their screens immediately shifted to the scene that was frantically flooding Tin Man's brain, surging and grinding inside him.

Reznik leaned back in his chair and piled his big feet up on the desk they shared. He pretended to be eating popcorn from a bowl on his lap. He grinned and fluttered his fingers, as if he was digging in.

He tossed an imaginary kernel up in the air and caught it in his mouth, chewing with exaggerated vigor.

A small square in the lower right-hand corner of their screens continued to follow what was happening in the alley. The video was supplied by the drones making their grim, endless circles in the drab sky over Old Earth.

Reznik tossed another fake kernel up in the air. Snap, chew.

Violet rolled her eyes.

"Cut it out, Rez," she snapped. "Don't be a jerk."

He snickered. *Hopeless,* Violet thought. *Expecting Rez to act mature—that's a lost cause. Totally.*

They watched their screens. The Intercept had selected one of Tin Man's memories from a decade ago and fed it back into his brain.

It was tearing him to pieces.

Molly Tolliver, aged five years, three days, four hours, twenty-two minutes, and eight seconds, lies in the ill-lit, foul-smelling room. She is too light to leave an indentation on the thin mattress. Her pale body, covered by a wispy blue rag that doubles as her dress, is cocooned in sweat.

An odor of decay rises from her. The vapors are thick and shimmering. Most of the bad scents are not produced organically by her body but by the artificial enzymes that have been pumped into her for three days now, in a frantic attempt to save her. The enzymes, as they break down, induce an accelerated tumble toward death. Sometimes—not often, but sometimes, or so the theory goes—the free fall of decay will reach a critical point and then use its accumulated energy to kick-start a rally in the opposite direction. *You never know,* someone had said about the fever's lethal whimsy and the possibility of a turnaround. That someone was a fellow scavenger, sharing their hollowed-out, roofless house. *Worth a shot.*

It didn't work. Now the stink is tremendous. It's bigger than she is. Molly is long past being embarrassed by it. But for her family—which means her mother, Delia, and her older brother, whose real name is Tommy but who is mostly known by the nickname Molly gave him, Tin Man—the reality is that they cannot *not* notice the rancid smell. This isn't fair. It isn't right that their last memory of Molly is wreathed in a disgusting, vomit-calling smell, an abomination that's like the mingling of dog shit and cat shit and rotten fruit and moldy basement and a shotgun-spray of farts. It's disrespectful.

Tin Man blinks. He reaches out to touch his sister's forehead, not knowing if her skin will be hot or cold.

It's both.

How can it be both? He doesn't know. But it is.

Before she got sick they were together all the time, he and Molly. They played, they ran, they chased each other across the broken streets of Old Earth, running and giggling, stealing what they could find to steal, darting through the wet, cold, smelly alleys. Molly was quick and small, and she could scoot into places that most people couldn't, like a sleek letter opener sliding under the sealed flap of an envelope. That's how Tin Man described it once to their mother. He knows about letter openers. He's swiped a few from the smashed cabinets in the abandoned houses. There's always junk left behind by the people rich enough to have scored a ticket to New Earth. Letters, packages, catalogs—they had made a big comeback in the mid-2280s. People realized that they missed running their hands across real paper. Missed folding it. Missed the elegant ritual of dealing with it. Thus letter openers became a hot item. The fancier, the better. Electronic mail is quicker, yes, but it doesn't *mean* anything. It doesn't seem to satisfy a certain longing in the soul. So on New Earth, the volume of Touch Mail is rising. And letter openers are easy to sell to New Earth tourists who sneak down here for a walk on the wild side.

A few days ago, Molly coughed. She covered her mouth. She pulled her hand away and looked at her small palm. Sticky orange webs of phlegm were strung between her fingers like cobwebs in a corner.

This is Missip Fever—named after a river called the Mississippi, a river that dried up a long time ago. Notorious viruses are christened for the trickling remnants of once-mighty rivers along whose raggedy, germ-sown banks they first gain a deadly foothold.

It's a week later and here she is.

Dying.

And doing it both too fast and too slow.

Tin Man watches. He draws back his hand, having grazed her forehead and found it both hot and cold. Inside his own body, he is aware of an excruciating pain, a pain made up of a savage mix of emotions: anguish, helplessness, fear, puzzlement. These feelings have squatted right down in the center of his brain and won't budge. He'd swear his mind is exploding, over and over again, each explosion igniting the next one in line, and then the one after that. He can't turn away from the pain any more than he can turn away from Molly.

The pain isn't just inside him. The pain *is* him. He is all pain, everywhere.

His sister parts her tiny white lips. She whimpers softly, like a pet seeking treats. Watching her, hearing her, Tin Man feels as if every cell in his body is being dragged in a separate direction, fingernails scraping the ground as the cells twist and writhe, fighting their fate. He wants to scream. He wants to hit something, smash it, destroy it. He wants to cause physical pain to himself, so as to balance out the emotional pain, the pain in his head. He is silent. He does not move. He believes in nothing.

Molly Tolliver takes a small sip of breath.

Lets it out.

Takes another breath.

Lets it out.

Takes another breath.

This time, she doesn't let it out. Her eyes are glassy, fixed.

She's gone.

She is five years, three days, four hours, twenty-two minutes, and eleven seconds old.

As Tin Man squirmed on his backside in a filthy alley in the midst of a cold rain, his curled finger tensed against the crude trigger of his slab gun, he was engulfed by the memory.

The sadness raced across his brain, showing up from out of nowhere—or so it felt to him—as he aimed his weapon at the cop who had chased him here.

The remembered scene rushed at him: Molly in the bed, Molly stinking, Molly dying. The images attacked him like his worst enemy would. They pierced him, paralyzing his trigger finger and the rest of his body, too.

His sister's waxy sunken cheeks.

Her eyes, orange and staring.

The sour smell of her—the smell of death, of ruined and rotting things, of the Absolute and Final End.

And then the realization that she was dead. *Dead*. He would never talk to her again. Never hear her laugh. Never watch her run.

Ever.

Ever.

All of it invaded him, overwhelmed him, plunging its tentacles deep into the tender pink core of his brain and rooting there, refusing to be dislodged.

Instantly Tin Man was sick. The nausea blotted and coated his throat, locking it shut, bubbling up in a thick bath of black acid. He was sheathed in pain. Shackled by it. His logical mind was swamped by what he was feeling. He was hurled aloft onto a gigantic and terrifying wave of toxic pain, a pain that roared and climbed and then twisted back around again, crashing down on him, smothering him, trapping him inside an endless, edgeless, boundless, all-over agony.

Tin Man couldn't see. He couldn't breathe. His body felt as if it were splitting into a hundred billion sharp-edged little pieces. He was hollowed out by the pain. Scraped raw by it. He was reeling and he was helpless.

Violet switched her attention from the Intercept feed—the record of what Tin Man was enduring inside his busy furnace of a brain—to the drone's real-time recording of the drama in the alley.

Tin Man was sobbing. Spit foamed over his lips. He was shaking so badly that the slab gun vibrated right out of his hand, falling to the bricks with a sad little clatter.

Danny kicked it away, far out of Tin Man's reach. He looked over at the drone that had dropped and roosted amid the greasy welter of garbage cans. Knowing they were watching him from New Earth, he smiled a crooked half smile. Not a smile of triumph—a smile of relief. He saluted the camera as he silently mouthed the word: *Thanks.*

Violet blushed. She felt the warmth rising in her cheeks. There was a small flash of blue in the crook of her left elbow.

It had all happened in a smattering of seconds.

Reznik grunted.

"I don't like that guy," he muttered.

Tell me something I don't *know,* Violet thought. Reznik did his job—he would save Danny's life when it needed saving—but that didn't mean he had to like it.

"He's just a big show-off," Reznik added. "And a selfish jerk."

She wasn't going to argue with him. "We're just about finished," she said. "Then we can move on to another sector."

"Great. As long as I don't have to look at Mayhew's stupid face anymore."

The trouble was, of course, that Rez had a right to be resentful. Danny caused a lot of trouble for a lot of people. No question about it.

While Reznik punched in the resolution codes, Violet kept her eyes on the screen, zeroing in on Danny's dark, wet face. Her feelings were all mixed up again. The quick rush of joy she'd felt when Danny smiled at her—okay, at both of them—had faded. Now she was back to being mad at him. But her anger, too, was changing just as fast as the joy had. It was dissipating into something else, another feeling. She didn't want her anger to soften; he had broken rules, risked his life. Sometimes, though, an emotion had a mind of its own.

Part of her was afraid Danny would never know how she felt about him. Another part was afraid he already did.

And still another part was afraid, period. Afraid of having experienced the feeling in the first place.

Because the moment an emotion was born inside her, it wasn't hers anymore. Well, it was hers—but not *exclusively* hers. Within the elegant infrastructure of the Intercept, a new entry in her file had just been created. A series of blunt facts had been inscribed upon an already crowded digital tablet:

CROWLEY, V. V. [VIOLET VERONICA]. Citizen No. 4612-97-8A-QRZ12.7. MOMENT OF RECOGNITION NO. 327 OF INTENSE AFFECTION FOR MAYHEW, D. A. [DANIEL ANDREW]. CITIZEN No. 7414-82-7D-QFP14.9.

SYMPTOMS: EXCESSIVE EXCRETION OF SWEAT IN PALMS, SHORTNESS OF BREATH, DIFFICULTY FOCUSING ON TASK. HEART RATE INCREASE FLUCTUATING BETWEEN 15 AND 19 PERCENT. BRIEF BUT INTENSE.

Moment No. 327.

It was the 327th time she had felt that way about Danny.

And each time she did, the Intercept created a record of the emotion. The moment was gathered up, time-stamped, sorted by intensity, verified by a match against the accompanying physiological changes also supplied by the chip. It was distributed into a category—love or pain, or hate or fear, or surprise or regret or jealousy or melancholy, or boredom or despair or delight.

Or it might be one of those intricate blends of emotions. Moments when you were happy *and* sad, or scared *and* excited. The new incident was added to the record. Information was piled atop information.

The Intercept systematically captured and cataloged every flicker of every feeling, every stray inclination or brief fancy or moment of curiosity, every irritation, every disappointment, every passion. As the machinery clicked and shimmied, as its digital apertures opened, the emotions of the world's population—both worlds, the Old and the New—rushed into its trillions of eager receptors. These emotions might be daily annoyances—exasperation, frustration, mild disappointment—or they might be intense, volcanic feelings that brought about towering, ravaging agony, from love to guilt to grief to the haunting helplessness of remorse.

Emotions were harvested from person after person after person. It might be seething anger at a friend's betrayal, or the golden exhilaration of finally understanding quadratic equations, or the blue-hued sadness of a Sunday afternoon. Emotions were routinely ransacked from soul after soul after soul, just after the feeling flared.

First one feeling

And then another

And then another

And then another . . .

Each time an emotion spiked, an electrical signal was generated in the brain. The emotion was inscribed on the chip embedded in the crook of the left elbow. Then the chip transferred a record of that emotion—through a Wi-Fi connection—to the murmuring computers that spread out beneath Protocol Hall and then on through the branching network laid out beneath the streets of New Earth, mile after mile after mile. The Intercept caught the signals one by one by one, like line drives snagged by a trillion-handed shortstop, and archived them.

And there the emotion waited. Waited for the Intercept to call it forth when it was required. This storehouse was always at the ready. When deployed back into the individual, the returning emotion created another small blue flash in the crook of the left elbow.

But Violet couldn't think about that all the time. If she did, she made herself crazy. She got so hyperaware of everything she was feeling, second by second, and of how the Intercept was eavesdropping on her deepest emotions, that she tripped over shoes she'd left on her bedroom floor or forgot to charge her wrist console overnight. She became totally self-conscious. So she tried not to think about it.

True, when she came to work each day here in Protocol Hall she *had* to focus on the Intercept. It was a job requirement. When her shift ended, though, she'd close that door in her mind. She'd taught herself how to do that. She couldn't lock it shut—but she could close it.

"After a while," Violet once said to Rez, "you sort of forget about the Intercept."

Rez didn't reply, but Violet knew what he was thinking—because she was thinking it, too:

Yeah, but the Intercept never, ever forgets about you.

2

Danny's Secret

Hey."

Violet flinched. She was totally focused on what she was writing and so the voice startled her. When she flinched, her hand jerked and she very nearly dropped her black tablet onto the floor of her workstation.

It was him.

A tiny blue flash winked in the crook of her left elbow. *God, I hope* he *didn't see that.* Her sleeve almost covered it, so probably not. *Close one.*

"What's going on?" Danny said. He let his bag slide off his shoulder. He moved closer to Violet. He was standing and she was sitting, so it was even more awkward than usual. A few hours ago she had rescued him from imminent peril; now here he was, as if nothing extraordinary had happened.

Most of the afternoon workers had already gone home. The people assigned to night shift were still milling around in small groups, enjoying their last few minutes of freedom before they sat down at their computers to monitor the Intercept feeds.

As dusk fell, Protocol Hall took on a new atmosphere. The

same number of people were at work in the vast honeycomb of cubicles, because the Intercept ran twenty-four/seven. But there was a different feel to this glass-walled citadel. Through those walls, the rest of New Earth—its spires rising against the coming dark—was visible. Tomorrow at sunrise its six cities would come alive again, with people making their way to work. Here at Protocol Hall, the sun's light would touch the glass walls like a magic wand in a fairy tale, anointing row after row after row of the stacked cubicles in which the Intercept was administered. The building quivered ever so slightly as the vast machinery of the Intercept clicked through its endless progressions, whirling and spinning. And watching.

Seeing Danny's face when she wasn't expecting to, Violet needed a moment to readjust. She had to remind herself that this was the *real* Danny—and not an image on her computer screen. He was here. *Right here.*

Something shifted inside her. She didn't want to identify it, but it was fuzzy and warm. It was also sort of scary.

And then her anger came slashing back, crowding out the soft things she'd been feeling. She didn't care what the Intercept did with her emotions right now. To hell with the Intercept. To hell with everything.

Too little time had passed since Violet had monitored Danny's close brush with death down on Old Earth. He had put her in the terrible position of seeing him almost get pan-fried by a slab gun, and she was furious.

"You could've *died*." Her voice was clipped and brittle. "You know that, right? You could've taken a direct hit."

"But I didn't." A hint of a grin. "Here I am—safe and sound."

"You got lucky."

Danny nodded. "No argument there. You and Rez had my back. Hey—where's Rez, anyway? That's why I came by. To thank you guys again. In person this time."

He glanced around the compact space, as if Rez might be crouching behind the other chair or hiding under one of the monitors.

"Don't know," Violet said impatiently. Her tone said something else: *I'm not his keeper.* "He took off when our shift ended."

"But you're still here."

"I've got some stuff to do." She didn't want to tell him what it was, because—well, because it was none of his business. She liked to keep some things all to herself. And the truth was, she was studying Old Earth history, more than what she'd learned in school. She had so many questions about the place where her parents had been born—questions that nobody on New Earth seemed to want to answer. She had pleaded with her father to let her visit Old Earth. He had stared at her a long time before he replied, "Absolutely *not,*" in a way that let Violet know she'd better not bring it up again.

She would, of course. But not right away.

Danny had been born on Old Earth, too. But that had nothing to do with her curiosity about the place. *Really,* she told herself. *It doesn't.*

"You look exhausted," she said. He hadn't changed his clothes yet. He was damp and rumpled-looking, and there was a gray, ashy tinge to his skin. The area around his eyes was smudged with fatigue. He looked tired right down to his bones. *And no wonder,* Violet thought. The round trip between New Earth and Old Earth was jarring and draining. It took a ferocious toll on the body.

"Yeah. I kind of am," he said.

"I guess there's a reason they tell people not to go down there more than once or twice a year."

"Yeah." He shrugged.

"And you'll do what they say, right? I mean—you'll follow the advice they give to people who go to Old Earth too often? Get a physical? A bone-density scan and all the other tests?"

Danny had made four unauthorized trips back in the past month. And those were just the times she knew about. There might have been more.

Oh, there were more, Violet told herself with weary certainty. *For sure.*

Because, after all, this was Danny.

He shrugged again. All at once she realized just how close to her he was standing. If she moved her chair even slightly, she'd be touching him. That caused a fierce scramble of contradictory emotions to start up inside her. Some of these feelings were wonderful; some of them were not so wonderful. But all of them were intense. The swirling mix reminded her of a passage in a book she'd been assigned to read back in her WordArt class—*Persuasion,* by an Old Earth author named Jane Austen: "It was agitation, pain, pleasure, a something between delight and misery." That's how the main character described her feelings when she saw this guy she really liked.

Violet could totally relate. Jane Austen, she thought, would've given her Intercept chip quite a workout.

But no matter what else Violet felt about Danny, she was still mad at him. The righteous anger kept slamming up against the other thing inside her—the mushy thing. The two feelings were like a couple of asteroids that hit and bounced off each other and then hit again, until they were both so nicked and frayed they could barely limp their way across the galaxy.

She decided that she couldn't stand this polite chitchat a minute longer.

"So why'd you go down there again?" she asked, blurting it out. This wasn't the first time she had posed the question. She knew what his answer would be—the answer would be a nonanswer—but she had to ask.

Because just as he was Danny Mayhew, she was Violet Crowley. She was just as stubborn as he was—although her stubbornness showed up as a fierce curiosity, while his was reflected in his mysterious trips to a forbidden place.

She kept on talking. "You were almost suspended last month for the same thing, right? And then you turned around today and went back. Without permission. What's the deal?"

Danny shrugged.

"It's complicated," he said.

"That's what you always say."

He was quiet for a moment. "Someday," he finally replied, "I'll be able to explain it to you. Until then—"

"What? Until then—*what*?"

"Until then, you'll just have to trust me."

"Trust you."

"Yeah. Trust me." He shifted his weight from one foot to the other. *His legs must be aching,* Violet thought. *All that running down on Old Earth. All that tension—confronting an armed criminal, knowing that you're seconds from death.*

Danny was still talking, his voice measured and sincere. "I hope you can do that, Violet. And I hope you can say to yourself, 'Well, I don't understand, but it's Danny, and so—so I *know* it's fine, and he must have a good reason. I can just let things be for a while.'"

"It was a pretty close call," she murmured.

"Yeah. Definitely."

Violet was still mad at him, but what could she do? He wasn't going to answer her questions. And his request had been clear.

Trust me.

But why did he do it? Why did he keep slipping back down to Old Earth without official authorization? What drew him to that bleak and broken place?

True, she wanted to go—but that was because she'd never been there. He *had* been there. He knew firsthand what she knew only from drone feeds: It was filthy and scarred and treacherous. Nasty things crawled along its broken streets and slithered up the scorched bricks of its shattered buildings. Danny knew that sad, battered surface all too well. He had to be haunted by his grim memories of its blasted-out towns and poisoned oceans and skeletal trees and stark, wind-mauled landscapes.

Yet back he went, every chance he got.

Why?

When he'd first started his backdoor visits down to Old Earth, Violet had guessed that maybe it was just homesickness. Old Earth might be ugly and depressing, but it was where he'd come from. It was the starting place for all his memories. Memories of life with his brother, Kendall.

Or maybe it was even simpler. Maybe he was attracted to Old Earth because somebody had told him *not* to go. And Danny was a rebel. A rule breaker. He did things his own way.

Violet could totally relate to *that,* too.

But each time he sneaked down, he increased the chances that something bad was going to happen. Something dangerous. And maybe fatal. Violet had a powerful recollection of Tin Man's hate-filled scowl as he aimed the slab gun.

"I hope they locked up that guy," she said.

"Yeah, they did. Callahan sent some officers down. They hauled him off to an Old Earth prison. That's what she told me." Michelle Callahan was the police chief. Danny's boss. "He didn't put up any resistance. The Intercept left him in tatters. Weak as a kitten."

"So you talked to the chief."

"Yeah. Stopped by on my way over here. Had to pick up my gear." He used his toe to nudge his bag on the floor. He looked a little sheepish. "She pulled me into her office. I had to watch the playback of the Intercept feed—with her sitting right next to me."

"Bet that was awkward. She's got a good reason to hate slab guns."

It was common knowledge that the chief's husband, Paul Stark, had been severely injured by a slab gun attack back on Old Earth. He would never again walk under his own power.

"Yeah, she was pretty pissed off," Danny said. "You know the chief—she gets intense. But she's giving me a second chance."

"I thought you'd already gotten a second chance."

"I did. This is my second chance at a second chance." He smiled.

Violet didn't smile back. She couldn't forget the dank, shadowy alley back on Old Earth and the sight of Danny in danger.

"It just seems to me," she said, "that it was sort of an amazing coincidence. You coming across a drug dealer down there, I mean. Totally accidentally."

He stared at her. "What do you mean?"

"Old Earth's a big place. The chances of you just bumping into a crime scene like that are pretty slim."

"Guess so." He shrugged. "My lucky day."

Lucky? That's what Violet wanted to say back to him. Yell it, even. *Lucky? You almost DIED.*

But she didn't say it. He already knew. He didn't need her to point it out yet again. Besides, talking that way would make her sound like a wheedling coward—something that Violet Crowley would *never* be. She was tough. And brave. As tough and brave as Danny was, actually, even if she hadn't broken as many rules as he had.

Yet.

"Good thing we have the Intercept," she said.

He paused. "Yeah. Right."

His hesitation surprised her. So did his tone. It almost sounded as if Danny was being sarcastic. As if he had some doubts about the Intercept, about the amazing technology that made New Earth secure, day after day. About the system that kept everything running smoothly.

But that was impossible. Because his own brother had invented it. Kendall Mayhew had died a year and a half ago. The Intercept was his legacy. And to Danny, nothing was more important than loyalty to his brother's memory.

Violet knew that for sure. There might be a ton of things she *didn't* know about Danny—such as why he couldn't stay away from Old Earth—but his love for his brother was beyond question.

What, then, accounted for the odd note in his voice just now? Maybe, she thought, he'd been hearing the same whispers about the Intercept. The speculation swirled in the winds that were pumped perpetually through the atmosphere of New Earth from the giant turbines in Farraday. It rode in the mild rumble beneath the floor of Protocol Hall.

"So what do you think about the rumors?" she said.

He looked at her sharply. "What rumors?"

"That there's something wrong with the Intercept. A weak spot."

Danny shook his head. "Can't be. My brother didn't make any mistakes."

"Yeah, but maybe there's something he didn't fore—"

"No. No matter what you've heard, the Intercept works fine. It will always work fine. It's perfect. It's always going to be there. We'll never lose it." His voice had a funny edge to it.

"You don't actually sound too thrilled about that."

"Why wouldn't I be thrilled? It saved my life." And with that, Danny brushed at some dirt on the sleeve of his tunic, even though Violet didn't see anything in that particular spot that needed removal. It almost seemed like he was buying time while he figured out what to say next. "Anyway," he went on, "along with telling you guys how grateful I am, I also came by to see how it's going. Getting ready for your Intercept intervention and all."

"It's okay. I can handle it."

"I know you can." He glanced away from her again, a sure sign that he was going to say something important. Something that made it hard for him to look at her when he said it. "Everything's good, Violet. Like I said—just trust me, okay?"

"I do. I mean it. You know that."

And she did mean it. Mostly.

Because in spite of it all—in spite of the regulations he ignored and the people he pissed off and the trouble he made for Chief Callahan and for her father, in spite of the annoyance and hurt she felt because he wouldn't tell her why he kept running back down to Old Earth every chance he got—yes, she trusted him. On some mysterious level that transcended all her doubts, Violet trusted Danny.

But couldn't you trust somebody *and* be worried that maybe he was in trouble? Couldn't you trust him *and* need to find out why he was doing something that might get him hurt or killed?

Sometimes Violet didn't like the fact that she had such intense feelings for him. She hated being dependent on anybody. *Ever.* In every other realm of her life, she was capable, confident, self-assured. Some people might even call her cocky. Because she was smart and she knew it. Because she was attractive in a casual, sporty, unfussy sort of way—and she knew that, too.

Around Danny, though, Violet was off-balance, uncertain. And clumsy. It made her wonder if liking somebody would always make her feel so . . . *stupid.* Or if someday—when she was older—she would turn around and realize that the emotion was making her feel stronger, not weaker. Making her behave like her real self. Not like some disgusting idiot who was obsessed all the time by the fear that somebody might figure out her true feelings. One day, she might look forward to that little blue flash.

Feelings. They had such urgent, scary power—which was the point, of course, of the Intercept in the first place. That was the key. That was why it worked so well. Such had been Kendall Mayhew's great inspiration: to use the vast coiled might of recollected emotions to control behavior, to force people into doing what they should have been doing in the first place.

Feelings made people so astonishingly vulnerable. The Intercept proved that every day, every minute. The idea of life without it—of a civilization that could somehow function without the collection and re-deployment of emotions—was unthinkable now.

"So," Danny said. "Wish I had time to grab a coffee or something. But I've got a few things to do."

You always have things to do, Violet thought grumpily. *What things?*

"Sure," she said.

"See you later, okay?"

"Sounds good." She always pretended that it didn't matter to her one way or another whether they got together or not. It was a matter of pride.

Could Danny see through her fake-cool attitude? She wasn't sure. And that made her wonder, in turn, how an emotion such as uncertainty might register on the Intercept—in shades of gray, maybe, with a lot of squiggly lines heading in different directions?

"Okay," he said. "And hey, listen—thanks again."

"Sure." Her next words came out in a rush. She was as surprised by them as he was. She didn't know she was going to say them until she did. "When you go back down there, is it—is it the same? The same as when you left?"

Violet's voice was full of wonder. She had a sharp hunger to know about the strange world he had left behind.

Fleetingly, she thought about the Intercept, and what it might do with her deep desire to experience Old Earth, a desire that was re-kindled over and over again. How would that emotion register on the Intercept? As an endless longing, she supposed. As a kind of fevered yearning.

Danny didn't answer right away. She waited. He was still here, yes, but in another way, it felt to Violet as if he was very far away, too. Even if she tried to make contact with him, she had the notion that he would always be—like his image on her screen earlier today—forever out of her reach.

"It's the same," he said, in a quiet voice. "But it's also *not* the same, you know? Not at all."

"I bet you miss it."

"Come on, Violet." Now his voice was scoffing. "It's terrible down there. You've seen the pictures. Dirt, hunger, disease—you know what it's like. It was bad when my brother and I left and it's worse now. How could anybody miss *that*?"

"I didn't ask about anybody. I asked about you."

He closed his eyes. Then he opened them again. "Okay," he said. He wasn't scoffing anymore. Violet had the distinct sense that a knot inside him had just loosened a little bit. "I do, actually," he said. "Sometimes—yeah. I miss it. Even as ugly and awful as it is, I miss it. Funny how you get that. I don't think anybody else ever has."

"I don't know about Old Earth. But I know about missing things."

"Yeah," Danny said. She could tell by the way he looked at her that he was waiting for more—waiting for more questions about why he risked so much to return as often as he did. Questions he was ready to ignore or deflect. His guard was up again; the shields had returned to their regular positions.

But she didn't ask anything else. She'd asked him enough for one day.

"So I get that," Violet said.

Their eyes locked. The moment was awkward—and the moment *wasn't* awkward, too, at exactly the same time. Violet had never felt anything quite like it with anybody other than him. On the one hand, she was nervous, fluttery, uncomfortable—but on the other, she'd never felt more relaxed. Or happier.

Was Danny feeling that way, too? Unless he decided to tell her, she couldn't know. Only the Intercept knew, based on history and probability.

"I'd better get going," he said.

"Yeah."

Violet picked up her tablet as if she was going back to her reading. She didn't want him to know she'd be watching him leave. But that's exactly what she planned to do.

As soon as he began his swift, long-legged stride across the wide expanse of white marble on the floor of Protocol Hall, Violet stood up so that she could follow his movements. Looking down from her workstation, she could easily keep track of his progress through the crowd. For one thing, only field cops wore dark blue uniforms. And Danny was taller and leaner than a lot of people. He reached the big glass double doors and waited a brief second for them to swish open. In another minute he would be crossing the plaza in front of Protocol Hall. The plaza, the main meeting spot for people her age on New Earth, was a large flagstone square surrounded by a low stone wall where people sat or leaned while they talked and laughed or read and drank coffee or just thoughtfully watched the sky. There was always a great deal of sky-watching on New Earth. The colors changed all the time.

Now that she was no longer distracted by Danny's close physical presence, the questions came back to her with fresh intensity, questions she wished she'd had the courage to ask him—instead of putting up with his evasions. He had asked her to trust him. But how could she do that, when his actions didn't make sense?

Why can't you just stay away from Old Earth? I wish you'd tell me. Or tell me why you can't *tell me. Why are you risking so much to keep going down there?*

Sometimes she had an inkling that—by not answering her questions—he thought he was protecting her. But from *what*?

From himself, maybe. From a secret he held deep inside, a secret he gripped so tightly that it had grown right into his soul, indistinguishable from his very being.

Or maybe it was something else entirely.

A new suspicion had recently occurred to her, a terrible hunch that had nothing to do with his soul. It could explain all too well why Danny kept sneaking down to Old Earth.

And the thought of it made her go cold inside.

The Very Bad Detective

She knew that what she was doing was weird. She knew that it bordered on stalker territory. She could hear Shura's voice in her head: *BORDERS on stalker territory? Um—I think you're actually* crossing *the border at this point, girl.*

She knew Danny would be angry if he ever found out. He would say it meant she didn't trust him, after all. Which—yeah, okay—it sort of did.

But Violet had to do it, anyway. She had to know why Danny kept risking his career and his future by going down to Old Earth. And she had to know right now.

She didn't know *why* she had to know right now—after all, she'd put up with the mystery for months now, and it was getting dark outside—but she did. Sometimes it happened like that for her: A situation was fine, fine, fine, and then suddenly it *wasn't* fine—in fact, it was unbearable—and she couldn't suffer through it for one more second.

She slapped a hand on the desk. The slap was like putting a period at the end of a sentence—and the sentence was this: *I'm going to follow him.*

Violet switched off her computer. She grabbed her bag. Moments later she was crossing the plaza just as Danny had done before her. She wove her way around the food carts. She cut through the lines of people waiting their turn to step up to the little windows to order their meals.

She tried to keep her head down, in case he spotted her, but she also needed to be alert and observant so that *she* could spot *him*. She couldn't move fast; fast movement in a crowd was too noticeable. She had to be casual but also deliberate. It was dark now but it wasn't *that* dark. Streetlights would be switching on any minute.

People streamed past her in all directions. She heard snatches of their conversations and scraps of their laughter, but she felt very distant from it all. She was focused on catching up with Danny so that she could track him. And figure out what he was up to.

The last faint remnants of sunlight glimmered in the distance. It had been a beautiful day. But that wasn't surprising. All the days on New Earth were beautiful. It was always summer, and the air was always spiced with a tender blend of growing things. It was a subtle fragrance made up of oranges and jasmine and cinnamon and freshly mown grass and a rich bottom note of oaky crispness. The odor had been specifically chosen for New Earth. When Violet's father had conceived of this place, he knew that things like smells would be very important, and that they were the things most likely to be overlooked by the engineers. Engineers cared about structural integrity and metallurgical stresses and optimal environmental sustainability. Not smells. And so Ogden Crowley had hired a crew of Scent Blenders— experts in botany and neurophysiology and psychology who understood what people needed to have wafting past them in order to feel at home. To feel balanced and whole.

Violet was barely aware of the smell anymore. Hardly anyone was. It was just a natural part of this world. They'd notice if it *wasn't* there, her father had explained to her, but they didn't notice that it was.

She did notice, however, the way the ground beneath her feet trembled and shifted with a constant vibration, like a lullaby with no words. That was the machinery of the Intercept doing its work, collecting and sorting, labeling and targeting.

All at once, Violet's heart gave a funny little lurch.

There he is.

Danny was about twenty yards ahead of her, stepping off the curb at the edge of the plaza, heading toward Curie Street. His apartment was on Curie Street.

It had to be him. Dark hair. Slender build. Dark tunic. Black boots.

But wait. He was stopping. Something had spooked him. Slowly, slowly, he began to turn back toward the plaza.

In one more second he's going to be looking straight in my direction.

Violet froze. She quickly realized, however, that freezing was an ineffective strategy when you were attempting to avoid visual surveillance and when you were, unfortunately, right out in the open. And so she jumped sideways. That put her behind one of the trees arranged along the plaza's western border. It was a ginormous sugar maple, so thick around the middle that three Violets, all in a row, could have successfully hidden behind it.

She pressed her back against the craggy and pitted gray bark, breathing in and out, and in and out again, trying to calm herself.

Had he seen her?

And if he *had* seen her and if he confronted her—what would he say to her? *Stop following me, you very, VERY weird girl. You perv.*

Well, he wouldn't say *that*. He was too polite. But he might *think* it, and that was bad enough. That was enough to make her cringe. She closed her eyes, expecting to hear Danny's pissed-off voice any second. He'd march up to the tree—for surely he'd caught a glimpse of her before she leapt out of his line of sight—and peer around it and stare at her, sadly shaking his head.

Maybe he'd even call the police.

Wait. He IS the police.

But it would still be bad. Very bad. And very embarrassing. So bad and so embarrassing that when Violet tried to envision the rest of her life, all she could see was misery and isolation. She'd hide herself away from everybody she cared about and from everybody who (foolishly, it was now clear) cared about *her*. She'd stop showing up for work at Protocol Hall, and then she'd get some menial job that she could do in the dark so that nobody would ever have to look at her, and she'd slink around in shame and humiliation, and then she'd get old, and even Shura would shun her and finally forget about her, and . . .

Nobody came.

Nothing was happening. Absolutely nothing. She opened her eyes. She leaned out to one side, twisting her neck so that she could see around the tree.

In the distance Danny was on the move once more, passing the sign for Curie Street and moving toward Bohr Boulevard.

Then it struck her: *That's not Danny.* His dark hair was longer than Danny's. And curlier. The tunic was black, not dark blue, which meant he worked for Intercept Security, not the police department.

So maybe it *was* too dark to follow somebody. Or maybe her guilt and her nervousness had gotten the better of her. Clouded her judgment. And her eyesight, too.

Violet slunk out from behind the tree. Now she was sure that she'd lost him. Too much time had passed. Squinting, looking hard into every face that threaded past her, she turned in a complete circle so that she could check in all directions. And then she turned one more time, going the other way, just for good measure. She saw a lot of people—shift change at Protocol Hall was always a mob scene, with some people coming and other people going, and all of it creating a rich and colorful cross-weave of humanity.

But no Danny.

Well, maybe that was for the best. What if she'd gotten her wish and actually been able to follow him? What if she'd ended up witnessing something she didn't really want to see?

What if her new suspicion about Danny—the one so awful that she hadn't even shared it yet with Shura and maybe never would—was confirmed?

Warm as it was, Violet shivered. She wondered how the Intercept would label the emotion that had—just now—officially colonized her brain. What category would it choose? In which of its drawers would the Intercept file away this feeling she couldn't seem to shake?

What would it do with dread?

4

The Darkening Day

Following Danny—or trying to—had left Violet with a very bad headache. And put her in a very bad mood. Along with the dread, she felt antsy and sour and sort of hollow. And confused. And more distraught than ever. Her emotions were on the loose, rattling around inside her, unattached to anything solid or dependable. She wanted to yell at somebody. She wanted to take a vow of silence. She wanted to run very fast, and she wanted to stand still. All at the same time. A series of small blue flashes crackled in the crook of her elbow.

She decided to do what she always did when she was a mess.

She called Shura.

"Be there in, like, two minutes," Shura said, which was exactly what Violet knew she would say, and which was, of course, the precise reason why Violet had called her. There were definitely Best Friend Rules, and Rule Number One was: When a Best Friend calls, you go. Even when the Best Friend—in this case, Violet—had given no details whatsoever about the reason for her distress and only blurted out a few ragged words about needing Shura *right now*.

Violet switched off her wrist console. She already felt better. Shura would hop a tram and meet her in Perey Park, which was just a short walk from Protocol Hall. That was where they always hung out.

Shura was an artist. A really good one. Her paintings were so wonderful that sometimes Violet forgot that anyone had painted them at all; they seemed like natural facts in the universe, random fragments of reality that somebody had cut out and framed. Some of them chronicled the sights of New Earth—the way the streets ran as straight and equally spaced as cello strings, right to the edge of the horizon, or the way the skies looked when the Color Corps over in Farraday was in the midst of its nightly shade-mixing ritual—but some of them showed scenes that had never happened before, anywhere. Those were the paintings Violet liked best.

Once she had asked Shura about it. They were standing in front of a painting her friend had just finished. The painting, propped on a paint-spattered easel in a corner of Shura's bedroom, showed a long field of smooth mossy green, framed by swirls and dabs of brown and orange and yellow. A football peeked up out of the grass.

It didn't look like any place Violet had ever seen before.

"The place in the painting—it's not real, right?" Violet said. "It never existed."

"Right," Shura said. "But it will."

That picture now hung in Violet's bedroom. Shura had given it to her for her sixteenth birthday.

Shura's parents didn't like the fact that their daughter was an artist. They didn't try to hide it, either. Violet and Shura had talked about it many, many times, because it was so hurtful to Shura, and also so important.

Her mother, Anna Lu, was an attorney who specialized in the rights of immigrants on New Earth. Her father, Edgar Lu, performed maintenance work for the Intercept. They were serious people—almost as serious as Violet's father, the most serious person Violet knew. They didn't want Shura to be a painter. They wanted her to be an engineer or an architect or a scientist or a lawyer, like Anna Lu was. Or a doctor, like Violet's mother had been.

Her parents thought art was frivolous, Shura had explained to Violet, and they thought that only frivolous people would want to have anything to do with it. "It's not that they're mean," Shura added. "They're actually pretty great. They're just worried. They know that art is about emotion. And with the Intercept and all—" She didn't finish her sentence. It wasn't necessary. Violet knew exactly what she meant: The emotions created by art—both making it and beholding it—would just be more raw material for the Intercept. More ammunition.

"They want me to do something practical," Shura had said. "They want me to be safe."

Safe.

That was a word Violet knew all too well.

Perey Park was a giant arena of green with a round marble fountain in the center. The fountain was spectacular. Six tubes jutting from its inner rim sent identical arcs of sparkling water leaping high into the air. The streetlights illuminated each arc, turning them into separate sprays of rippling diamonds.

Here and there, patches of flamboyant flowers burst up from the soil like another kind of fountain, the living kind, along with carefully spaced trees. The frizzy tops of those trees swayed and trembled in the light but persistent breeze. Along the park's outer edge was a series of wrought-iron benches, connected like the links of a chain necklace. Violet loved every inch of it.

She picked a bench that wasn't near any other occupied benches and sat down. She didn't have long to wait. Shura showed up right away. She usually wore her straight black hair pulled back tight in a ponytail, but tonight it was hanging loose around her face. Violet couldn't quite see her eyes, and not just because of the darkness.

"So," Shura said. She plopped down beside Violet. "You sounded terrible on the phone. Are you worried about the intervention?"

Everyone working in Protocol Hall had to undergo an Intercept intervention, so they would know what manner of temporary chaos they were inflicting on others. The tricky part was that you never knew when it was coming. The element of surprise was a crucial part of the experience, because if you knew when the Intercept would be slinging one of your emotions back at you, you could prepare yourself; you could grit your teeth and get through it.

So Violet didn't know when it was coming. It could happen next week or next month or ten minutes from now. At any moment, she might be hit with a memory: something so intense and vivid that it would be temporarily debilitating.

Just as debilitating as the image of his sister's death had been for Tin Man.

"That's not it," Violet said. "I mean, I'm not exactly looking forward to it—but that's not it."

"So what's going on?"

"I followed Danny."

"You *what*?"

"I followed him."

"When?"

"Just now. And so I feel—well, ashamed, I guess. A little bit. But mainly frustrated. Because I lost him. He could be *anywhere* now." Violet gestured toward the enormous glass structure in the near distance, a blaze of cool angular radiance set against the dark horizon of New Earth. "He came by Protocol Hall when my shift was over and we talked and I asked him—like I always do—why he keeps going down to Old Earth. He did it again today, okay? And he almost *died* this time." Violet quickly summarized the incident in the alley with Tin Man. Shura winced when she heard the words *slab gun*.

"And so I just lost it," Violet continued. "The second he left my workstation, I thought, *Screw it—I'm going to get to the bottom of this myself.* Maybe he was on his way to meet somebody. And maybe he'd tell them why he keeps being so stupid. And maybe I'd be able to eavesdrop and then I'd know why he's doing it, and then maybe—"

"And then maybe," Shura said, interrupting her, "he'd catch you spying on him and never speak to you again. Is that what you want?"

Violet crossed her arms and slumped back against the bench. This wasn't how she thought the conversation was going to go.

"So how long did you tail him?" Shura said.

"Not long. I didn't even get past the plaza. Too risky. And too dark."

"Good."

"Good?"

"Yeah. Good. Because following him was wrong." Shura shook her head. "For a smart girl, you can do some pretty dumb things."

Coming from anybody else, Violet thought, those words would have caused so much heated resentment to rush and boil inside her that her Intercept file would probably explode. Coming from Shura, though, it was okay. Best friends could get by with saying things that other people can't.

Especially when those things happened to be true.

"I know, I know," Violet conceded. "It's just *eating* at me, though. Danny won't stop going to Old Earth. And he refuses to tell me why he won't stop going." She thrust out her right foot as if she were kicking an invisible soccer ball. She'd needed something to do with all the frustration-fueled energy that was stacking up inside her. "They won't put up with it much longer, you know? One of these days, Chief Callahan is just going to fire him. And then what?"

"Not your problem."

Violet gave her a long, meaningful look.

"Okay," Shura said. "I get it. It *is* your problem. In a way. Because of how you feel. But you can't spy on him. That's not the answer. You know that. Right?"

Neither one of them spoke for a few minutes. The park was busy, even after dark; there was a lot going on, and that was good, because it made the silence seem not like silence but simply a break to watch the action. Thanks to the streetlights, a visit to the park was a spectator sport.

Two young girls punted a football back and forth. An old lady was doing some sort of original dance with a scarf and a stick, bending and twirling, lifting one knee and then the other while she hummed and chanted. Some people walked dogs along the track that ringed the space. Violet watched a basset hound who couldn't be moving any faster than an inch an hour, his long brown ears dusting the ground. The owner, a woman in a pink jumpsuit with pearl-white hair, was very patient. She never tugged on the leash. She let the old dog set his own pace.

Violet wondered how patience would register on the Intercept. Or maybe patience wasn't an emotion. Maybe it was a behavior that just reflected an emotion.

Patience.

The word made her think of Marguerite Perey, the physicist from Old Earth whom the park was named for. Perey died three centuries ago, in the Old Earth country of France, but Violet had loved learning about her back in history class. After years of tedious, painstaking work, Perey discovered an element called francium—the last natural element. There was less than an ounce of it in the crust of Old Earth, and it decayed in about twenty minutes, but it was real. And its existence was known only because Perey had been patient enough to find it.

All at once, Violet's ruminations on Perey came to a halt. She'd heard a snuffling sound.

To her surprise, when she looked over at Shura she saw that her friend seemed to be . . . *crying.* She was doing it silently, except for that snuffle, but she was crying, all right. And as Violet peered closer, she noticed what she hadn't noticed before—because she'd been so caught up in her own problems. This wasn't the first time Shura had cried tonight. That's why she'd pulled her hair forward.

So that Violet couldn't get a close look at her eyes and see how red and puffy they were.

"Hey," Violet said. "What's going on?"

"I wasn't going to talk about it," Shura said. "I didn't want to bring it up, because *you're* the one who called *me*. This is, like, *your* crisis. And so I didn't want to—"

"Tell me." Violet's voice was firm.

"It's my mother."

"Is she—is she sick or something?" Violet asked. She had to. But she was afraid to hear the answer, because she knew what it felt like to lose a parent.

"No. It's not that." Shura swallowed hard. "You know what some people are saying, right? That somebody's found a way to get past the Intercept? To escape it?"

So here it was again. The rumor that wouldn't go away.

"Yeah," Violet said. She tried to make her tone light, dismissive. "But people are always gossiping. You know that."

"This is different." Shura's face was grave. "My mother has been getting threats. And it may be related to the breach of the Intercept— or at least what people are saying *might* be a breach." She needed a deep breath before she could go on. "I only know this stuff because I heard her talking to my dad about it. And it's scary, Violet. Really scary. I can't—" The tears started up again. Shura rubbed her eyes.

"What does that have to do with your mom?"

"I don't know," Shura said. She'd managed to stop the tears. "I don't think my parents do, either. They're just starting to put a few things together. Trying to figure out what's going on. All I know for sure is that my mom's scared. And she's *never* scared. So it's got to be really bad." Shura's face changed. A small smile appeared. "You know what's funny? You've seen me and my mom fight, right? We argue over everything these days—all the time. Any little thing can set us off. But when I think about something happening to her, I just—I can't—"

Violet slung an arm around her friend's small shoulder. She gave her a very short hug, probably one of the shortest hugs in the history of human civilization. Because Violet wasn't a hugger. But this was an unusual occasion, and so she felt the need to break her rule. *Fine: I can hug. See?*

Sitting beside Shura this way, Violet felt the same emotion she'd been feeling at various moments in the past few weeks. It was a new one for her. It was foreboding, yes—but there were other emotions mixed in with it, too.

Like fear.

Like sadness.

The sadness wasn't attached to anything specific. It just *was*. Yes, Violet missed her mother every day, every minute, and yes, she wished she could get closer to her father, but this kind of sadness wasn't related to any of that. It was bigger. And somehow it was less personal, too. There was a lot more at stake than just her own mixed-up feelings.

The world was shifting. Transforming itself from one thing into another thing. Life was becoming volatile and unsettled—not only in their own lives, as she and Shura moved ever closer to their seventeenth birthdays and to being considered adults, but on New Earth in general, too. Violet had the sense that important events were happening in hidden places these days, that vast shapes were rearranging themselves just behind the visible spectrum.

"I know how you feel," Violet said. "Until my mother got sick, I never thought my life was going to change. And then everything changed."

"I'm just so worried about her." Shura shivered.

"Any idea who's threatening her?"

"Only a hunch. You know she deals with immigrants, right?"

"Yeah. The people from Old Earth who are allowed in, a few at a time—your mom gets them settled." Violet's face clouded over. "An *immigrant* is threatening her? But she's *helping* them. Why would somebody—"

"No. That's not it. I think maybe it's related to the fact that my mom is back on Old Earth a lot. Four or five times a year. Sometimes more. She meets with her clients before they get up here."

"Right."

"Well, I heard my mom and dad talking late last night in the kitchen. I came back downstairs. They thought I was asleep. They were talking about the threats my mom's been getting. There's some group—some secret group—that claims it's just about figured out how to get around the Intercept. They call themselves the Rebels of Light. And they want my mom to help them."

"Help them how?"

"I don't know. But it has something to do with her trips back down to Old Earth. I tried to find out more, but they caught me listening. And they shut up. I know my parents—they don't want me to worry about it. They're always trying to protect me."

"Has your mom told the police?"

"No." Shura's voice was blunt. "No, she wouldn't do that."

"Why?"

"She thinks the cops are out to get new immigrants. That they're looking for any excuse to deport them. And so they'd use the threats against my mom as a way to justify rounding up a bunch of them to ship them back."

Might happen, Violet thought. A lot of the cops—not Danny, of course, because he was a recent immigrant himself—were suspicious of the new arrivals. So were many of the citizens of New Earth. They feared that the people from Old Earth were out to get the best jobs, or would refuse to work at all, straining resources.

"So what's your mom going to do?"

"No idea. My dad's been driving her to work. Sticking close to her if we're out shopping or whatever. I didn't even notice, can you believe it?"

"Yeah, I can. And it's okay. You love your mom. But you've got your own life. And she *wants* you to have your own life. She wouldn't want you worrying about her all the time."

Shura nodded. Then something occurred to her. "Listen—you can't say anything to anybody about this."

"Of *course* not. Come on. You don't have to tell me that."

"I know. I know. I'm just kind of nervous these days. About getting my parents in some kind of trouble. And your dad is—well, you know. He's Ogden Crowley."

"Like I could ever forget." Violet made a grunting sound. "People think it's so great to be the president's daughter." She packed as much sarcasm into her voice as it could hold. "Right. *So* cool. *So* many special privileges. But you and I both know what it really means—it means that people are always nervous around me. They think they have to watch everything they say and do. Every minute. Or they're going to get in big trouble."

Darkness had completed its takeover of the park. Only a few streetlights were still left on, to guide people on their way home. Yet it was not a menacing darkness. It was not a hard darkness that had fallen all at once, but a gradual and tender one. The darkness had a soft texture to it. The park was transformed, its edges blurred. The fountain in the middle was no longer visible and thus it existed now only as sound, as the timed jets of water plashed back into it, one by one by one.

The sound caused a sudden sweet memory to rise in Violet's mind:

When she was five years old, her mother had taken her to this park almost every day. One afternoon, Violet leaned over the low lip of the fountain and touched the water. She heard the soft slap of each jumping curve of water as it struck the surface. *One, two, three, four, five, six.* Violet recalled counting them in her mind, and being very proud of herself for knowing her numbers. And then the pride melted into something else. Another feeling. She turned to her mother and asked, "Do you know what that sound is, Mommy?"

Lucretia Crowley said, "Tell me, sweetheart."

And Violet replied, "It's what happiness sounds like."

She didn't tell Shura about this memory. It was a special one, a private one, one that belonged only to her. It had belonged to her mother, too, of course, but now that her mother was gone, Violet had the total responsibility for keeping it.

Another thought flared in her mind, an irksome one: The memory really wasn't private at all. Even though the Intercept had not been installed until Violet was eleven, the memory lived in her. And once the Intercept was online, it had grabbed that moment of happiness straight out of her brain, just like a shoplifter, and carried it off to Protocol Hall and jammed it into her file. It *knew*.

Her best friend didn't know about that day and the emotion it had kindled in her—but the Intercept did.

It also, as of now, had a record of how annoyed this realization had just made her. She didn't need to check for a small blue flash to have that verified.

Violet had had such an epiphany before. She knew that no emotion was truly private on New Earth—it couldn't be, her father had explained to her, because private thoughts led to conspiracies and crimes—but usually that dismay had accompanied the momentous times, the swelling of the big emotions: love, hate, joy, despair. Her sometimes-out-of-control crush on Danny.

This, though, was a small thing—a small, perfect moment between her and her mother. And the Intercept had come along and put its hands all over *that* one, too.

"Do you think it could be true?" Shura said. "Do you think somebody could really have figured out a way to outsmart the Intercept?"

"I don't know. It sounds pretty far-fetched," Violet replied. "Then again, the Intercept itself probably seemed unlikely, too. When they first installed it, I mean. Like—impossible. And it's here." She realized that wasn't very reassuring. "But hey—listen, okay? If somebody *has* found a way to get around it, that doesn't mean they'll get away with it. They won't. They're going to be in for a fight."

Violet visualized her father's face. The grim set of his jaw. The hard knots he made of his fists. The flinty look in his eyes. He had devoted his life to creating New Earth, and then to hooking up the Intercept to preserve it. Nobody wanted to cross Ogden Crowley. No one dared stand between him and his desires.

She cared deeply for her father. But she was also a little bit afraid of him—and not because he'd ever hurt her, or ever *would* hurt her. She was afraid of his dreams and what he would do to protect them. To keep everyone safe.

Violet gazed out across the darkness of Perey Park. There was now a chill in the air. Only a slight one, but Violet felt as if she could almost see its arrival, as it moved across the tops of the trees and settled onto New Earth in a clinging mist.

"Anyway," Shura said. "I guess there's nothing we can do about it. I just want my mom to be safe. In fact, I want everybody I care about to be safe—and happy. Including you." She gave Violet a sideways glance. "You won't follow Danny again, right? Because that could backfire on you. Big-time. Promise me right now that you'll quit playing detective."

"Um—sure."

"Violet. Come on."

"I said I would."

"Doesn't sound like you mean it."

Shura knew her well. Sometimes, she knew her *too* well.

"I solemnly swear," Violet said, drawing out the words so that they sounded grand and extra-dramatic, "that I won't follow Danny anymore."

"Good."

"Satisfied?"

"Yeah."

Violet wasn't really lying to her friend. That's what she told herself, anyway, when the guilt started to trickle in. She didn't have any plans to follow Danny again. Following him had been stupid. Impulsive. And it hadn't worked, anyway.

So she wouldn't follow him.

But she might do *other* things.

Because she couldn't give up. Not yet. Not while she felt the mystery moving through her blood, haunting her thoughts. She didn't want Shura to worry about her—but Violet knew, as surely as she knew anything, that the first chance that came along, she'd find another way.

She had another plan. And if *that* one didn't work, she had one more idea left for getting to the bottom of Danny's secret.

The only downside was that she'd need Reznik's help to pull off Option Number Three. And that, in turn, would mean she'd have to take advantage of Reznik's crush on her—which made Violet feel even sneakier and shadier than she did already.

Over the Edge

No lights were visible in the living room. That didn't matter. Violet didn't need any lights to know her father was there. She could hear his breathing: raspy, heavy, clotted. He was sitting in the massive leather armchair. That was where he always sat.

She switched on the floor lamp. His big head didn't move. He wasn't asleep—his eyes were open—but he didn't react.

"Dad?"

Her voice seemed to reanimate him, in a way that neither the opening and closing of the front door nor the sudden light had. He lifted his gnarled, scarred hands from the armrests, stretched out his fingers, and then gripped the armrests once again.

"Hi, sweetheart." Ogden Crowley shifted his legs.

Well, one leg: the left. The right was a hollow husk. If he wanted to move it, he had to pick it up and place it in the new position. "How was work?"

"Good."

Violet watched as he rearranged himself in the chair. She liked the ruggedness of his face, its deep lines and crevices. Ogden Crowley was a broad, solid man with a crown of unruly white hair.

His damaged hands and his bad leg were the result of wounds suffered long ago, when he was a young boy on Old Earth. He had described their origin to Violet, once he thought she was old enough
to hear it and not be upset by it.

Thirteen-year-old Ogden Crowley had been trapped in the cross-
fire during the Second Mineral War. He was the sole survivor of
an attack that killed his parents and their friends when their hiding place was discovered. His lungs had been injured by all the
smoke, which was why his breathing, to this day, was loud and rattling. Radiation burns had short-circuited the nerves in his right
leg, leaving those nerves useless and dangling, like the strings of a
broken harp. The flesh on his leg, lacking its living nets of infrastructure, had shriveled.

The best doctors on New Earth had proposed ways to fix his dead
leg—but those remedies involved replacing what was left of it with a
prosthetic made of thermoplastic polymer. And Ogden said no. He
wanted to keep the last remnants of his real leg. He wanted to remind
the people of New Earth of what happened when a world was allowed
to disintegrate. His dead leg was a symbol of the worst-case scenario.
If he replaced it with a shiny new leg, the lesson would be lost.

When he put even the slightest bit of pressure on his leg, he told
Violet, it felt as if a million or so supernova suns were exploding
underneath his skin, each one instantly triggering the one right next
to it, snapping and rippling, until he wondered how such a worn,
flimsy flap of skin could possibly contain all that pain, all those
repeated scalding surges.

He rejected medication, because he needed to be sharp and alert.
And he never acted as if he felt the pain. All Violet ever saw was a
slight tightening of his jaw. Or a tremor in his hands, when he gripped
the armrests a bit more firmly.

"Would you like some dinner?" he asked her. "We could go out.
Or perhaps—"

"I'm good, Dad. Really." Violet collapsed onto the couch. She unstrapped her orange wrist console and dropped it on the end table. She tucked her legs up under herself. "What's going on? You're hardly ever home this early."

"My office was too busy to get any thinking done. I have a lot on my mind."

She waited for him to elaborate. It was unlikely, but she waited anyway, just in case.

Sometimes she wished her father would tell her more about his work. When she thought about it for any length of time, though, she was glad he didn't. His job was always complicated and usually depressing. He had too much responsibility for too many things on New Earth. Violet had figured out that when he kept her on the outside of his problems, it was just his way of protecting her.

Which was basically fine, because she had her own problems to think about.

Her father smiled. He was trying to be cordial, even though his mind, Violet knew, was struggling with something massive and vexing. It always was. "How's Shura?" he asked. "And your colleague— Reznik, isn't it? Steve Reznik?"

"Fine, Dad. Everybody's fine." Once a parent knew the names of your friends, you were doomed; they used the names in a nightly Q and A to show they were paying attention to your life. Even though they really weren't. Names made it too easy for them.

"It should be coming up soon, right?" he said. "Your Intercept intervention?"

"Yeah. Although you never know for sure just when it will be."

"Doesn't matter. You'll do well. I'm sure your friends—the ones who've already been through it—have told you that."

Not really, she wanted to answer. Nobody wanted to discuss it, to talk about how it felt to have a pungent memory stuffed back into your consciousness against your will.

"Sure," Violet said. She didn't want her dad to worry about her and how nervous she was. There was nothing wrong with a little fib.

"In any case, it's important for you and the rest of the Intercept monitoring team to understand what you're dealing with," he said. "The strength of it. The awesome power. It'll be something to keep in mind when you initiate an intervention."

She nodded. She was just about to confess that she *was* kind of nervous about having an emotion loaded back into her brain.

But she never got the chance. Her father's face changed. Something had occurred to him.

He raised a pale twisted hand to his forehead and rubbed at a spot an inch above his right eyebrow. Violet had seen him do that many times, especially after her mother died.

"I just remembered," he said. "Chief Callahan asked if we'd join her and her husband for dinner this week. I can't possibly accept— there's simply too much work to do. Too much going on. I thought you might be willing to go. In my stead."

Violet liked Michelle Callahan. But she had a suspicion that, whether her father was present or not, the conversation would quickly settle on one topic and stay there:

Danny.

The police chief knew that Violet and Danny were friends. She'd seen Violet come by the station to walk him home sometimes when his shift was over. And so even though it was a social occasion, Callahan would probably put Violet on the spot and ask her to talk some sense into him. Get him to stop violating direct orders by sneaking down to Old Earth. The chief had tried threats and even a brief suspension. Nothing seemed to work. And because of Danny's special status—he was Kendall Mayhew's brother—Callahan would never be able to kick him off the force for good. Not that she wanted to: He was her best officer.

Violet's first impulse was to tell her father she couldn't attend the dinner. It wasn't convenient. She had other plans.

But then she took a long look at his haggard, care-creased features. Weariness seemed to tug at his face, dragging it down. He worked very hard and he didn't really ask a lot of her. And there was, Violet reminded herself, a special responsibility to being the daughter of Ogden Crowley, founder and president of New Earth. Her mother was dead; now there was only Violet. Her father needed her to take care of things sometimes. To deal with social obligations when he couldn't.

"Okay," she said. She'd go to the stupid dinner. And when Chief Callahan brought up the fact that Danny was making his supervisors mad, and maybe even imperiling his life, Violet would let her know right away that nobody—*nobody*—told Danny Mayhew what to do.

Just like nobody told Violet Crowley what to do.

Well—except for her dad, when he asked her to go to dinner at the chief's house. But that was different, right? He was her dad.

"I appreciate it, sweetheart," he said. "And maybe you'll surprise yourself and have a good time."

"Unlikely."

"I owe you one, then."

"Do you mean it?"

His remark had been intended casually, which Violet knew very well. But she had to take what she could get.

"I do," he said. There was wariness in his tone.

"Good. So maybe we can make a trade. I go to dinner at the chief's house—and you let me go to Old Earth. Just for a short visit. Just to see what it looks like."

He was silent.

"Dad?"

"No."

"But why won't you even consider—"

"We've been over this, Violet. Many, many times. It's too dangerous. I can't allow it. The discussion is closed." Odgen Crowley's word was law in Violet's world—just as it was law throughout New Earth.

Had her father heard about Danny's latest trip down to Old Earth?

The one that almost left him in sizzling-hot shreds after a hit from a slab gun?

Probably not, she decided. Ogden Crowley was in charge of the entire population of New Earth. He'd hardly have time to keep track of a single rogue cop, even if that cop happened to be the brother of Kendall Mayhew. Her father rarely had a moment to eat or sleep.

"I'll go to the chief's house," she said. "If it helps you, I'll do it."

"Good. Glad to hear it."

He was drifting away from her again, his mind returning to its many burdens. She could tell. She always knew when she was losing him. She wondered if he was thinking about the rumors. The gossip that said the Intercept was in trouble.

Had someone really managed to short-circuit it? She had asked him about it briefly last week. He dismissed it. But that meant nothing. He would always try to protect her from bad news.

It was time for her to go to her bedroom—which did not mean she was ready to sleep. Violet liked to end her days by reading her mother's journal, picking a day here, a day there, and luxuriating in Lucretia Crowley's voice and observations. Violet stored only one thing on top of her dresser: her mother's black medical bag. Between the bag and the journal, she kept her mother's memory alive in her heart.

She rose and walked over to her father's chair. She leaned down and kissed his cheek. It was as cold and hard as marble. It made her think of Protocol Hall and its cool stone floor, the white slab beneath which was sealed the Intercept's complex systems.

In the crook of her left elbow, a tiny blue starburst came and went, synchronized with the surge of love she felt for her father. The Intercept, Violet thought, would have a simple job classifying that one. Because love was the easiest emotion to categorize.

"Good night, Dad," she said. "Hope you sleep okay."

He didn't answer. She hadn't expected him to. He was already far away from her, his brain rapidly synthesizing all the problems of New

Earth and Old Earth, too, problems and issues that clicked along as relentlessly as the work of the Intercept itself.

And then Violet had a wild impulse. She felt a sudden, totally irrational desire to talk to her father about Danny, about how she felt when she saw him or thought about him, about how anxious she was each time he disobeyed orders—all the things she would've shared with her mother if her mother were still alive.

"One more thing, Dad."

"Yes?"

She was just about do it—just about to bring up Danny. She stopped herself just in time. *I'm not* that *crazy.* Now she would have to cover.

"I'm just—I guess I'm just feeling extra nervous about the intervention," Violet said hastily. "That's all. I want to do well."

"You will. Don't worry."

As much as she loved her father, she could not talk with him about Danny. Because (1) he was her dad, not her mom, and (2) he was Ogden Crowley, president of New Earth. He didn't have time for her problems. He had the problems of millions of people to worry about. But the most important reason was (3) her father didn't like Danny.

He'd never said so out loud, but it was easy to figure out. Violet had watched his face when she mentioned Danny's name, the way he held back a frown. Kendall Mayhew was the one her father had admired—and now mourned. Danny was the opposite of his fragile, luminously gifted brother. Danny was tough. And volatile. And passionate about things, unlike the cool, rational Kendall. Danny represented some of the very elements that Ogden Crowley wanted to keep out of New Earth: Spontaneity and risk. Fire and intensity.

Her father's dislike of Danny wasn't personal. And it wasn't mean. He just wanted to keep everyone safe. Especially her.

Standing next to his chair right now, in a room cushioned by darkness, Violet felt a wave of compassion for her father, for all his struggles, and gratitude for all that he did on behalf of others. She looked down at his big white head. She stroked the hair on one side. It was stiff and coarse, like the bristles of an old brush. Violet let her hand linger there for a few extra seconds. She almost believed she could feel heat rising from her father's head, a heat generated by the fierceness of his ruminations.

There was a deep abiding sadness in Ogden Crowley. It was the residue of all that he had endured, the pain and the losses and his ferocious hope for New Earth, a hope that was always under siege. Violet knew she couldn't fix his sadness. It was out of her reach. The only one who had ever been able to do anything about her father's sadness was her mother. And she was gone.

Violet murmured another good night. She knew that this one, too, would not be answered.

And with that, she left him alone with the impossibly heavy burden of keeping New Earth safe.

That night, Violet dreamed about the Intercept.

She'd had trouble getting to sleep. She punched at her pillow and changed her position, turning onto her side, then turning onto her other side, then drawing up her knees and cinching her hands around them. She was hot, and so she slipped out of her T-shirt, and then she was cold, and so she groped around the floor beside her bed and found the wadded-up T-shirt and put it back on again.

As she twisted and shifted in her bed, very tired but unfortunately still very wide awake, she only made things worse by letting her mind go over her memories again and again.

She kept returning to a pivotal moment in her past: the day in third grade when she first learned that New Earth was her father's invention.

The class was called New Earth history. And nine-year-old Violet—a little stunned, a little scared, a little upset, and slightly embarrassed—heard the teacher say that Ogden Crowley created New Earth. The idea filled her with wonder.

My daddy, she thought. *My daddy made this world.*

It seemed so—so unlikely. Preposterous, even—which was a word that Violet didn't know back then, but if she'd known it, she would have used it.

Her own *father*? The founder of all this?

The man who sat across the dinner table from her every night and drank his coffee? Really?

When she came home from school that day, Violet had asked her mother about it. Her mother was working in her lab. She took Violet's hand and led her into her father's study. She told him that Violet had something she needed to know.

"Is it true, Daddy? Did you—did you make all this? Was it all your idea?"

Her father had frowned. He put down the tablet he'd been furiously writing on. He pushed his chair away from his desk so that he could turn in Violet's direction. His injury made it hard for him to move, but he seemed to want to be looking at her when he talked.

And he told her the story.

First, he said, she needed to understand something. "The idea isn't the hard part," he declared. "Anyone can have an idea. People have ideas all day long—good ones, bad ones, in-between ones. Crazy ones and clever ones. The true challenge is turning an idea into reality. Going from the daydream stage, when you stroke your chin and you sigh deeply"—and here he had sighed in a flamboyant, theatrical way, which made Violet giggle, as was his intention—"to the moment when you make blueprints and materials lists and deal with nuts-and-bolts realities."

Nuts and bolts.

The phrase had enchanted Violet, even though she didn't know what it meant. Nuts? Bolts? Her parents had been born on Old Earth, and sometimes they used strange combinations of words. That day, her father told her the meaning, told her about putting things together and making them work.

And he also told her about how he'd created New Earth. The notion had come to him many years ago as he stood amid the wreckage of Old Earth, despairing over the fast-forward destruction of the world, its headlong slide into disaster.

Saving the world was simple: Split it in two.

Simply divide the population. Not according to country or skin color or political philosophy or language or god—but by the number of possessions. By intelligence. By money and property.

It would be logical. No gray areas. No troubling ambiguities. The rich and the brilliant go in one direction—up—and the poor and the ordinary stay where they are, back on Old Earth, fighting over the scraps and ashes and crumbs of a dying planet.

Some people agreed with him in principle, he explained to Violet, but they argued for another solution. *Find a suitable planet to serve as a second Earth,* they proposed. *Relocate the chosen ones* there. *In a place far away from the mess of this torn and bleeding world.*

But Ogden Crowley said no. He insisted that they must stay tethered to *this* planet. They must use Old Earth as a pedestal. A base. A stepping-off point. That way, the shock would be lessened. They wouldn't be leaving their home totally behind—but they wouldn't be staying there, either, to sink into the abyss.

New Earth was an astonishing technical feat, a marvel—that's what he explained to Violet that day, with a bright note of pride in his voice.

New Earth was constructed of hybrid amalgams that were lighter and stronger than any materials known on Old Earth. It was kept aloft by an elaborate system of gravitational leverage—a quantum lock-and-dam system—and sustained by its manufactured atmosphere, by its own food and energy sources. New Earth had highways and houses and driveways and cars and street signs and yards and bicycles and trees and town squares and parks and ponds and buses and schools and businesses and mountains and windmills and solar farms and the bright green promise of tomorrow.

Its six cities were named Hawking, Higgsville, Franklinton, Mendeleev Crossing, L'Engletown, and Farraday. The capital was Hawking. That was where Violet lived with her parents.

He told her about the Great Migration. He told her about the moment when the last pod lifted up from the cracked and pitted surface of Old Earth, bound for the silver streets of New Earth. He told her how the people left behind had shielded their eyes from the flash and then settled back to make what they could of their lives in a cold, dark, desperate place.

Meanwhile, the approved groups that had been transported to New Earth beheld a sky that shimmered and grass that sparkled and rivers that ran clear. Most of the New Earth streets didn't even have names at that point. Each fresh batch of arrivals walked around for the first day or so, awed and grateful, blinking at the gleam and the dazzle and the wild unlikeliness of it all.

Some wept, her father recalled, and Violet tried to imagine it: grown-ups crying openly in front of other grown-ups. *Weird.*

Some fell to their knees and bent over and kissed the imported dirt. Some couldn't even talk for a time. Eventually they recovered, of course, and it was as if a communal held breath was suddenly let out and a certain word was chanted like a prayer:

Safe. Safe. Safe.

Old Earth, bleak and lost, seemed very far away. Even if you stood at the outer rim of New Earth and looked down, her father had warned her, you couldn't really see it. It was only a furious gray-black swirl of filth and mist, as if the clouds themselves were in a very bad mood. That's why few people on New Earth ever bothered to look over the edge.

What was the point? Old Earth was a place they wanted to forget. Old Earth was a world marked by hunger, danger, and happenstance.

Happenstance. That was another word Violet didn't understand at the time. But she didn't ask her father right then what it meant. She could figure it out later. She didn't want to interrupt him. She wanted him to go on with his story.

She wanted to know.

No: She *had* to know. She had to know about Old Earth—the birthplace of her parents, and her friends' parents, and every generation before hers.

Old Earth, he explained, was a treeless and meager world. A world of grim, jaundiced sunrises. A world of rusty rain. A world run by hustlers and scavengers.

But that wasn't the worst part. The worst part was that when the people of Old Earth looked up, they could sometimes see New Earth. Really *see* it—visible now and again when the black, rain-gorged clouds momentarily parted.

And during those brief moments, New Earth surely seemed within their grasp.

Maybe, Violet thought, those left behind would gather on the tops of the highest hills of Old Earth, and they would reach and reach. Maybe they put small children up on their shoulders and told them to reach, too. And to dream.

New Earth was so near. It should have been theirs for the taking.

But it wasn't. Violet could imagine their crushing disappointment when the truth struck them: New Earth wasn't close at all. It might as well have been a million miles away.

Several years later, her father discovered the existence of a new technology called the Intercept. He was enthralled. It was, he told her, the Next Great Step. It was the answer to everything. It was the only way to keep New Earth truly safe. Forever.

But that was another story.

In Violet's dreams that night, the Intercept was a living thing. It wasn't just a machine anymore.

It spun. It tumbled. It glowed a bold red. It reached deep into her brain, yanking out her feelings by their scraggly roots, and then tossed those emotions into hundreds of different baskets. It could reach in and retrieve them and fling them back at her, whenever it wanted to.

Thrashing in the dark net of her dreams, Violet twisted under her blanket. She pushed her pillow away. She was half aware that it had begun to rain outside. Technically, rain never needed to fall on New Earth. But her father had realized, back in the early days of New Earth, that people missed it. They craved varieties in weather, especially in a place where it was always summer. And so rain was programmed into the weather mix, added to the atmospherics controlled by the giant electromagnetic turbines in Farraday. Rain was put on shuffle play, so as to be unpredictable, like real rain.

Usually New Earth rain was gentle, comforting. But tonight, the angry raindrops slapped her bedroom window with a sinister intensity.

Nothing was the way it was supposed to be anymore. Not even the rain.

6

Rebels of Light

While Violet slept her moody and troubled sleep, the streets of New Earth glowed bright silver in the moonlight. The low rhythmic hum under the streets continued, as the Intercept did its work. The rain pestered the ground like tiny white arrows.

A few miles away from the apartment where Violet and her father lived, a man paused in front of a small brick building set well back from the street. The building was grimy and run-down, with a sagging strip of dark green awning and an old wooden door. The door was cracked and split.

The rain made the building seem far more forlorn than usual. Even on the clearest of nights, however, it looked very different from the mammoth, gleaming architecture that thrived all around it, the soaring towers, the elegant plazas. When the planners selected by Ogden Crowley designed New Earth, they realized that having everything look new could be just as oppressive as having everything look old. And so, once again using an algorithm that simulated randomness, they stuck in some dilapidated places, places built out of scraps and deliberately scarred and weathered materials. They intended these places to remain vacant, like the fake storefronts in movie studios in the long-ago twentieth and twenty-first centuries. They were here for contrast with all the surrounding magnificence, nothing more.

But this one was not vacant.

The man, his face anxious and sweaty, twisted the knob. He closed the door behind him. It made a single solemn click.

A few minutes later, a woman arrived at the same door from the opposite direction.

She glanced around furtively. She drew up the blue scarf around her neck until it covered the lower half of her face. Then she, too, put a hand on the knob. She slipped inside.

Another bit of time passed, and then a third person, another woman, approached the door, and she, too, shot hurried glances to her right and her left before opening it and entering. She carried a sack, an old and threadbare one.

Inside, there was total darkness.

As soon as the door closed behind the final arrival, the rest of the group emerged from their standing positions at the edges of the room. They stepped forward to form a ragged, practiced circle. They were young and old, male and female, black and white and brown—but that didn't matter here, because the darkness was so profound. They were only voices.

"You're late." It was an accusation, not an observation, from a male voice.

"I did my best," said the woman who'd been the last to get there. "I can't take the same express tram from Higgsville every time. Bound to look suspicious."

"We've discussed that. They're not watching this shack. They don't even know it's being used. As far as they know, it's just an empty shell. So you don't need to worry."

"I'll worry if I want to." She didn't mind standing up to him.

"Whatever. Just try to make it on time tomorrow night, okay?"

"Gotcha." The woman uttered a disgusted-sounding snort. She

didn't like being lectured. She was seventeen, one of the younger ones. "But don't talk to *me* about security, pal. *You're* the one who's living dangerously."

"We're all living dangerously."

She had no reply to that.

By now they had learned to feel their way in the darkness. Most of them—there were nineteen in all—operated in the darkness better than they did in the light, because they'd trained and honed their senses to do so. Light was a distraction. In its absence, they had cultivated other senses, other ways of seeing. It made them stronger, more resourceful.

The air was stippled with tense expectation. For a moment or so the only sounds were the communal ones of their overlapping breathing. Some of the breathing was loud and had a regular rhythm. The rest was sporadic, with fear woven into it. One person coughed. There was a nervous shuffling of feet. The heel of a shoe scraped the floor with a quick rasp. In the solid darkness, even the most ordinary sound stood out.

The latecomer lifted her sack and shook it briskly. The objects inside it clacked and rattled against one another. It was a signal for the ritual to begin. She called out a name and the summoned person reached out a hand, the palm open and slightly curved. The woman placed the wrist console in her or his hand—a hand she couldn't see, but somehow sensed the location of—and then went on to the next name, the next curved palm. Burner consoles were switched out every other day, to reduce the chance that they'd be traced.

"Status reports," said the man who had accosted the late-arriving woman. Authority rang in his voice. "Supply officer, you can start us out."

"Stockpiles are low. We need an infusion."

"Noted," the man in charge replied. "Research and development," he said, addressing someone else in the circle. They knew he'd shifted his head because the direction of his voice changed.

"Doing our best." The woman's voice was apologetic. "We've been hit by a few snags lately. Setbacks. It's tricky—you know that. We're only protected for a short period of time, and if we miscalculate, if we're off by even the tiniest fraction, they'll be onto us. Crowley's no fool. We're working in borrowed labs with substandard equipment. The conditions are primitive." She wanted to end on a more upbeat note. "But we're hanging in there. We've just got to be patient."

"*Patient?*" The word came out as a roar, not a word, from the leader. "*Patient?* Do you understand what the stakes are? Do you have the *slightest clue* what we're up against?"

No one answered, because of course they did. They were risking their lives by even showing up here. They were glad to have this outpost, grateful for the cover it provided, but they were also fully aware that one misstep, one careless gesture, one light left on at the wrong moment could bring them all down.

"Patient," the leader repeated. He'd settled down, but barely. "Don't talk to me about being patient. The odds against us are *staggering*. We have no weapons. We have no power. We're running out of raw materials. We don't know from day to day—we don't know from *hour to hour*—if we're about to be exposed. We could be raided at any second. Or tomorrow. Or next week. If they find out who we are, we're *doomed*."

He brought his rant to a dead stop. He settled himself. These people looked up to him. They trusted him. They needed his skills, his heart. Not his wrath. And besides, it was never a good idea to let your emotions control you. Why do the Intercept's work?

"Okay," he said. "I'll take care of replenishing the stock." His voice softened, but only marginally. "I don't mean to be hard on you. But we're so close now. We can't back down. We've got to keep pushing forward."

"What if we don't want to?" The voice belonged to a man directly across the circle from him. The voice sounded tired and sour and belligerent. Fed up.

"What are you talking about?" the leader asked.

"I'm talking about shutting this down. Going back to our lives."

"No." The leader was moving around the room now, behind the standing people, so that his message would encircle them, rally them, lift them up. "We've got to keep going. Keep fighting. Because everything we believe in is at stake. Our freedom. The freedom of our loved ones. *Everything*. We can't stop now."

"We're losing." The man's voice was flat, absolute.

"We are *not* losing." The leader was adamant. "We've had some setbacks, that's all. We expected that."

"Yeah? Really? Well, I don't see any progress. All I see is danger. They know about us now. They may not know *who* we are, specifically— but they know we're out here. The rumors are everywhere. They know what we're trying to do. They know the special power we've discovered. So they're on the lookout. They're pissed at these little stunts we've been pulling and they're ready for us. Sooner or later, you're going to get caught, and when you do—"

"No. That won't happen. And you know why."

"We can't go on like this."

"We can—and we will." The leader took a deep breath. It was time. He couldn't lose them. So he had no choice. "I didn't want to talk about this yet. It's not a fully formed plan. But it's close."

"What are you talking about?" The skeptical man was still skeptical. But there was an edge of interest in his voice. He couldn't help himself. He was curious.

"Something big," the leader declared. "It's going to change everything. It's almost time."

The others absorbed the information in silence. But he knew they were listening. They always listened to him. He had seen far more than the rest of them had seen. Suffered more. He wasn't one to bluff.

He didn't make false promises. He didn't exaggerate. He chose his words very carefully. They knew that.

If he used a word like *big,* he did it on purpose.

It could mean only one thing.

"The endgame," a woman stated. There was awe in her voice, and fear, too. The leader was actually glad to hear that pinch of fear. Fear kept them sharp. Alert.

He felt a quick, hot surge of affection for these people. In the darkness he couldn't see their faces, but he knew what those faces looked like, and the memory moved him. He cared deeply for these men and women, no matter how rough his manner. He knew what they sacrificed to join him, to be here, reviewing strategy, planning their missions, fanning out across the six cities of New Earth to do what he asked them to do. Lying to their families—because their families would've tried to talk them out of it.

People who love you, he told them, always want you to be safe. But sometimes safety is the most dangerous thing of all.

"Yes," the leader said. "You could think of it as the endgame. We've been hiding in the shadows too long. So it's almost time. Just a few more details to nail down—and then we strike."

He could sense their excitement. They were with him. Even the man who'd challenged him—he was generally always the one who challenged him, because he was young and hungry—was with him again. The leader could pick out the sound of the challenger's breathing from the breathing that emanated from the rest of them. The leader's hearing was that acute. And the challenger's breathing was quicker now, eager with anticipation. He was back on board.

The leader thrust out his right hand into the middle of the circle. The others sensed it rather than saw it. Person by person, they thrust out their right hands, too, one hand placed atop another, until there was a stack of hands rising up and up and up, a living tower.

"Rebels of Light," the leader said.

"Rebels of Light," the others murmured in unison back to him.

He gave them their instructions, the maneuvers that would initiate the final fury, and then he dismissed them. No one said "Good luck" to anyone else. Luck had no part in this.

They left one by one, first pausing at the door to check out the wet silver street, their eyes moving quickly in all directions. Their senses were sharp. Then they flattened themselves against the sides of the buildings as they threaded out across the calm nocturnal landscape of New Earth.

The Very Bad Detective Strikes Again

Three days later, Violet sat cross-legged on the low stone wall outside Protocol Hall. It was just before noon. The air was sweet and bright; the sky was dotted with tiny clouds arranged with careful randomness across the surpassingly beautiful blue. The sparkling glass tip of Protocol Hall reached eagerly into that sky.

Violet still had an hour before her shift started. Her bag was on the ground beside her. Nestled in her joined-up palms was a cup of hot black coffee.

She was here early because of her new plan.

The plan pleased her. It also made her very nervous.

If it worked, she'd finally have the answers she craved about Danny. If it *didn't* work—well, then it was on to Option Number Three.

Danny might be in trouble. Wait: He already *was* in trouble. But he might be in even *bigger* trouble than just putting up with a stern talking-to by the boss, if Violet's latest theory was right. She had to get to the bottom of her new suspicion.

Following him the other day had been a really dumb idea.

So she'd decided to come at the problem from another angle. Rez had taught her that. It was the way he worked with computers. "If you can't solve something head-on," he advised her, "try the side door. If that doesn't work, try the back door. If that doesn't work, try a window. If *that* doesn't work, climb up on the roof and bust out the skylight."

Violet was in a skylight-busting mood these days, for sure.

She looked down into her cup, at the oily black coffee. It seemed to move, ever so slightly. The quiver was a result of the vibration transferred up from the ground as, just below the surface, the Intercept went about its endless collection and storage.

The coffee was way too hot to drink. That didn't matter. She had no intention of drinking it. She didn't like the taste of coffee. But it was an essential part of her plan.

She'd bought it at the small red cart outside Protocol Hall. Nobody knew the name of the man who worked there, but she could tell from his soiled, too-big clothes and from the way he stooped and hunched that Coffee Cart Guy was a new immigrant from Old Earth. He had passed her the cup with a trembling hand and taken her money and then instantly ducked his head, avoiding her eyes. He clasped his hands in front of his gray tunic and held very still, as if awaiting her permission to go on to the next customer. He acted the same way—cowering and cringing—with everybody.

Violet hated that. Why did he treat her like she was a princess or something? Why did he have to act all weird and deferential? She was a person, just like he was. But Coffee Cart Guy's behavior was typical of most new people from Old Earth. They were nervous all the time.

Maybe, Violet thought, they were afraid of being sent back. Or maybe it was because of the bad memories they carried, as surely as if they stored them in the inner folds of their dirty tunics. They'd seen things in person—terrible things, unbearable things—that Violet had seen only on a screen. From a safe distance. In a nice comfortable workstation on New Earth.

Maybe if you carried bad memories around long enough, they started to change how you walked, how you talked. How you thought.

The plaza was crowded, like always. A few minutes after Violet sat down with her coffee cup, she saw a friend named Sara Verity moving through the big glass doors. They slid shut behind her.

Sara was interning in transport logistics. She was short, round, and rumpled. She wore rectangular black glasses and had energetic-looking red hair that always reminded Violet of a series of exclamation points.

"Anything yet?" Sara said.

Violet knew what she meant, because she'd heard the question from just about everybody lately: *Did you have your intervention?*

"Nope."

"I bet the waiting is the toughest part. That's what they say, anyway." Sara's plaid bag was slung across her shoulder, leaving her hands free. With her right one, she absentmindedly stroked the tiny scar in the crook of her left elbow.

"Want to sit down?" Violet asked. She followed up the invitation with a silent burst of internal passion: *Please say no, please please.* Her desperation had nothing to do with not liking Sara. It came from the fact that she planned to meet Danny here before her shift started—and in order for her scheme to work, she needed to be alone with him. Violet wanted to be polite to her friend—but she fervently hoped that Sara would turn her down.

Sara shook her head. "Sorry. Can't. I've got to get going. But thanks. Maybe I'll see you later."

"Sure."

Sara waved and moved on, merging with the people on the plaza.

Violet watched the crowd for another few minutes. She shifted the position of her hands around the cup. Doubts had begun to slide into her thoughts, slowly at first but faster now, the longer she waited.

Maybe she should just give up. Abandon her plan. Stop asking questions. Forget about trying to find out why Danny kept breaking the rules. Honor his request to be patient. And just trust him.

It would be so much easier that way.

She was about half a second from canceling the whole thing—she could dump out the coffee and tell Danny she didn't actually have time for a walk today before work—when he showed up.

Violet's heart did that funny lurching thing it always did when she saw him. She'd worn long sleeves today. No worries over the tiny blue flash.

"Hey," she said.

"Hey," he said. He took the spot next to her on the low wall.

Danny didn't have his uniform on because he wasn't working today. He wore the clothes he'd brought from Old Earth: a faded brown work shirt and brown pants. Neither were quite right for him. The shirt was too big and the pants were too short. There was a time, when she'd first met him, that Violet almost said something to him about his Old Earth clothes. She'd seriously considered pointing out that he could fit in better—blend in—if he dressed like the people of New Earth.

Then the truth had struck her: Danny didn't *want* to fit in. He didn't *want* to blend in. Not at first, anyway. He and his brother were refugees, new immigrants, but they weren't ashamed of it—not in the way that Coffee Cart Guy was. They never shuffled their feet or hung their heads. They spoke up when they wanted to. They didn't care who knew they were from Old Earth. In fact, they seemed proud of it.

"Glad you called," Danny said. "I thought you were still mad at me."

"I am."

"But you said you wanted to get together."

"Well," she said, "maybe I'm mad—*and* I want to get together. They're not mutually exclusive, Mayhew."

He laughed. "You're complicated. Guess I'll never figure you out."

She lifted her coffee cup. "You want this? I haven't had a drop."

He looked puzzled. "Why'd you buy it? You hate coffee. You're a tea girl."

"It's all they had. And I like having something hot to wrap my hands around." She blushed. She hadn't meant to sound flirty—in fact she had an excellent reason for buying hot coffee on a warm day, one that she would never disclose to Danny—but the moment the words were out of her mouth, she realized they sounded like a dirty joke.

"This is New Earth. It's eighty-two degrees."

"Like you said—I'm complicated." She handed him the cup. She moved too fast, spilling a small drop on his sleeve. "Sorry," she said, dabbing at the fabric.

"No problem."

"Come on," Violet said. "I've got to get some exercise before my shift." She picked up her bag, flung the strap over her shoulder, and rose.

"Sounds good." He stood up, too, finishing the cup in two long swallows.

"Wow," Violet said. "That was, like, *really* hot coffee. How'd you drink it like that?"

"It's just a matter of ignoring the shreds of melted flesh hanging from the roof of your mouth."

She grinned. These were the moments she loved: just spending time with Danny. Enjoying the bright simple pleasure of his company and feeling that he was enjoying her company as well. No emotional baggage. No mysteries. Only the soul-deep satisfaction of being in the presence of someone you really liked.

Sometimes she wondered why it couldn't be like this all the time: Hanging out. Talking and laughing. Kidding around. Being serious and then not being serious. Discussing the stars and the planets and the books they were reading and too-hot coffee.

But deep inside, she knew why.

Because he was Danny Mayhew.

Because he was Kendall Mayhew's brother, and because Kendall Mayhew had invented the Intercept.

Because she was Violet Crowley, and because her father was Ogden Crowley, president of New Earth. Both she and Danny were tangled up in all kinds of things that had nothing to do with them— not really—and yet they couldn't break free of those things. They couldn't *not* be part of their families. They couldn't be anybody else other than who they were.

And because Danny wouldn't stop going down to Old Earth.

And because Violet had to find out why.

"So—no intervention yet," he said. "Must be pretty nerve-racking."

"Yeah. Maybe that's why I've been having trouble sleeping."

"Makes sense."

They had paused in front of the Cab, one of Violet's favorite buildings. It was composed of a cluster of giant white pipes of varying heights that were punctured by small octagonal windows. The pipes jutted up so high that each time she leaned her head back to see just how tall they actually were, she got a neck-ache.

"Cab" stood for Central Administration Building. Like a lot of acronyms, though, it had long ago broken free of the dry dock of its original meaning and now was known exclusively by its shorthand initials. It was the Cab. Nobody called it the "Central Administration Building" anymore. If somebody did, other people would stare, wondering what they were talking about.

On the walk here, Violet and Danny had discussed everything from the novel she had taken from her father's bookshelf and started reading—it was about five centuries old and the title was the main guy's name, *David Copperfield,* and it was okay, she said, but way too long—to Danny's description of the new fitness regulations Callahan had put in place a few weeks ago. The chief thought her officers were getting fat and sloppy, he explained. The Intercept was doing their work for them. They were slacking off. "But it's not really like that," he added. "I mean, we still have to go and secure the scene, you know? Make sure the perp's in cuffs and the victims are safe. It's not like we can just sit in front of a screen all day." A sheepish smile. "No offense to you guys in Protocol Hall."

Violet laughed. "Oh, come on. Takes more than that to rile me up. But I still get a free shot as payback."

She punched his arm playfully, and he punched hers back. At this moment, she felt completely relaxed and happy. She had another fleeting impulse to ditch her little scheme. She wanted to sink inside this day and pull it over her head like the soft warm covers of her bed, and sort of float away on the feeling.

But she couldn't. Because no matter how serene she felt right now, she knew her curiosity wouldn't leave her alone. Danny would do it again. Tomorrow, the next day, the day after that—he'd go back to Old Earth. He always did.

And Violet *had* to know why.

By the time they reached the Cab, she was ready.

"When people mention the Intercept," she said, trying to make her voice sound casual, as if the question had just occurred to her, "does it hit you? Is it like—'Hey, my brother *invented* that.' Does it ever feel weird that way?"

"Sure. Sometimes."

"And?"

"And—what?"

"And so what do you *do*? The memories—don't they ever—well, bother you? Memories of Kendall, I mean."

Danny looked out across the gardens that surrounded the Cab. That was why people lingered here; the gardens were the most sumptuous ones on New Earth, unspooling in a color-rich, texture-varied, scent-infused medley of thick leaves and wild blossoms and nodding ferns. The gardens looked random but really weren't. In fact, they were about as far from random as you could get. The gardens had been meticulously planned, right down to the precise placement of the ladybugs on the hosta leaves—leaves that had been propagated to grow to precisely the eye level of a person of average height.

Violet's choice of a conversational topic wasn't random either.

But she hoped Danny would think it was.

"Sometimes it's really painful," he said. "But I don't want to forget him. So I *need* those memories. They're all I have of him now. So even if they hurt—I'll put up with it."

Violet didn't know a lot about Kendall Mayhew. She only knew what everybody else knew: the story of his genius and then his tragic early death. She and Danny had talked about Kendall now and again, but she'd never pushed for details. That's why she felt okay about asking the questions today. If Danny wanted to talk about his brother, fine. If not—well, that was fine, too.

Or so he'd think.

Danny and Kendall had been invited to New Earth four years ago. Only a handful of new immigrants were allowed to enter these days, but the Mayhew brothers were special—because Kendall Mayhew, after years of work in a scruffy, makeshift lab back on Old Earth, a place filled with jury-rigged equipment and ragtag, scavenged materials, had invented the Intercept. And it was a package deal: If Kendall came, then Danny got to come, too.

Danny was not like his brother. He was smart, yes, but no genius. Whereas Kendall definitely *was* a genius. Danny's preference—he had told Violet this many times—was not to spend long, motionless hours staring at a batch of computers, watching code dump itself out on a screen like breakfast cereal shaken out of a box.

Danny was restless. He craved action and change. He'd rejected Kendall's world of advanced biostatistics and molecular genetics and diffuse axonal transfiguration. "And of sitting on my butt in front of a computer screen until it grows right into the chair," Danny had

added, as he and Violet talked about it during one of their long walks
across New Earth. Violet understood. That butt-growing-into-the-
chair thing—it pretty much described her job at Protocol Hall. She
knew what Danny meant. Sometimes she got restless, too, just
sitting there.

So Danny became a cop. The training was rigorous and demanding, although in some ways that training didn't make a lot of sense
anymore. With the Intercept now fully functional, cops had few
chances these days of putting it to the test.

A year and a half ago, Kendall had died of a drug overdose. He'd
slipped back down to Old Earth, tracked down a dealer, and took a
lethal dose of deckle. His body was found sprawled in a wet, cold,
lonely alley. No one had known about his drug use. Not even his
brother.

Kendall's death was a mystery that had settled over Danny's life
like a gray fog. That's how he described it to Violet, the few times they
talked about it. He couldn't shake it off. It was as if the grief had been
absorbed by his skin. It was a part of him now. It moved when he
moved. Breathed when he breathed.

And that was how she had come up with her awful, terrifying,
unthinkable but oddly plausible theory about why Danny kept
going down to Old Earth. That was why she was ready to deploy
Option Number Two in her quest to discover the secret of Danny's
stubbornness.

They began walking again, backtracking toward Protocol Hall.
Violet was nervous. She had to be very delicate. Also somewhat
devious, which didn't feel good at all.

"What was he like?" she asked.

"What do you mean?"

"Your brother. I've never asked you before because I didn't want
to be like everybody else. I mean, people are always coming at you
with questions about Kendall, right?"

"Yeah. They are." Danny hesitated. "Kendall was a genius."

"I don't want to know about the genius part. I want to know about the brother part."

This time the hesitation went on even longer. "It's hard to talk about him," Danny said. And then he seemed to rally. He'd give it a try. "My brother was funny and brave. He had a sense of adventure. He was—he was a great brother." There was a trace of hoarseness in Danny's voice, and it was softer than normal, but Violet could hear him perfectly well. It was as if his words had carved out a little cave in the middle of the day, a small, perfect place with room enough for just the two of them. "He was the best."

The moment had arrived, Violet realized. If she didn't go for it right now—when their conversation was close and easy, when his defenses were down—she'd lose her nerve.

"Danny."

"Yeah?"

It was harder than she'd thought it would be. It was almost impossible to get the words out. But her hunch wouldn't leave her alone.

To the question she'd been asking herself for months now—*What's on Old Earth that you can't get on New Earth?*—she'd finally come up with a possible answer:

Deckle. The drug that had killed Kendall Mayhew.

Or maybe another illegal drug. Maybe tumult or trekinol, one of the other mind-scrambling, mood-shifting, life-threatening substances bought and sold daily on the ravaged streets of Old Earth. Hard to get on New Earth—but depressingly easy to buy down there.

She blurted it out, eager to get the questions over with as soon as possible: "Are you—are you taking deckle, Danny? Like Kendall did? Is that why you go down there? To get more?"

His answer came almost before she'd finished the question. "No," Danny said.

She believed him. She knew he was telling her the truth. She just knew it. But she also knew that she'd needed to ask the question.

Because some people didn't show the symptoms of illegal drug use until it was much too late. It had been too late for Kendall.

If Danny had answered yes, if he had admitted to being in that kind of trouble, then she would have done whatever she could for him. She would not have abandoned him. And she would not have stopped loving him.

You didn't love someone because he was perfect. You loved him because you loved him.

"I'm sorry you even had to think that," Danny went on. "For even a second. I'm sorry that anything I've done made you go there. I'm not taking deckle. I've never taken an illegal drug in my life. That's something I would never—" He swallowed hard. "Never. Never. I would *never* do that. And not just because of what happened to Kendall. Because it's wrong."

He turned to face her. There was sadness in his eyes, and a kind of weary, beaten-down disillusionment, too. All at once, he looked almost as exhausted as he'd looked when he last returned from Old Earth, after all the shaking and jarring.

But this time, it was another kind of jarring that had taken its toll on him. The emotional kind. He had just realized that her choice of topic wasn't accidental.

"So that's why you wanted to talk about Kendall," he snapped. "That's why you were asking me about my brother. You were—what? Trying to soften me up? Hoping to trick me into confessing that I'm a drug addict, too? Was that it, Violet? I asked you to trust me. To just be patient and trust me. But you couldn't do that. You had to keep pushing.

"By the way—I saw you," he continued. Resentment hardened his voice. "When you followed me. You didn't see me, but I saw you. I saw you going after that guy you thought was me. And now you're doing it again. Snooping around.

"Next time," he said brusquely, "don't pretend you just want to take a walk, okay? Don't try to fool me."

He bolted away before she could figure out what to say. By the time she did, he was so far away that she had to raise her voice. "Danny—wait—it's not—"

He didn't turn back.

Great. She'd hurt him. She'd wounded and disappointed somebody she cared about. And she wasn't one bit closer to solving the mystery.

Violet gritted her teeth in frustration. She hiked the strap of her bag higher up on her shoulder. She watched Danny's fast-moving figure until he was just a brown blur, a blur that merged with the midday colors of the horizon of New Earth. She was upset with him for taking off like that, and she was annoyed with herself, and she was worried that, unless she ran all the way back to Protocol Hall, she was going to be late for her shift.

Mixed in with all of *those* feelings was yet another one: simple relief. So drugs weren't the reason Danny kept doing what he did. Drugs didn't make him hop down to Old Earth every chance he got, infuriating Chief Callahan, imperiling everything he'd achieved since he and Kendall had come to New Earth, everything he'd worked for, everything that mattered to him.

But if *that* wasn't the real reason, then what was?

Violet had one more trick up her sleeve to help her discover the truth about Danny. Option Number Three was far more drastic and intrusive. She'd really hoped she wouldn't have to use it.

That hope was now officially gone.

The Intercept Strikes

I t hit.

It happened the next morning. Violet had just finished breakfast. She was back in her room with a glass of orange juice, sitting cross-legged on her unmade bed, using her wrist console to catch up on the news.

Her father was already gone; he always left for work when it was still dark outside. A big black car picked him up at the curb in front of their apartment and ferried him away to his office.

Violet twisted the small dial on the side of her console. She rarely paused to read more than a headline before racing on to the next, the next, the next, the next.

She saw a flash of color in front of her eyes.

Blue.

No—red.

Okay: blue *and* red.

And purple. And yellow.

Wait—green. Yes, green. Green! Green, brown, black, pink, white, gold—and swirling combinations of other colors, too, chopped and blended into spinning frenzies. The colors seethed and hovered and then zipped away, as if they had pressing business elsewhere.

Violet was suddenly dizzy. The dizziness seemed to grip her temples and shake her head from side to side. Her limbs were hot, buzzing. Her console felt unbearably heavy, too heavy for her arm. Her stomach was queasy. It lurched and it churned. The orange juice she'd swallowed felt like a burning knife, thrusting itself back up into her throat. She was afraid that she was going to throw up all over her sheets.

The Intercept, Violet thought. *It's really happening. It's starting* RIGHT NOW.

And with that, the present melted, losing its firm shape, becoming . . . something else.

Six years ago:

A bedroom.

Her mother's bedroom. The thick green curtains hang in a series of symmetrical folds at either side of the tall leaded window. Books are stacked on every surface.

The bed.

The smell of death.

Her mother lies in the middle of that bed, covered only by a flimsy white nightgown. Her long red hair is spread out around her head in a soft wavy fan. She is sweating. The heat rises from her in twitchy little waves. Even the gossamer-light garment seems to torment her everywhere it touches.

Lucretia Crowley's skin is orange. Her arms are straight at her sides. Her eyes are open, and Violet can see that the whites of her eyes are now orange, too.

Missip Fever.

Violet is ten years old. She feels a stabbing pain, as if someone is hammering a nail into the center of her stomach. She even looks down to check. But, no. Nothing there. What she feels is the unfathomable pain of watching her mother die.

Her mother has just returned from one of her trips to Old Earth. Lucretia is a doctor. She has long been upset by the fact that few nurses or doctors live on Old Earth anymore. She cares about the people down there, and she would have stayed permanently to treat them, Violet knows, were it not for her love for her and her father. As it is, she goes back much too often, helping as many patients as she can. Lucretia repeatedly visits the worst parts of Old Earth, the rawest, roughest, and most dangerous places, and treats the sick and the dying.

But now those risks have caught up with her.

The first symptoms of Missip Fever appeared an hour after her return this time. Now, Violet's beautiful mother is in the final throes of the terrifying disease: the crushing fatigue, the sheet-soaking sweats, the cough, the bright orange phlegm, the overripe-fruit smell of the breath, signaling the breakneck disintegration of the lungs, the liver, the kidneys, pancreas, the heart. Name your organ, and Missip Fever shreds and dissolves it.

Her mother's lips move. She is trying to say something.

Violet leans over. She puts her lips next to her mother's ear. She can feel the intense heat of her mother's body, the disease-stoked furnace that is destroying her at a ferocious pace.

"Mom. Mom, I'm here," Violet whispers.

The smell is horrific. To be dying amid such a foul, rancid odor is an indignity, Violet thinks. It's as if her mother is being mocked. But there's nothing anyone can do about it.

"Vi . . . Vi . . . Violet . . ." Lucretia's lips are cracked and split. Watching them as they try to form a word is excruciating.

Where is her father? Violet looks around. There he is: back in the corner, hunched over, clutching the knob of his cane with his trembling right hand, the other hand locked into a fist, his face a tight mask of fierceness. Ogden Crowley has said his good-byes. He wants Violet to have this moment with her mother.

"Mom," Violet says. "Mom, I love you."

Lucretia's eyes slide up and over to meet her daughter's eyes. She is too weak to move any other part of her body. Her lips flutter again. There is something she must say:

"Ta . . . take. Care. Of . . . of your fath . . . your father. He . . . he needs you."

"I will, Mom. I promise," Violet replies, even though she can't imagine Ogden Crowley ever needing anyone—except for the woman who is dying in front of their eyes.

Violet feels the tears wetting her cheeks. She didn't know she was weeping. But she is. She's been weeping for the past hour. Maybe longer. She didn't realize she had this many tears inside her.

With the last bit of strength she can summon, Lucretia blinks. It means, Violet believes, that her mother hears her, that she's aware of Violet's promise. They have exchanged precious gifts in this moment: To Violet, Lucretia has given the gift of her trust; to her mother, Violet has given the gift of being worthy of that trust.

Lucretia's body is rocked by a spasm. When the spasm is finally over, she lies still. Her eyes seem to be looking past Violet, past this room, past this moment, past love and pain and disease, into the heart of a distance that the living will never visit.

No, Violet thinks. She is gripped by panic. *No, this CANNOT be happening. No, no, no.*

She needs to do something—to yell at somebody, to insist, to cajole. To pray, to threaten, to beg, to plead, to swear, to scream, to demand. To hit somebody. There's been a mistake. A terrible, terrible mistake.

But she doesn't do anything. Because there is nothing to be done. There is no escape from this moment. No way out.

Violet is quiet. She looks at the body in the bed, her gaze moving fitfully up and down and sideways, trying to take it all in, every inch of her mother, for the last time. She sees the lacy trim across the bottom hem of the nightgown. She sees the horrid orange skin. She sees her mother's red hair. She sees her mother's feet—such tender, intimate things, feet are. Violet reaches down to pull the sheet over those feet. Funny how most people want to cover the face, but for Violet, it's the feet that seem most private, most deserving of her protection.

Wait—did her mother twitch?

Oh my God—is she still alive? Do I have another minute with her, another few seconds, one second?

I'll take it, Violet thinks, frantic with joy. *I'll take it. Is she—?*

No. It's an illusion. Her mother is gone. Forever.

That truth is like a savage blow. Violet staggers backward. It is unendurable. She can't go on. But she must.

And now, right now, right here, it was happening all over again, the massive sadness that was like a great black wall, blocking every direction in which she tried to turn her mind, to move her thoughts. She couldn't get away from it. No matter where she went, no matter how fast she ran, it would still be with her.

It *was* her.

I can't stand this feeling. Those are the words that crowded through Violet's entire being. Right now, those were the only words she recognized. They struck her mind one by one, a heavy bell's grim tolling:

I

Can't

Stand

This

Feeling

And yet she had to. She had no choice. It was part of her, this anguish. A vital part. It ran in her blood. It sent its threads groping deep into her bones to find a place to root. It branched throughout her body.

There is no escape.

She couldn't move or breathe. She couldn't think. The emotion thickened, coarsened, swelled up, so that it was even more powerful now than it had been the first time around, when she actually *experienced* it. She had no more will, no more fight left in her. She couldn't win against an enemy that was inside her. That *was* her. She was helpless.

Which was the point all along.

And so the Intercept had beaten her. It had beaten her without firing a shot or heaving a rock or even making a threat. It had won.

It always did.

Holdup

"Hey—so how was it?"

Shura was waiting for Violet outside the giant glass doors of Protocol Hall. Violet had just finished her shift. The sky was a lemony yellow, tailing off to olive green at the edges.

Just before her shift started, Violet had sent Shura a quick message from her console: *Done.* Shura would understand. They had discussed a long time ago how Violet would let Shura know it had happened.

And then Violet had added a brief coda to her note: *Meet in plaza after work.*

Shura followed up her greeting by tucking an arm around Violet's arm and bumping against her hip. They walked in casual lockstep across the crowded plaza, turning as a twosome when they needed to turn, zigging and zagging through the crowd. "Okay," Shura went on. "Was it, like—was it *unbearable*? Or sort of okay? Or *what*?"

"Rough." Violet couldn't think of what else to say right then.

But that was the beauty of a best friend. A best friend didn't always need words to get what you were saying.

"So we guessed right," Shura said. "It was about your mom. The Intercept picked the day your mom died."

"Yeah."

"Are you okay?"

"Yeah." And she was. Well—she would be okay. Eventually. First she needed to scrape off the residue of the memory, the feeling of grief and sadness that still clung to her.

The day's only bright spot—and it surprised her—had come when Reznik offered to finish up the last few minutes of their shift by himself. It was a slow day, and he could handle the resolution codes single-handedly. He knew Violet had gone through her intervention that morning; the Intercept activation was part of the official archive now.

"I was thinking about you all day," Shura said. "Wondering, I mean. About how it went. Was it—was it close to the real thing? To how it felt when she—" She paused. Her curiosity was at war with her concern for her friend.

"Yeah," Violet said. She knew she'd practically worn out that word, just in the last few minutes. "Actually, it was worse."

"Worse?"

"It's like it comes back even stronger. The feeling, I mean. Like it picks up speed or something on its way back—speed and force." Violet was talking rapidly now. "You think you can handle it and you're doing okay—and then you're *not* doing okay at all. It's too much." She had to stop talking about it. She didn't want to get emotional. Not here, right out in the open.

"At least it wasn't real. It was just the Intercept."

Violet stopped walking. She detached herself from Shura's arm, moved a step away. "What do you mean—'It wasn't real'? Of course it was real. I was *there*. My mother died."

"I mean the intervention. It wasn't the real thing. It was just a simulation."

"A simulation." Violet shook her head. She was surprised at how little Shura seemed to understand. "No. It was the real thing. It happened all over again. It wasn't like a play, like something based on that day. It *was* that day. Although, if anything, it was harder than that day. The day it happened, the first time around."

"But how—"

"I don't know. But it was." Violet wasn't mad. She was just sort of . . . shocked. Shocked that Shura didn't get it.

They started walking again. Neither of them said, "Let's start walking again, okay?" They just did it, both at the same time. And somehow they knew they were going to Perey Park.

Which was another quality shared by best friends, even best friends you were currently disappointed with. Little synchronicities like that happened all on their own. Violet instantly forgave her. You couldn't expect someone to comprehend an intervention unless she'd been through it.

"Have you talked to Danny about it yet?" Shura asked.

"No."

"I just thought that—because of Kendall Mayhew and all—you'd, like, maybe want to discuss it with him, and tell him about how his brother's machine had—"

"No." It came out sharper than Violet had intended it to.

"What's going on, Violet?" Now it was Shura's turn to stop.

With all these stops, Violet thought ruefully, *we'll never make it home.*

"What do you mean?"

"I mean that you're acting weird," Shura declared. "I know the intervention was difficult. And I know how much you loved your mother. But this is something else. Is it about Danny? Promise me you're not still following him."

"I'm not."

"But it *is* about him, right?"

The area around the park had grown even darker now. They had not passed anyone in several minutes. They were deep into their conversation and so neither of them saw the wiry figure until it had leaped out of the shrubbery lining the path and lunged at them.

Shura screamed.

And Violet realized—initially with more surprise than fear, although the fear wasn't far behind—that the object being thrust repeatedly at her face was the ugly snout of a slab gun.

Writhing black hair.

Thin, haggard face.

A snarled rat's nest of curses, uttered in a low continuous mumble.

Those were Violet's impressions of their assailant. She felt a quick crease of fear in her belly, but then that feeling, like the surprise, vanished.

The man didn't have a chance.

He made a wild grab for Shura's bag. Before his hand could close around the strap, his head snapped back. He looked as if he'd been zapped with an electrical charge, although nothing and no one had touched him. He staggered backward, flailing wildly as he flopped onto the ground.

The slab gun flew out of his hand. His body stretched and folded and stretched and folded again like an amped-up accordion. He bucked and he shook. His words came out in bitten-off shrieks of panic:

"No, Buster, no! Bad dog! Bad dog! NO! DON'T! Don't run out in front of the car! Buster—No!—You can't—"

He exploded into sobs, sobs that seemed to be clawing their way out of his throat in a frenzy of grief. He pulled at his hair, yanking it out in greasy black hunks. Spittle foamed over his lower lip. He pounded the ground with his fists.

Violet had seen the Intercept in action multiple times—she'd lost count, frankly, given her job—but each time, she was surprised all over again by its speed and power and efficiency. Emotions were more dangerous, more self-destructive, than guns or knives, than bombs or poison, than sticks or rocks or ropes. They were killers.

She touched her wrist console. Reznik's face popped up on her screen.

"You guys okay?" he said.

"We're fine. Right?" Violet looked over at Shura. Shura was breathing heavily, and she was obviously shaken up, but she gave Violet a thumbs-up, all the same. Violet's eyes came back to her console. "Good work, Rez," she said.

"Not a problem. I'm just glad I stayed late tonight. They asked me to help out with park surveillance. Everything's under control." Rez tucked his bottom lip under the upper one. He gave Violet a small, honest smile. "It was hard to see you in that kind of situation," he went on. "Vulnerable, I mean. Even though I knew there was no real danger—not with Steve Reznik on the job." Then he blushed. Violet saw it clearly on her console.

When someone liked you a lot more than you liked him, it wasn't a good situation. It didn't make you feel at all superior. Violet was uncomfortably aware of the imbalance in her relationship with Rez.

And yet—she couldn't stop the thought from coming—she fully intended to exploit it in the near future. To take advantage of his technical skills for her own purposes. Did that make her a terrible person?

Okay, maybe it sort of does. Whatever.

Rez was still talking. "Hey—do you guys want to see the guy's Intercept feed?"

"Yeah," Violet said. "Actually, I do." She was always interested in what lay waiting in the dank basements of people's memories, ready to reach up and strike them. She wanted to see what had taken down their assailant.

"Hold on. I'll send it to your console. Turns out it was a childhood memory."

Childhood memories were always the most pungent, Violet knew. They slipped between the neuronal cracks, finding nooks and niches to use as hiding places. And there the memories waited. They waited until they were reawakened, freshly harrowing, by the Intercept.

"Thanks, Rez. See you around."

"Yeah." He nodded. "Sending the feed right now."

While Violet was speaking with Rez, two cops had arrived to perform the post-incident maneuvers. Their blue tunics were smooth and clean. Each took an arm, carrying off the trembling, babbling attacker and hoisting him into the back of the police van. He would be processed into a secure facility. Eventually he would regain his emotional poise. He'd stop sobbing. Stop ripping out his hair. But the newly revived memory, like burned flesh, would go on hurting him for a very long time, scalding its way down through all the layers.

Violet switched her console to reception mode. The man's Intercept feed flared to life on the screen.

At the moment he jumped at them, a surveillance drone had picked up the disruption. Reznik, watching from Protocol Hall, initiated the intervention. The assailant's brain was marinated in a memory. Violet watched his emotions as they swept over him:

The feel of Buster's square brown head as the dog rests it on his knee.

The warmth of the dog's heavy, steady breathing.

The tender devotion in the animal's soft brown eyes.

And then come the sounds of fast-moving traffic on a nearby road, the raucous rumbles and metallic screeches that catch Buster's attention. The dog wants to investigate, he *has* to check it out, and so he hoists himself up on all fours and he runs at full stride and he—

"No, Buster, no! Don't—please—Buster, no!"

A startled, helpless medley of car horns.

Every nuance—the dog's big body flipping into the air when he is struck, the yelp of surprise, the nasty thump when the body hits the pavement and splits open, a mess of meat and fur and bone—is present in the man's mind.

Violet can see it on her console just as the man had seen it, blooming in his brain over and over and over again.

And over and over and over and *OVER AND OVER AND*

It is his only reality. He cannot turn away from it. The memory singes him. Engulfs him. He cannot *not* see it, cannot *not* know it. He cannot *not* feel it.

It is tearing him to shreds.

"Wow," Shura murmured. She'd moved closer to Violet so that she could see the feed, too, on the bright screen of her friend's console. "Kind of hard to watch. All that he's feeling. All that pain."

Violet was struck by the same realization that was troubling Shura: The man's suffering seemed out of proportion to his potential crime. But she couldn't reveal that to anyone. Not even Shura.

"Yeah, I guess so," Violet said. She hoped her brusqueness would cover up her uncertainty. "But he broke the law, right? He's a criminal. And if the police had done it the way they used to do it on Old Earth—rushing in and shooting and trying to take him down, going after his slab gun—we might've been injured. Other people, too."

Reznik wasn't a mean person, or an insensitive one. And neither was she. They protected people. They kept the world peaceful and safe. If Violet had been working tonight and this same incident had occurred, involving two other innocent people walking home in the park, she would've done precisely what Reznik had done: Initiate the Intercept. Disable the attacker.

They did their jobs. There was nothing more to it than that.

Right?

10

A Memory of Christmas Morning

From its place on her bedside table, Violet's console played a soft, three-note chime. She knew the ringtone well: *Danny.*

She wasn't sure what time it was, but her room was entirely dark. She had been lying in the darkness, thinking about him and the Intercept, and about a lot of other things, too. Sometimes insomnia was terrible; sometimes, though, it wasn't so bad. Darkness was a good background for deep thinking.

Violet waited for her heart rate to resume its normal rhythm and then she touched the screen to accept the call—but only on audio. She was wearing her usual T-shirt and sweats in bed, with the lights off. She didn't want him to know that.

"Hey," she said.

"Hey. I heard about what happened tonight in the park. It was in the end-of-shift report on the day's criminal activity." His voice was more agitated than she'd ever heard it. "Are you okay? Did he hurt you? How's Shura?"

"We're fine," Violet said. "She's probably asleep by now. It was no big deal."

Danny let out a long breath.

"I know the Intercept is everywhere," he said, "and I know it works and all, but when it's somebody you know—somebody you—" He stopped. "Look, Violet. I'm sorry I got so mad at you. And just walked away like that."

"You were right. I shouldn't have tried to trick you."

"I know it's frustrating. I mean, I know *I'm* frustrating. But I just can't—" Danny took another deep breath. "Someday. Someday, okay? I promise—someday I'll tell you everything. Until then, you've just got to—"

"I've just got to trust you," Violet said, interrupting him. "Right. Got it." She was massively disappointed. She had really thought that, in the aftermath of the attack on her and Shura, in the midst of his concern for her, he might relent. Let her inside his mind.

But—no.

Still no answers.

"Yeah," he said.

"Okay." *Fine,* Violet thought. The third and final option she'd come up with to figure out Danny—the one for which she needed Rez's help—was looking better and better.

"Okay," Danny said. Even though they were sort of quarreling, he didn't want the conversation to end. Violet could tell. Because she didn't want it to end, either. "Sorry to call so late," he added. "I just had to check."

"It's fine. I wasn't asleep yet. It was a rough day even before the guy jumped out at us. I had my intervention."

"Wow. How was it?"

"Rough. Like I said." She was still miffed. She didn't want to talk about it with him right now.

He didn't push her to say more than she wanted to. He never did. "Well, I guess I'd better go," Danny said. "I'm still at the station. Had another little session with Callahan."

Violet didn't need to ask why. It could be about only one thing: Danny's defiance of the rules about trips to Old Earth.

"How'd it go?"

"Not too bad." That was his standard nonanswer answer. "She's pissed, but that's always the case."

"I'll put in a good word for you."

"What do you mean?"

"I'm supposed to have dinner with the chief and her husband. As a substitute for my dad. He's way too busy. Tell you the truth, though, I think they're going to be a little disappointed. They think they're getting the chief executive—and they get me instead."

"I wouldn't be disappointed."

Before Violet had a chance to respond, Danny was speaking again. Hurriedly. "You're sure you're okay," he said.

"Totally sure. You know how it works. That guy never touched us. The Intercept won't allow it. But you know what? Even with the work I do every day at Protocol Hall, it's still hard to watch an intervention in person. Seeing those emotions on the attack—it's pretty awful. Emotions can be so—so brutal, you know? So overwhelming."

He didn't answer right away. When he did, his voice was filled with quiet awe.

"I saw them once," he said.

"Saw what?"

"Emotions."

"Oh. Okay, yeah," Violet said. "On the screen, you mean. During an Intercept. You saw a feed."

"No. Not then. Before."

"Before," she repeated. She didn't know what he was talking about.

"Yeah. In the lab. Back on Old Earth. When Kendall was first laying the groundwork for the Intercept. Your father hadn't come down there yet. Nobody had any idea what Kendall was up to. There wasn't any Intercept. It was all just an idea in my brother's head. A crazy theory of his."

She didn't say anything, because she wanted Danny to go on. After a moment, he did.

"So Kendall called me into the lab one night. He was pretty excited. I didn't know what he was working on. I only knew that whatever it was, he'd been working on it for *years*—year after year. He barely slept anymore. He just worked. And that night, he asked me to stand in front of this big, funny-looking machine he'd mashed together from a bunch of old parts he'd swiped from other machines, things people had thrown away or forgotten about. It was connected to his computers and to the test tubes he'd lined up on dozens and dozens of shelves. They were filled with this bubbling purple stuff. Smelled awful.

"Now, to me, that machine looked like a big pile of rusty, useless junk—but if Kendall had put it together, I knew it couldn't be junk. It had to be something really special. Something *important*.

"And then he told me to close my eyes. So I did." Danny took a deep breath. Violet could hear it plainly through her console. The memory before him seemed to be like a beautiful flower, and he wanted to take it in all at once, with a great inhalation of scented air.

"When I opened them again," he went on, "Kendall was standing next to the machine. There were these funny little electrodes attached to both sides of his head, with coils running from the electrodes to the machine. And then—rising out of the top of the machine—was a big glass bowl that looked like some kind of weird aquarium. It had gloppy stuff inside it. Pink, red, blue, orange—all swirled together, rotating. Making this humming noise. And the gloppy stuff sort of twisted and . . . sort of *shimmered,* too, I guess I'd call it. Like a snow globe somebody shook up and all the little bits are flying around. Only this wasn't made up of *things*. It wasn't *objects*. It was colors. And energy. And light. It looked like it might become objects at some point—but right now it was just a kind of chaos. You could tell it needed a lot more work to become what it needed to be."

"What was it?" Violet said. She was so caught up in his story that she almost whispered it, afraid to break the spell.

"That's what I asked Kendall. And he said, 'Christmas morning, 2280.'" Danny swallowed hard. "Our mom and dad were killed a month later. And as I looked at those colors dancing around inside the glass, and I realized they'd come directly from Kendall's memory and that somehow he'd transformed the energy of his thoughts into this *other* kind of energy, which he then would be able to transfer *back* into his thoughts again—I also realized that that Christmas morning was the last time my brother and I were truly happy."

Violet leaned back against the headboard of her bed. While listening to Danny she had pulled up her knees to her chin, wrapping her arms around them. She was feeling the force of his story, the texture and density of his recollection from long ago—really, two recollections: the memory of a precious Christmas morning, and the memory of *seeing* the memory of a precious Christmas morning as it emerged from a ramshackle machine, transformed into pure energy.

Energy that would soon be repurposed. Reborn as a powerful weapon, against which there was no defense.

What Kendall had revealed to his brother that day in the lab was the first step toward his destiny. A few steps later, the Intercept was born.

11

Division 12

At night, the streets of New Earth breathed.

If Violet concentrated on it, she'd swear she could hear the ground inhaling and exhaling. It was a sort of subterranean pulse, a soothing rhythm that created a slight but persistent tremor under her feet.

The first time Violet felt it, she'd thought: *It's like a heartbeat. But no. Not a heartbeat. It's like . . . breathing. Yes.*

It wasn't steady, like a heartbeat. It was looser, more haphazard, like an on-again, off-again breeze. When she listened hard, it seemed to weave in and out of her consciousness, like something she'd known long ago but thought she'd forgotten—the lyrics of a lullaby, the faint sound of a faraway voice calling her home, a color she couldn't quite describe—and now it returned to her, as if that's just what it had planned to do, all along.

Part of it, she knew, was the vibration from the Intercept, doing its work beneath the surface of New Earth. But part of it was something else. Something magical.

Violet was walking to the Callahan home for dinner. It was just before dusk. There was a dwindling, butterscotch-colored light in the sky as the sun sagged lower and lower behind the horizon. She loved this time of day. And she loved that tremor. She loved the sensation that New Earth itself was thinking right along with her. Especially when she had a lot to think about.

Like, for instance, the memory of her mother, which was so intense right now, because of the intervention. And like, for instance, the rumor that wouldn't go away, the rumor that someone had found a way to breach the Intercept.

She knew the way to Chief Callahan's apartment, but she took a few wrong turns on purpose. Violet liked to walk. Running was best of all, but she couldn't arrive there sweaty and panting, so walking would have to do.

Sometimes, when she walked, she let herself be lulled into a sort of fugue-like state that was like dreaming while you were still awake. On she would go, led forward by the quiet breathing of these streets, the soft incessant quiver.

I wish Mom had lived long enough to meet Danny.

That was how her grief for her mother struck her sometimes. It had gone from the sweepingly general—*Mom, oh my God, I can't believe you're not here anymore, I miss you so much that I don't think I can't stand it even one more second*—to the small and specific, the particular:

I just wish I could talk to you about Coffee Cart Guy. Or how much Rez loves code. Or about how much I don't love David Copperfield. Or the rumors about the Intercept breach. Or about . . . Danny.

Her mother would understand. Violet was certain of that.

If you'd ever had a chance to meet him, Mom, you'd know why I fell in love with him. And you could've helped me explain it to Dad. He'd listen to you.

She walked on. The streets breathed in and out.

Michelle Callahan was old. She was almost as old as Violet's father, and he was *really* old. She had gray hair that she tied back into a small knob. Her eyes were gray, too. And yet there was a lightness to her, a nimbleness, that had somehow survived the pileup of all those years.

She had yet to change out of her police tunic. Violet figured that probably meant she'd had a very long day and had just arrived home. Callahan, like her dad, spent more time at work than anywhere else.

"Hi, Violet. Come on in," Callahan said. "Sorry your father couldn't make it, but we're really glad to have you join us tonight."

She took Violet's jacket and led her into the living room. Paul Stark, Callahan's husband, was sitting in an easy chair. Violet had always found him vaguely creepy, and she hoped it wasn't because of the HoverUp and its incessant *whish-whoosh* sound—which would make her a very bad person, of course. Someone who couldn't get past the superficial.

The apartment looked a lot like the one in which Violet and her father lived. It was square and beige, with pieces of furniture occupying the spots you would expect them to. New Earth was a place of careful ratios and balance and proportionality. The sole exception to that rule, Violet thought with pleasure, was her father's library; it was a beautiful mess. It was also the only room she had ever known that could surprise her.

Stark directed his HoverUp closer to Violet in order to shake her hand. The *whish-whoosh* sound intensified as he did so. Newer models of the HoverUp were completely silent, but the originals made that distinctive sound, the sound of air rushing through hundreds of millions of tiny silicon coils as the device propelled itself. Stark had been one of the first to use one.

Violet's father had told her Paul Stark's story. He had once been a hotshot cop, young and brash and fearless, a legend on Old Earth. Marked for great things. Headstrong. Rebellious. The way her father described him, he sounded a bit like Danny Mayhew.

No, Violet had corrected herself. *A lot like Danny Mayhew.*

"When it came time to install Intercept chips in the population of Old Earth," Ogden had said, continuing the tale, "I assumed we would meet strong resistance. The people down there just don't know what's good for them. So I sent the toughest cop I knew to head up the unit—Paul Stark. He'd worked a lot of years on Old Earth before New Earth was constructed. And that's when it happened."

"What?" Violet had asked.

"He was chasing down a man who'd refused the chip insertion. Paul had just caught up with him when the man pulled out a slab gun. One shot. That's all it took. The lower half of Paul's spinal cord instantly melted. His legs—" Ogden had paused, as the memory of the horror overtook him. He shook his head and continued. "He died at the scene."

"Died?" Violet had said. "But—"

"He was revived in seconds by his partner. He hadn't been dead long enough for any brain damage and thus he was fully able to comprehend—even as he lay there, writhing in silent agony, once his breathing resumed—that his life was irreparably altered now. He was half of what he'd been. Half of him still had skin and bone and muscle. Half of him still responded to his will. The other half was a gelatinous mass, a boiling puddle that spread across that dirty pavement. I'm sorry to be so graphic, Violet, but you need to know what a slab gun can do. You need to know why the Intercept is worth it—so that in the future, a good man like Paul Stark won't have to go through that kind of hell. Ever, ever again."

Violet nodded. The words indeed had been hard to hear. But she was glad her father had trusted her with the story. She wasn't a child anymore. He was right: She needed to know.

"It kind of makes you wonder," she had said to her father that day, thinking aloud, "if the partner who brought him back to life really did him a favor, after all."

Ogden nodded. "That partner was his wife. It was Chief Callahan."

"Paul made his specialty for us tonight," Callahan said. "Tomato basil soup. Right, dear?"

There was an awkward silence.

"Yeah," Stark finally said.

Violet realized, with the kind of intuition that came naturally to her, that both of them were lying. Stark had not made the soup. He was supposed to have, but he hadn't gotten around to it, and when Violet rang the doorbell, they were probably arguing fiercely about it.

"I'm going back in the kitchen to finish up some things," Callahan said. "Paul, I'll let you entertain Violet for a few minutes."

Um, thanks, Violet thought. *Great.* She wondered if the Intercept had a special category for sarcasm-fueled feelings. She'd never checked.

"Have a seat," Stark said. His sour tone didn't match the welcome of his words.

Violet gave him her best fake smile as she sat.

"Michelle's mad at me because I didn't cook dinner," Stark said casually. "I told her I would."

"Oh." Violet didn't know what to say. Was she supposed to be on his side? Tell him it was okay? It wasn't okay. Based on what her father told her, Chief Callahan worked tremendously hard. The least her husband could do was cook a meal for company.

"I got busy," Stark said, as if she'd asked the question out loud. There was petulance, not apology, in his tone.

"Okay."

The only sound in the room for a long time was the *whish-whoosh* of his HoverUp. Violet had never really looked at him before. Now she did. His hair was gray, like his wife's hair, but he wore it so short that the color was only visible in a series of dots covering his scalp. A cop's hairstyle, blunt and simple. Only he wasn't a cop.

Not anymore.

He was still a relatively handsome man—before his accident, he was everybody's pick for Sexiest Cop in Division 12 on Old Earth— but the years of dealing with pain and frustration had carved deep grooves on his face and left a kind of hollowness around his eyes. Those eyes were cloudy now. The chiseled chin sagged, having collapsed without a fight into the flesh of his neck. It was the dull gray stamp of despondency.

A HoverUp looked like a small shoebox on which Stark stood while millions of powerful air jets directed his artificial legs and his arms and his torso, pushing them, lifting them, arranging them, enabling his body to move on its own in response to his silent mental commands. Sometimes Violet could completely miss the fact that the person was hurt at all—that's how smoothly a HoverUp did what it did. She sort of forgot about the small humming rectangle attached to the bottom of the feet. All she saw was fleetness and freedom. The HoverUp meant that somebody like Stark wasn't stuck in a wheelchair—yet from the way he acted, Violet thought, he must still feel stuck. Only now he was stuck in his life. And it showed on his face.

She knew other people who used HoverUps as a result of injuries and they weren't like Paul Stark. They weren't bitter. They didn't think of their lives as something lesser, something different and inferior. It made her realize that his real problem, whatever it was, had nothing to do with the HoverUp.

She wondered what Stark had been like back when he was a rugged young cop like Danny. Back when he saw himself as whole. Back when he could run. Back when he had hope.

A few days after her father told her about Stark's accident, he had told her the rest of the story.

"On Old Earth," Ogden said, "cops are all that stand between the people and total chaos." He was sitting in his armchair that night, a stack of reports on his lap. He had looked up from his work when Violet came home from Protocol Hall and asked her to draw up a chair next to him.

"They had to keep the peace in a place where the criminals had nothing to lose—and still don't," Ogden went on. "That's what made Stark and Callahan so special. They stayed above the fray. They didn't let that stinking, dangerous world down there ever get to them. Old Earth people—they're like feral cats. When strangers come along they instantly scatter and hiss, escaping into cracks and crevices. They can disappear in seconds. And then all you hear is the wind moaning through those cold streets." Violet thought she spotted a small shiver in her father's shoulders after he said that.

"But no matter how bad it was down there," he went on, "I knew Callahan and Stark would get the job done. They'd get a chip inserted in every last person. It was our only hope of retaining some small bit of control over that place. So the two of them poked through piles of garbage and turned giant spotlights into the narrow passageways leading to attics and basements and caves. They stormed every potential hideout. They rounded up a great many citizens of Old Earth. They sedated them and implanted them with chips. And then they let them go.

"They could let them go because there was no longer any need to detain their physical bodies in order to correct bad behavior. We had their minds. We certainly weren't going to waste our time monitoring Old Earth all the time, but when we needed to—we were firmly in control." At that point Ogden had given Violet a satisfied smile. The smile faded again. "Then came the terrible day when Stark and Callahan were chasing one of the last holdouts. A man who'd refused his chip. I have watched that particular feed myself, many times. Stark was in the lead. The man suddenly stopped, twisted around, and pulled out a slab gun, aiming for Stark's lower torso. There was a flash of light. A crisp sizzling sound."

Now it was Violet's turn to shiver.

"Too much?" her father had said. He reached out his gnarled hand.

"No. I want to know about it, Dad." She held his hand while he continued.

"If Stark had had another partner, if it had been anybody other than Michelle Callahan with him that day, he surely would've died," Ogden declared. "Another cop would have been frozen with horror.

But Callahan can compartmentalize. And she was able to cordon off the part of her mind that was reeling from the shock of seeing him that way—fallen, totally helpless, the bottom half of his body a hot gurgling mess—and to save his life."

"How do you know all of this?"

"Callahan told me herself. And I'm telling you so that you'll know what Old Earth is really like. And maybe you'll stop asking me to go."

Nice try, Dad, Violet had thought. *I think they call that a scare tactic. And it won't work. I'll see it one day. Just you wait.*

The dinner was turning out to be so dull that Violet thought she might scream, just to liven things up.

She didn't. Instead she smiled a polite, practiced, *this-is-me-smiling* smile and watched as Callahan ladled red soup into three white bowls. The large pot was placed on a square ceramic tile; the tile was placed in the center of the round table. As Callahan finished filling a bowl, she passed it on. Violet was impressed: The chief didn't spill a drop.

Stark sat across the table from his wife. Violet was on Callahan's left. As Stark had joined them at the table, Violet watched him with grudging admiration. Sitting down was one of the most challenging maneuvers of all to learn in a HoverUp—the transfer from standing upright to bending the body at the waist and the artificial knees so that you could slide into a chair. Stark made it look easy.

"So I wanted to ask you about Danny Mayhew," Callahan said. "I know you two are good friends."

Smooth, Violet thought. *Real subtle.* She hadn't even had time to take her first sip of soup.

"What about him?"

Callahan picked up on the defensiveness in her tone. "Don't worry. I won't ask you to tell me any secrets about your friend."

Good. Because I won't. Violet tasted the soup. It was actually pretty good, a fact that she found annoying. It would've been easier to keep her resentment going if the soup was gross.

"I'd just like to know if you have any idea," Callahan said, "why he keeps going down to Old Earth."

"No."

"As I'm sure you've heard, we're at a critical point right now. You know what we're facing—a group of traitors who are trying to take down the Intercept. I need all of my officers to be focused on the crisis at hand."

Before Violet could think of a good nonanswer answer, Callahan abruptly addressed her husband: "Paul, is the soup too hot?"

He seemed startled. He'd probably zoned out when his wife had begun interrogating Violet—that was the verb Violet chose for it, because she felt as if she might as well be down at the station—and apparently didn't realize he would be forced to express an opinion.

He took a sip. "No."

So the chief's zero for two, Violet thought with a sneaky feeling of vindication. *Everywhere she goes, it's a big fat "No."*

Callahan turned back to her. "Let me be clear," she said. "I like Danny. A lot. He's one of the finest cops I've ever worked with—on Old *or* New Earth. I'm trying to help him."

"Okay." Violet looked down at her bowl. She didn't want to look at Callahan.

"I was hoping," the chief continued, "that maybe you could talk to him. Make him understand that if he doesn't stop, he's severely jeopardizing his future. I'm doing my best, but I don't know if I can protect him anymore. Not after so many times."

So I was right, Violet thought. *This whole thing was a setup. She knew my father would be too busy to come to dinner and he'd send me instead—and I'd have to sit here and listen. If I won't be a snitch, she hopes I'll be some kind of messenger or go-between or whatever.*

Being right didn't feel nearly as good as it was supposed to.

Callahan was still going. "I've known Danny since he first set foot on New Earth, did you know that? I was right there on the day when the Mayhew brothers first arrived."

"Really." Violet swallowed another mouthful of soup.

"Oh, yes. I was working border security back then." Callahan went on with her story, a story about the two young men who stepped shyly out of the rusty two-man pod. They had, she recalled, thin, famished cheeks, sunken eyes, dark hair, and bewildered expressions. You knew instantly that they were brothers, she said. They were the most important people ever to cross the threshold of New Earth—well, Kendall was, anyway—but at that moment, they were just two scared-looking teenagers among a few other scared-looking teen-agers, shuffling and murmuring, nervous and uncertain, their lives on the brink of profound change.

"Sometimes it's still hard to imagine, you know?" Callahan said. "How little we knew back then. When it was first installed, nobody really understood what Kendall Mayhew's invention was going to do for New Earth. Nobody could've predicted—no matter what they say now. Even your father wasn't sure. That's why he waited so long to bring them here, I think. He wanted to be certain that the Intercept really worked the way Kendall said it would. If it was a total disaster, he didn't want the inventor around as a constant reminder of failure."

Stark decided to join the conversation. He snickered—a mean snicker, with no amusement in it. He grinned at his wife. "Yeah," he said. "There you were, you and all those other cops, doing all those searches at the New Earth portals, looking for bombs and guns and drugs and chemical weapons. And along comes Kendall Mayhew—the guy responsible for bringing in the most dangerous weapon that either world has ever known. The Intercept. Right under your noses."

Callahan gave him a puzzled look. "Dangerous? That's a funny way to put it."

"Just trying to help you get a read on the kid," Stark said quickly. "Trying to help you figure out what's eating him. I mean, it was bound to have a big impact on Danny, right? On his work? His behavior? His brother's genius, I mean. And then Kendall Mayhew's death, coming only a couple of years after they got here. I'm just saying that you can't look at Danny the way you look at the rest of your squad. He's got some emotional baggage that we'll never understand. His problems with authority? There's your cause, right there. He's got a lot going on inside him. That crap he's always pulling—it might be his way of dealing with all those internal storms." Stark tapped the tabletop with a finger. "You can only do so much for him, Michelle. At some point, you might just have to stand down and let him get the punishment he deserves."

Violet watched the two of them facing off against each other across the table. It was as if they'd forgotten she was here.

"Abandon him, you mean," Callahan said sharply. "Let them suspend him. Maybe even fire him."

Stark shrugged. "If that's their decision, then—yeah. I know you're loyal to your squad. But at a certain point, you've got to let go."

"No. I don't."

"He's beyond any help you can give him."

"I can try, can't I?"

"Your belief in him is admirable," Stark said. "But it's not working. And it's not fair to the rest of your squad. What happens to them while you're focusing so hard on Danny Mayhew?"

"So now you're saying I'm not doing my job?"

"I'm saying that you could be doing a *better* job if you didn't spend most of your time trying to save one stubborn kid who doesn't know how good he's got it up here."

Callahan started to answer—Violet watched her lean forward, a retort at the ready—but at the last moment, she held up.

The *whish-whoosh* of Stark's HoverUp was the only sound in the room. The machine kept up its odd music even when it was at rest. Husband and wife had both put down their spoons. The soup was cooling, but neither one of them cared. Violet realized that the argument was continuing, but silently now, with their eyes alone doing the dueling.

Emotions ran roughshod over humanity, Violet reminded herself. Even the most intelligent people were helpless when caught in the vortex of those whirling, unpredictable forces. Even the toughest, hardiest, most resolute individuals could be brought low by intense feelings—by passionate love or soul-scouring grief or a hot furnace of hatred. Kings and queens who had ruled long ago on Old Earth, tyrants who had controlled the destinies of millions, had been undone by their emotions—by a passing infatuation or a sudden twist of envy or a quick knife-thrust of intense hatred. Violet had read about it. She knew.

So were emotions good things or bad things?

They were like fire, Violet decided. Fire could burn down your house or cook your tomato basil soup. Emotions could save you. Or they could destroy you.

But no matter what they did, they were *yours*. They belonged to you.

Not to the Intercept.

She was startled by that last thought. It had come unbidden, sort of sliding in sideways while her thoughts were looking the other way. It was the first time she had put it to herself quite that bluntly: Your feelings were *yours*. They were, in effect, possessions—like tablets or consoles.

Nobody had the right to take them from you without your permission.

Did they?

Callahan's voice brought her back.

"All I want you to understand, Violet," the chief said, "is that I'm in Danny's corner. I want what's best for him, too. And so if you have any idea why he keeps going down to Old Earth without authoriza—"

"Like I said, I don't." Violet's interruption came quickly. "I don't.

Really. I mean, I've told him the same thing—that it's a bad idea. But he does what he wants to do."

Callahan nodded, but she didn't seem convinced. Violet was tired of the scrutiny, tired of having a cop's eyes on her as she tried to finish her dinner. So she looked over at Stark.

His face was closed up and shut down, like usual. But she saw something stirring behind that tight mask. Or at least she thought she did.

If Violet had been forced to name it, she would have said that it was a combination of sadness and restlessness and another element, too, a furtive and forlorn one, as if Stark secretly believed he wasn't worthy of his wife's belief in him, or her love.

Or maybe, Violet thought, giving herself a little internal talking-to, *I'm just tired and I don't really want to be here and so I'm seeing things. Making stuff up. So give it a rest, girl. Finish your soup and then you can go home.*

"Okay, well—thanks," Violet said. "Really, I had a great time." She shook Callahan's outstretched hand. She turned to Stark and nodded. She hoped they couldn't sense her deep relief at the prospect of getting out of here. Words like *escape* and *freedom* were pinwheeling through Violet's mind.

They stood by the front door. Violet had just accepted her coat from Callahan and was draping it across her forearm. She had no idea why she'd brought a coat. It was warm outside. She wouldn't need a coat for the walk home—a walk she was really looking forward to, after being trapped with two old people for what seemed like a millennium. She might even run.

Yeah. I feel like running. Definitely.

Violet had almost made it out the door when everything changed.

The brash, clanging alarm was long and loud, instantly enveloping the apartment and the hall—and the world beyond, Violet surmised—

in a thrash of raucous noise. She knew what the sound was. She had heard it before, although not often; general alarms, the kind audible all across New Earth, were rare.

Callahan twitched as if she were hooked to a generator and somebody had hit MAX POWER. Her eyes went right to her console. She read the message. Then she whipped around to address Violet and Stark.

"Breach at Protocol Hall," the chief said, snapping off the words. "I have to go. Paul, can you take Violet home?"

Violet felt a flame of outrage leaping inside her. *Take me home? Really?*

"What kind of breach?" she asked, ignoring the chief's implication that she was a helpless child who needed an escort.

Callahan was swinging on her long blue coat. "I can't discuss that. Paul?"

Stark nodded and took Violet's arm. Violet shook him off. She meant to do it lightly, but she wasn't sure she had achieved that goal. She was too upset over having been so gallingly insulted. And underestimated.

"Look," she said. "I'm not a kid. I work at the Hall, okay? I have a right to know what's going—"

"Fine." Callahan barked the word. She buttoned her coat. Her voice was cold with intensity. "You want to know? Fine. *Fine.* I'll tell you. Somebody infiltrated the main circuit of the Intercept."

Violet's face must have shown how startled she was, because Callahan quickly said, "I know. I know. It's *impossible*—but it happened. A million different safety triggers should have prohibited that—including the Intercept itself. It should've kept anybody from being able to break in. Everybody's got a chip. And so the Intercept should have recognized the approach of the saboteur and initiated an intervention. And that should have shut down the crime. We should be able to go into the chamber below Protocol Hall and find that hacker moaning and screaming on the floor—with his most painful memory sparking through his brain. He should be begging us to shut off his Intercept feed. Give him back control of his mind.

"But the message was from my officers on the scene—and guess what? They have *nothing*. Somebody got in and shut down the signal and got out—and now they're long gone. The server was only off-line for four seconds. But four seconds today can be four minutes tomorrow. And four minutes tomorrow..." The chief's voice had revved up and up and up. Now she let it trail off. She jammed her hands into the pockets of her coat, diverting her anger into another channel.

So it's true, Violet thought with alarm. *Somebody* has *figured out how to thwart the Intercept. How to put themselves beyond its reach.*

It was terrifying, but it was also...

Violet was afraid to envision the word, because if she let her excitement attach itself to the raw syllables, the Intercept would pick up on it. Excitement was an emotion. An emotion would send an electrical signal to the chip under the skin in the crook of her left elbow and, as indicated by that damned blue spark, the record of what she felt would go zipping off into her file at Protocol Hall. And it might be used against her later.

So she tried to think the word very calmly, very sedately:

The breach was terrifying, but it was also kind of *exhilarating*.

Her father had told her, over and over again, that the Intercept was all that stood between the horrors of Old Earth and the beauties of New Earth. It was the last barricade between civilization and catastrophe. Yet right now, the idea that someone had outsmarted the Intercept didn't frighten her.

It intrigued her.

Violet tried to switch off the feeling of being intrigued, like someone throwing a handkerchief over a lightbulb.

Callahan had regained her sense of purpose and now rushed past her, barreling out the door and toward the elevator at a pace that was just short of a sprint. She slammed a fist against the down button.

The moment the elevator arrived, she turned around to make a final comment to Violet. "Your father's at the crime scene. I'll tell him you're on your way home."

Stark edged his HoverUp into the apartment doorway. He wanted a final word with his wife.

"Any idea who did it?" he called out.

"Security found some graffiti scratched on the wall," Callahan said. "Same group that's done a lot of damage lately. They call themselves the Rebels of Light." She lunged into the elevator, eager to be on the job. The doors hissed to a quick close and she was gone.

The Color of Love

The trouble with being a painter, Shura had pointed out to Violet many times before, was that when you gave your best friend a present, she always knew what it was before she'd even opened it.

Case in point: right now.

"Big surprise, right?" Shura said. She rolled her eyes.

She gently set down the object she'd just carried into Violet's living room, bending down to lean it against the couch and then standing upright again and backing up a few steps to study it, hands on her hips. Violet stood beside her, also with her hands on her hips.

The object was wide and flat, and it was covered in brown paper wrapping and tied off with twine. Violet knew it was a painting. Duh. *Anybody* would've known it was a painting.

But what *kind* of painting? That was the question. With Shura, you never knew.

Shura's visit was a good diversion for Violet. New Earth was a nervous place this morning. Consoles had been dinging every few seconds with news alerts. Except for people like Violet, who worked at Protocol Hall, everyone had been told to stay home. The authorities wanted to keep the streets clear for their investigation. So far, they had found nothing. No clues. No traces of how the break-in had been accomplished. Violet had had a short console conversation with her father and he confirmed it: The trail was cold.

The mystery continued.

Just after breakfast Shura's face had showed up on Violet's console. She asked if she could come by because she had something to give her.

And here she was, standing in the middle of Violet's living room, eyeing the package she'd brought as if she thought it might sneak off if she didn't keep tabs on it. She was ready for the big unveiling.

"Is your dad here?" Shura asked.

"Nope. He didn't come home last night. He's working with the police. They're trying to track down the criminals who broke into the system."

"Well, I sort of wanted him to see this, too. It's for both of you. But that's okay. I'm glad I went ahead and brought it. We've been through so much lately—I mean, having that guy try to attack us in the park, and last night's Intercept breach, plus the stuff with my mom—I think we need it now." Shura looked slightly sheepish. "That sounds pretty arrogant, right? Like art is going to make everything all right again. Like art is going to change the world."

"It's the only thing that ever has," Violet said softly. "That's what you taught me."

They were quiet for a moment. Shura didn't like compliments. She didn't know how to handle them. Violet knew that, but sometimes she had to go there anyway.

To cover her embarrassment, Shura bolted forward, ripping off the brown wrapping paper.

"It's from a photo you showed me once. On your console," Shura said. "I hope it's—I hope it's right, you know? And that it captures her? Even just a little bit." She stepped back again, to give Violet a clear view.

Violet felt a warm whispery silkiness spread through her body, as if soft, busy feathers were starting at her stomach and radiating out toward her toes and her fingertips and the top of her head.

She couldn't speak. She could only feel.

The Intercept would know what to call this emotion and where to file it—but Violet didn't. Was it joy? Was it sadness? Was it yearning? At the moment, she didn't *care* that she didn't know what to call it. It was enough just to have it. She didn't have to assign it a category.

It was a portrait of her mother.

In simple brushstrokes and basic colors like cornflower blue and bone white and jade green and ruby red, Shura had captured her mother's radiance and intelligence and endless sense of fun. Those attributes all lived in her eyes. Lucretia, dressed in a white blouse and black pants, was looking back over her shoulder, urging an unseen someone to hurry up and catch up with her. Her red hair was held back with a long white ribbon. The dangling ends of the ribbon were fluttering, flying, meaning that the breeze was spirited and intense.

Just like the woman caught so joyfully in the midst of it.

Violet remembered very well the precise moment when her father had taken that photograph. And the person her mother was waiting for was herself. She was eight years old. She could still hear, from deep in a valley in her mind, the sound of her mother's voice: *Come on, sweetheart! You'll miss the sunset! Run to the top of the hill with me, Violet! Run!*

The sky was light purple. There were yellow daisies at her mother's feet.

Gradually Violet resurfaced into the present moment. She was in her living room, right? With Shura? Reluctantly she moved her eyes away from the painting.

"It's—it's beautiful," she said.

Shura nodded. She knew she was an excellent painter. That was one of the things Violet had always appreciated about her best friend: no false modesty.

"I wanted you to have it," Shura said, "because I might not be painting much anymore."

"What?"

Shura seemed to have trouble saying the next few sentences. "It's just that—well, with everything going on, I've decided to focus on something practical. This morning I put in my application for medical school. Painting will be a hobby. But not even that, for a while. Until I finish school."

Violet was stunned. "You love to paint. You need to paint."

"Yeah."

"So when you say '*I've* decided'—what you mean is that your *parents* decided, right?"

"No. I mean—yes. It's what they want." Shura paused. "But it's what I want, too."

"Your work makes people feel. It makes *me* feel. I can look at this painting and it's like opening the door to another world," Violet said. "A world that exists outside what happened to my mom. It's all about the moment. Not about what happened *after* the moment. Or *before* the moment. It's about the now. And now is all we have. Your work tells me that. It shows me that. It *proves* it to me, over and over again. So I want you to keep painting. I want you to—"

Her friend's voice was sharp. "Just stop it, Violet, okay? Lay off. It's my decision. Not yours. It's *my* family. And *my* life. With everything my mom's going through—I just thought it was something I could do for her. To make her happy. And anyway—what's wrong with being a doctor? Your mother was a doctor."

"I didn't say there was anything wrong with it. Not if it's what you want to do. It was definitely my mom's calling. But is it yours?"

Shura did not answer.

Violet reached out toward the portrait of her mother. She didn't touch it. She didn't need to. The act of reaching out to be closer to it gave her a sense of peace, one she'd not felt in a long, long time.

"You're right," Violet finally said. "It's none of my business. Thanks for this gift. I'll cherish it. I know my father will, too."

She felt a deep crater of sadness opening up inside her. She was losing Shura—the old Shura, that is, the best friend she'd had for all these years. The old Shura was slipping away. Violet would have to get used to the new Shura. The one who wasn't a painter.

"I guess I better go," Shura said.

Violet nodded. "Yeah. Me too. My shift's coming up. Everybody's supposed to stay where they are—except for those of us who work in Protocol Hall. Breach or no breach, there's still a job to do." It was early for her to be leaving, and so Violet added: "I've got to return something to Rez."

Shura didn't ask her what it was. There was a distance between them now. It wasn't a cold distance, but they didn't walk out the door side by side, the way they would have done before. Shura kept herself a few steps ahead.

All at once she spun around.

"It's too much, Violet," Shura said, her voice strained, ragged. "The emotions. All the feelings. I'd be stirring them up inside people. My paintings would, I mean. I'd just be giving the Intercept more to work with. I don't want to do that. I mean, I know the Intercept is a good thing and it keeps us all safe and your dad only wants the best for New Earth—but my paintings—they make me *feel*. My mother says it's too risky. I can't—" She cut herself off.

Violet had so much she wanted to say at this moment. She wanted to tell Shura to keep on painting. She wanted to tell her friend that tons of people could be doctors but only *she* could be a painter. *This* painter. She wanted to tell Shura that safety couldn't be the goal of life, that safety was a terrible thing to desire, that seeking safety was, in fact, the most dangerous thing you could ever do.

Violet hadn't known she felt that way. Not until the words to describe it had flared up in her, hot and true. She didn't even bother to check the crook of her elbow for a blue flash. She didn't care what the Intercept did with this feeling. She wanted to tell Shura to ignore her parents and just keep on painting, no matter what.

Violet's emotions kept spinning and bumping and crowding and crashing inside her—and so she did what she always did when there was too much to say. She said nothing.

Chip-jack

Reznik was already in their workstation. He was hunched over his keyboard, slamming the keys, glaring at a screen filled with spazzing code, frowning a frown so harsh that it made new dents and fresh creases in his chubby face. His hair looked as if it hadn't been combed since the First Mineral War. It stuck up in wheat-colored tufts. There was a wide stripe of grime on the back of his neck.

"Been here all night," he said. He didn't look up, only acknowledging her arrival with a vigorous head-bobble. "Running my own back trace. Trying to track down those jerks who hacked the system. Gonna find 'em. Gonna get 'em. *Guaranteed.*"

Violet dumped her bag on the floor. She pulled out her own chair and sat down.

"Any luck so far?" she said.

Another head-bobble. "Near as I can figure," he said, still not ripping his eyes away from the screen, "something blocked the Intercept signal."

"Like what?"

"Don't know. The signal is fine when it leaves Protocol Hall. But by the time it tries to reload the memory into the brains of the bad guys, something gets in the way. Like a shield. A shield that comes between the Intercept and the target. The block doesn't last long—but while it's on, it completely shuts down the signal."

"I thought that couldn't happen."

Reznik looked up from his screen. "Lots of things *can't* happen that somehow *do* happen. I'm just telling you what the numbers say. I didn't claim that it made any sense."

He coughed, a long, rattling cough that seemed to go along with pulling an all-nighter. He looked terrible, she thought. He looked like an old overcoat that had been stuffed in a garbage sack and left in a ditch for days. But that was one of the things she admired about Rez: He stuck with a problem until he solved it—no matter what he ended up looking like. Or smelling like.

"Can you take a break?" she said.

"Got to work."

"I know. But I wanted to give you back the chip-jack."

Rez sprang up from his seat. His eyes were round and huge.

"Not so loud!" he said in a fierce, appalled whisper. "Come on, Violet—you know better than that."

"Sorry." She was still so upset by Shura's decision to abandon her art that she'd forgotten her promise to Rez—that if he loaned her the homemade device he called a chip-jack, she would be discreet when talking about it.

Reznik risked a quick 360-degree glimpse around Protocol Hall. The workstations were all occupied. The glass walls meant that you could see what everyone else was doing—if you cared to look, which most people didn't. Their colleagues were sitting at their computers, trying to dig out a clue about last night's intruder. These investigations were on top of their usual work of monitoring the Intercept feeds. Orange code twisted across every screen; the atmosphere in Protocol Hall this afternoon was one of intense, almost robotic preoccupation. Violet had never seen everyone so focused. It was eerie.

But it was also totally understandable. The breach had rattled New Earth right down to its shimmering core.

No one seemed to have heard what she'd said. Nobody had heard her refer to the chip-jack.

Rez's shoulders rose and fell with a heavy sigh of relief. He plopped back down in his chair.

"Okay," he said. "But be cool, okay? Just give it to me slowly. I mean *slowly*. Don't make a big deal."

Pinching the tiny device between her thumb and index finger, Violet handed it back to him, placing it in his grubby palm. The black metal dot looked totally harmless.

It wasn't. In fact, it was the opposite of harmless: It was so dangerous that Violet was glad to be rid of it—almost as glad as she'd been to be able to use it.

"Thanks," she said. "I got it all set up."

"Did it work okay?"

Reznik's eyes were bright with eagerness. He was afraid to raise his voice—he was whispering again, which sounded weird to Violet, because usually Rez's voice was so loud the people at adjacent workstations complained about it—but he needed feedback. He craved compliments the way other people craved snacks. They were his fuel. As smart as he was, he was desperate for validation.

And not from just anybody. From *her*.

"I haven't initiated it yet," she said. "I did a preliminary test, though. Just a small one. Seems fine."

Reznik waited. He was wildly curious about why she'd asked him to borrow the chip-jack. But he didn't want to ask her outright. He wanted her to want to tell him.

She knew that, but she couldn't do it. Because it was related to Danny. And Rez would be jealous—jealous of her feelings for him. The jealousy was always there in the background when Danny's name came up, but it needed to *stay* in the background. As long as it was a low-level hum and not a crazy roar, Violet could handle it.

"So you'll let me know, right?" he said. "Once you try it?"

"Yeah."

He switched back to his usual self. "Wanna know how I did it? How I came up with the chip-jack?"

No, she didn't. Not really. But she owed him.

"Sure, Rez," Violet said.

Once again his eyes flew all around the vast hall, checking to make sure nobody was paying attention to them.

Nobody was.

He leaned forward. His voice was cautious, but there was a smugness in it, too. "I may not have invented the Intercept like your friend's brother," he said, "and I may not be able to figure out how those creeps are getting around it, but I *do* know pretty much every inch of it, okay? I know how the Intercept *thinks*. I've mapped its brain. I know its code protocol like I know my own name." Now he leaned back and crossed his arms. "That's how I came up with the chip-jack. It piggybacks onto the feed. If you touch the chip-jack to the skin over the Intercept chip you can sync both chips—and then you can access that person's feed. Spy on them." He pumped his fuzzy eyebrows up and down in triumph. Violet could've sworn she saw some lint tumble out. "It's like you're right there beside them, wherever they go," Rez said with a giant smirk. "Seeing what they see. Hearing what they hear."

Violet had a vivid memory of running the chip-jack against Danny's sleeve outside Protocol Hall the day she staged her won't-you-please-finish-my-coffee tactic. She had felt a little guilty about the trick, and a little queasy—but only a little.

The chip-jack was just for emergencies. She didn't really want to use it. It was altogether too sneaky, and too sinister.

But if she had to—she would.

"It only works temporarily, right?" Violet asked.

"Right. Once it's activated, the hijacked feed doesn't hold up for long. Just an hour or so. Sometimes a lot less. But sometimes, if you're lucky, the feed will pop back up again. Again—just for a few minutes. Depends on the air quality and the density of signal interference."

Violet nodded. No matter how obnoxious he was, Rez was also a friend. The chip-jack was illegal. Or at least it would be if the authorities knew about it. He had risked a lot to let her borrow it. And he hadn't even asked her what she wanted it for.

She decided to pay him back with the only currency he really cared about: her admiration. She didn't have to fake it.

"You really do know the Intercept, don't you?" Violet said. "I mean, you don't just monitor it, like the rest of us do. You *know* it. You can practically read its mind."

"Oh, yeah. I can do whatever I want to with it." With a flick of his thumb he gestured toward his screen, where the orange code waited for his next command. "I've got this baby down *cold.* If somebody gets hold of something they're not supposed to have, if somebody's not where they're supposed to be, if somebody's not who they say they are—I'm going to find out. First the Intercept knows and then *I* know. Okay? Simple as that. Like I told you, the chip-jack is like a back door into the Intercept. Nobody else could've figured that out. Nobody else knows the ins and outs of the Intercept like me. I know its moods. I know its secrets."

He leaned over and touched his computer, stroking its black plastic side with a couple of fingertips. It almost looked like someone touching the cheek of his beloved.

Had anybody but Steve Reznick done that, Violet would have been totally creeped out. But this was Rez. It was hard for him to reach outside himself and his own supercharged brain, she knew. The only human being he had ever really cared about—which happened to be her—didn't care about him in the same way. She never would.

And so he'd forged a link where he could. He'd found one that satisfied him. Sure, it was with the Intercept, and not a woman or a man, but it spoke to his soul. It made him feel whole. Part of the world.

Nothing creepy about that, Violet thought. *We all do what we have to do to feel human. To feel a real human connection.*

Which was a strange thing to say about somebody who'd fallen in love with a computer program. But then again, the world was full of strange things these days.

14

Prisoner No. 49878104-12-XHVB

Why do they call you Tin Man?"

Tin Man laughed. "You come all this way—and *that's* the question you wanna ask me?"

"One of them, yeah."

Danny and Tin Man faced each other across the cold, bare space. Tin Man appeared to be thinner and even scragglier than he'd been the last time Violet saw him, back in that rain-ruined, garbage-stacked alley.

That was barely a week ago, and so the transformation was surprising. Old Earth prison must be even worse than she'd imagined it would be.

Violet twisted the dial on her console up and down, and up and down again, trying to bring the scene into better focus. She was sitting cross-legged on her bed, her elbows perched on her upraised knees. She had been home from her shift for several hours. She hadn't heard from her father, which didn't surprise her; he would not rest until he had explored every last means of finding the intruders who had shut down the Intercept for a few scary seconds.

But the trouble was, she hadn't heard from Danny, either. And he hadn't answered his console. She knew his schedule, and she knew he wasn't on duty.

And so his silence could mean only one thing: He had gone to Old Earth.

Again.

So as soon as she arrived home, Violet had plugged in the password Reznik gave her. The password linked her to the chip-jack signal, the one that continued transmitting to her console even though she had returned the device.

A grainy, misty-looking picture wavered slowly into focus.

It was a small pocket of space chopped and gouged out of the depths of a mountain. Violet recognized the dimensions right away, from her criminal justice class: This was a prison cell. Carved into one of the craggy sides was the identity of the person assigned to it:

Prisoner No. 49878104-12-XHVB.

Violet knew him by another name:

Tin Man Tolliver.

But why was Danny visiting the drug dealer who had almost melted his face off with a slab gun?

She squinted at her console. She turned up the volume control.

"Okay," Tin Man was saying. "I steal tin. I mean—I *stole* tin, before they threw me in this stinking place. You know what metal's worth down here, right? I steal copper sometimes, too. But tin's my specialty. So I'm the Tin Man."

"Tell me the rest," Danny said. "There's got to be more."

Violet could hear their voices clearly, but the visuals continued to be distorted. She knew why. Reznik had explained to her that the chip-jack would work great everywhere—except on Old Earth, where the radiation lingering in the atmosphere from the last Mineral War might partially block the signal.

"Okay," Tin Man said. "So you want to know how I *really* got this nickname? It's simple. She liked the movie. It's a million years old, give or take, but it was still her favorite."

"Who? And what movie?"

"You know who," Tin Man scoffed. "And you know which movie. I'm not stupid, okay? I've got a good idea about how the Intercept works. I'm aware of the fact that you've seen my feed. All of you. All of you New Earth snobs and hypocrites." He sneered. "In *The Wizard of Oz,* he's the best character. Only one that works hard. Only one that's got a real tool. Carries an ax. Most little girls, they'd go for Dorothy or that candy-ass lion. Not Molly. She liked the Tin Man. So she started calling me that. Long time ago." He shrugged again, as if pronouncing his sister's name no longer pierced him.

Violet knew better. She remembered that alley, when the moment of Molly Tolliver's death had been fed back into Tin Man's brain. It had completely incapacitated him. It had turned him into jelly.

"Who *are* you, anyway?" Tin Man said. "And how'd you get here? Travel's restricted from New Earth."

"I've got my ways."

"So you're not going to tell me."

"No. I'm not going to tell you." Danny took a few steps around the space, looking left and right, up and down.

"What're you doing? Measuring for drapes?" Tin Man said, adding a cackle of laughter. With a dirty fingernail, he scratched vigorously in the crook of his left elbow.

Violet recognized the gesture, but it looked different when Tin Man did it. It wasn't a casual habit, like pushing your bangs out of your eyes. A lot of people on Old Earth, she knew, had tried repeatedly to dig out their Intercept chips with pocketknives, or sticks, or the sharpened edges of spoons—anything they could find. It was impossible. And you could do a lot of damage to yourself by trying. Tin Man had an ugly twisting scar there. When he dug at the spot, it was like he hoped to open up the wound all over again.

"Hell," Tin Man went on, staring scornfully at Danny. "You're just a kid. Like me. Didn't get a good look at you while you were chasing me—but now I see. I didn't need to run. I could've taken you, easy."

A column of dingy muted light dropped from an ancient bulb fitted into a metal socket chained to the craggy wall. Violet recalled the descriptions she had read. In Old Earth prisons, the light was never turned off. The prisoners couldn't see one another, but each knew that all the others were there, thousands of them, breathing, shuffling, moving around, moaning in their fevered sleep, slotted into identical pockets gouged out of the rock.

There were no iron bars in this prison. Outside, there were no high fences finished off with barbed wire. No guard towers. No guards. None of those things was necessary. Prisoners were monitored by a specialized Intercept unit up on New Earth. If trouble broke out—if a prisoner tried to escape, or even contemplated trying to escape— an intervention was initiated, and the prisoner would be instantly subdued by a stabbing, incapacitating grief. The last guard had left Old Earth in 2290, when the sixty-fifth prison was completed.

Tin Man was still talking. "You're an arrogant SOB, you know that?" He slapped a bicep and rubbed it hard, as if he wanted to polish his latest tattoo. Skull and crossbones, Violet noted. The classic. "Couldn't believe you followed me into that alley," he went on. "Stupid move, you know? Almost cost you, big-time. Two more seconds and I would've hit you with that slab gun. *Destroyed* you. You'd be in pieces. Dripping, smelly pieces." The image made him smile. "You know that, right? If it weren't for that damned Inter—"

"Yeah," Danny said. "I know."

"Still waiting to find out why you showed up here," Tin Man said. "What you're after."

"Information."

"Really." One side of Tin Man's mouth curled up. "And just what makes you think I'll talk? Doesn't look like you brought any weapons."

"I didn't. Not the kind you mean, anyway."

Violet was getting nervous. She tried to tamp down her nervous-ness, so the Intercept wouldn't take it and tally it, but it was difficult.

The silence spread out all around Danny and Tin Man. The silence was made more ominous for Violet by her awareness of how many millions of tons of rock were pressing down on top of Danny right now, a massive steady pressure.

"You're going to tell me," Danny said, "exactly what I want to know."

"Really."

"Yeah."

"And just why am I going to do that?"

"Because if you don't," Danny said, "you'll be seeing your little sister again. And you won't like it any better this time than you did the last time."

Tin Man's face crumpled. "No," he said, in a hoarse whisper. "No, *please.*"

He was backing away now, cringing and crouching, his palms out in front of him. His bravado was gone. His body—and Violet knew because she'd felt it herself—still carried the invisible imprint of the Intercept, a sense memory of the power that had messed with his nerves and menaced his brain. It took weeks, sometimes months, to flush out the aftershocks of an Intercept.

Tin Man had had only a few days. He was nowhere near being over it yet. Neither was she.

Tin Man's hands were shaking. He spoke rapidly. Fear and uncer-tainty sent his words slinging crazily into one another, bouncing around, out of control. "What do you want? You want slab guns? I can tell you where to get all the slab guns you could ever need. Totally untraceable. Or is it deckle? Is that what you're after? I can get you a source for that, too," he said in a pleading, wheedling voice. "I can. I swear. All you want. *All you want!* Is that it? Because I can help. I wasn't the only dealer, you know. Hell no. I know plenty of others. I can give you names. Streets. Safe times to go. Please. *Please.* Or tumult, maybe? Or trekinol? I can help you get those, too. No problem."

He squinted at Danny, trying to read his face, get a sense of his desires. "Anything. Name it."

Violet realized she hadn't taken a breath in a while. She, too, was waiting to hear Danny's answer. *Was* it drugs, after all? Was that why he was here? Had he lied to her?

She felt as if her whole future were teetering on the brink of whatever Danny said next.

"Like I told you," Danny replied, "what I want is information. I wish I didn't. I wish I could just leave you here, but you've got something I need. I wanted to get it from you in the alley that day, but it wasn't possible. Not once they spotted me from New Earth. So I had to come back."

Tin Man swallowed hard. "So if I cooperate, you'll keep the memory away from me?"

"Yeah."

Tin Man, tough guy, bad-ass drug dealer, nodded vigorously, like a kid who'd just been promised a second piece of candy. His head bobbed as the nod went on and on. Too long. He was too helpful, too obliging. That told Violet just how much pain he'd been in during the Intercept's visit. How desperate he was to avoid a repeat.

"All right, then," Danny said. "I'll tell you what I'm here for. I need you to—"

The picture on Violet's console faded. It flipped sideways. Then it winked out. She jiggled her wrist. The picture returned, but in another second it winked out again. Fuzzy static replaced the scene in Tin Man's prison cell.

The chip-jack signal was gone.

Violet was so frustrated that she had a sudden impulse to jump up, rip off her console, and fling it across the room. But she resisted. No use adding a trip to the console repair shop to her to-do list.

She was out of options. She'd tried following him (*check*), tricking him into revealing he was a drug addict (*check*), and using the chip-jack (*check*). Nothing worked. She still didn't know why Danny kept going down to Old Earth.

And now another mystery had been added on top of the original one: What kind of information did Danny want from Tin Man?

Glitch

That's weird."

Reznik leaned closer to his monitor. He was squinting.

"What's weird?" Violet said.

"This. Right here." He pointed to his screen with a stubby finger.

Violet leaned over to look. "Okay, so the numbers are elevated. For less than a second. Got to be an anomaly."

"Doesn't mean it's not important."

She had lingered for a few minutes past shift change. To her irritation, Reznik stuck around, too. He was having trouble with the light level on his screen. Ever since the Intercept breach, a variety of glitches and ghosts had bedeviled the computers, sparking a scraggle of small, persistent annoyances. No permanent damage had been done, apparently, although the Intercept maintenance team, led by Shura's dad, was still checking and rechecking.

And now Rez had seen something that made him curious.

Too curious.

Violet was fairly sure that the elevated levels had something to do with Danny and yet another trip to Old Earth. And she didn't want Reznik involved. As eager as she was to figure out Danny's agenda, it was her mystery to solve, not Reznik's. Besides, there were plenty of other mysteries to absorb Rez's attention.

The Intercept breach was still the primary topic of conversation around Protocol Hall. Theories as to the identities of the members of the Rebels of Light dipped and swirled around the vast space. How had anybody gotten past the Intercept long enough to pierce the mainframe? Any human presence would have been automatically detected, triggering a disabling intervention. There was no record of anything like that.

Thanks to the chip-jack, she knew Danny had made another round-trip to Old Earth. But she didn't want Rez to know that. If he knew, he'd be obligated to report it. That meant Danny would face another confrontation with Callahan.

"Wonder what it was," Rez murmured.

"Maybe it was a sunspot."

"A *sunspot*?" He snickered. "Really?"

"I was kidding."

"Sure you were." His grin faded. "Seriously, though, Violet. Take a look. The pattern fluctuated right here." Reznik pointed to the bottom right quadrant of his screen. "Unmistakable."

She looked again. Yes. At the precise mark when their shift had expired last night, the level had risen and fallen in a tiny red spike. A wrist console had been activated. And the only way the activation would register on the Intercept—because there were, after all, millions of console activations going on all around them every second, as people communicated with one another, and none of those routine activations mattered—was if the console in question was, at that precise moment, located outside the confines of New Earth.

And if it was located outside the confines of New Earth, there was only one other place it *could* be located:

Old Earth.

"Don't worry about it, Steve," Violet said. She said it in a low voice.

He looked at her. She never—well, almost never—called him by his first name.

"I'm supposed to report it," he said. "You know that. Especially after what happened the other night."

"Your screen's acting up. You said that yourself. You're having problems with your light level, remember? It could be a glitch." With an effort, she kept her voice calm and even. The members of the monitor team set to relieve them were still a good distance away, talking and laughing, glad for an extra minute or two of relaxation before they had to sit down in front of their screens and focus. They paid no attention to Violet's conversation with Reznik.

"A glitch," he repeated dubiously.

"Yeah."

"That's what you really believe."

"Well, it's a possibility, right?"

"I think I liked the sunspot theory better."

They both knew full well what the numbers meant. They meant that Danny had done it again. He'd gone down to Old Earth. But neither one of them was willing to say it out loud.

With all the numbers swooshing and diving through their days, the spikes coinciding with Danny's trips had not been noticed before—until, in the wake of the security breach, Rez dug in and gave extra attention to every single number on his screen. Now, though, it was clear what had happened. And Violet was slightly frantic.

"Maybe we could let it go," she said hastily. "We don't have to make a formal report. We could just ignore it."

"You're trying to protect him."

Violet didn't answer. The answer was obvious.

Once again she was taking advantage of Reznik's feelings for her, just as she had done when she'd asked for the chip-jack. She sort of hated herself for doing it—again. But she had to. Her loyalty was to Danny. It always would be.

"Those glitches—they happen, right?" Violet said.

"Yeah. Sure. Sure they do."

Three quick keystrokes later, he had logged out of his Intercept account. He wasn't going to make the report. There had really been no chance that he would, from the moment he understood the intensity of Violet's desire that he not do so. She sensed the emotions moving through him, all the feelings for her that she did not feel for him. And never would.

Knowing Steve Reznik as well as she did, she knew he hated this, hated the fact that love had the upper hand. Not even his magnificent brain was a match for his emotions.

"Yeah," he said. There was sadness in his voice, the sadness that came from acknowledging a weakness he couldn't do anything about. He might as well be trying to climb that rope in gym class again. "Sure. A glitch. Happens all the time."

16

Lucretia Crowley, M.D.

Violet opened the door to the apartment. Ogden Crowley was in his usual spot, rooted in the big leather armchair. One leg was propped on the ottoman. It was almost midnight.

Her father looked so alone. Alone in this room. Alone in the apartment. Alone with his responsibilities.

Alone in his life.

Classical music drifted from his console. It was a Chopin waltz. A treasure from Old Earth. Light rain had started up just after midnight, tiptoeing gently across the window.

"Hey, Dad."

Violet's voice made him smile. It always did. He turned his torso toward where she stood, in the arched threshold that linked the foyer to the living room. Much as he would've liked to rise and embrace her, he didn't get up—his right leg made that difficult, especially at the end of a long and tiring day. But he wanted her to know how glad he was to see her, so he put his welcome into his voice.

"Good evening, sweetheart," he said.

Sweetheart. When she was a little girl Violet didn't like it when he called her that. She didn't like it when her mother called her that, either. She wanted to be tough. So she'd roll her eyes, make a face. Now she didn't mind at all.

"I didn't hear you come in," he added.

"You never do. You get kind of preoccupied, Dad." She grinned at him. "Anyway, I tried to be quiet. Thought you might be in bed."

"No. No chance of that."

She didn't like the idea of sitting on the couch tonight. She wanted to be closer to him. And so she picked a spot on the floor next to his chair, sat down and crossed her legs. Her father touched the top of her head. He nodded knowingly at the dampness.

"You've been walking in the rain," he said. "Your mother loved to do that, too."

Violet didn't answer right away. Sometimes, late at night, they'd stay like this for a little while, not talking, her father's scarred hand on her head. His touch was light, trifling, barely there, but through its pressure she'd swear she could feel his sorrow. She'd told him so. It was always with him, he had explained to her, this constant pain at the loss of his wife. And the loss of other things, too. It was nothing that Violet or anybody else could do anything about. It was nothing you could grasp or fight, nothing you could get your arms around. It was like the mist rising in the wake of the rain: Even if it wasn't with you on a particular day, you always knew it would return.

"Any luck in tracking down the Rebels?" Violet said.

He shook his head gravely. "No. And we still don't know how they did it. How they managed to get past the Intercept itself. It's as if they're somehow able to resist it. Like they have temporary immunity. But that doesn't make sense."

He was so frustrated that he'd made his other hand into a fist, as if he wanted to find a wall he could batter, in hopes of finding the answer behind it. Violet reached up. She gently pulled his fingers apart until the fist disappeared.

"You need your sleep, Dad. Maybe a doctor could—"

"Violet."

"Okay. Okay." She knew better than to push him.

He had always refused medication that would help ratchet down the terrible pain in his leg. He was afraid it would dull the edges. He needed to be completely in control at all times. He was responsible for all of New Earth. He had to be alert.

"I never got a chance to ask you about dinner over at Michelle Callahan's," he said. "After the breach, everything else flew out of my head. How was it?"

"The soup was great." She wasn't really answering his question, and she knew it.

He waited. When she didn't add anything, he said, "She asked you about Danny Mayhew, I assume."

"Yeah."

"And that made you uncomfortable."

"He's my friend, Dad."

"And he's her employee."

Her father knew that she and Danny hung out. He had a general idea about her other friends, too; he knew about Shura Lu and Reznik, and he knew her work schedule. But unless she specifically brought up her personal life, he didn't pry. That way, he could pretend it wasn't real. He could pretend that she was still the same little girl who used to climb up on his lap and ask him to tell her a story about Old Earth, about the place where he'd lived when *he* was little.

One day when she was about five years old, Violet had walked up to his chair and lifted his ugly twisted hand with her tiny ones—it took both of her hands to lift one of his, because his hand was so big and heavy. She looked at him and said, "Is that where it happened to you, Daddy? On Old Earth? Is that where your hands and your leg got hurt? I don't like that place, Daddy. I don't ever want to go to the place that hurt you."

But now she was all grown up.

Sitting on the floor beside his chair, she saw the rain ooze slowly down the darkened window. The peace of this New Earth night settled in all around them. Peace: that was what the Intercept promised. The lure of that promise was what had caused Ogden Crowley to make his fateful trip down to Old Earth to track down a technology still only whispered about at the time.

Her father had told her the story over and over again. She always wanted to hear it just once more.

"It was raining like this, wasn't it?" Violet said. "The day you first met Kendall Mayhew in his lab? The whole place smelled gross." She laughed softly. "I remember you telling me that, when I was a kid."

He nodded. A faraway look came into his bloodshot eyes. He fell easily into the familiar rhythm of the tale. "I was worried about New Earth. Worried about how we'd keep control of the citizens—so that New Earth would never, *ever* turn into Old Earth, with all the violence and the mayhem, all those uncollected emotions on the loose. I had heard rumors about a fantastic invention that could help me do that. Help me keep control. So I went down to Old Earth to see for myself. That was the first time I saw Kendall Mayhew."

"What did he look like?" she asked.

"Well, I only saw half of his face. Less than half, really. He was wearing these enormous leather goggles to protect his eyes during experiments. They plainly didn't fit—they were way too big. He told me later that he'd scrounged them out of the trash. The lenses were so scratched and cloudy that I have no idea how he saw where he was going—much less created a technology that would save humanity. Anyway, I will always remember the sight of Kendall there in his lab. Yes, you're right—the place smelled *terrible.* It smelled like smoke and chemicals and something rotting behind the walls. But I could see the splendor of what he'd created, no matter the circumstances in which it had come to life. I offered him whatever price he named for this device he called the Intercept. And I told him he could come to New Earth and install it. Put on the finishing touches. Work out the last few kinks."

"What did he say?"

"He surprised me. I thought he'd jump at the chance. He'd have a new lab with anything he needed. The best of everything. He'd have absolute creative freedom. But he said, 'Not right away, President Crowley. You can have the Intercept—but I've got more experiments to do down here first. I'll come when I'm ready. And when I do, my brother comes, too.' Naturally I agreed. I would've agreed to any conditions. I wanted the Intercept. I had to have it. The future of our new civilization was at stake.

"Two years later," Ogden continued, "the Mayhew brothers finally came to New Earth. And then a year and a half ago, Kendall died of a drug overdose—but his Intercept lives on. It's doing exactly what I had hoped it would—save New Earth. And it does it efficiently and cost-effectively. There's no need for giant armies or expensive weapons. New Earth will never become like Old Earth."

At that point, Violet realized, the storyteller part of Ogden Crowley was giving way to the president part, the part that made speeches: "It will never be subject to the violence of Old Earth," he declared. "It will never fall victim to the terrible wars and the devastating plagues that come in the wake of wars. It will never sink beneath the weight of catastrophe. Its children will never see their limbs blasted away or their parents murdered or their dreams crushed. Here, everyone is safe."

Safe.

Violet had heard her father use that word so many times. Tonight she decided to take a chance. She would do more than just nod.

"So is that always a good thing?" she said.

"What?"

"Safety. Is that always the goal? I mean, isn't every great thing accomplished because somebody put something else *ahead* of safety? Like when you created New Earth. That wasn't safe. You had to take risks."

"Not the same."

"Why not?"

"You're a child, Violet. You have no idea what you're talking about."

"I'm *not* a child. I'm sixteen years old. And I think that—"

"ENOUGH!" He thundered the word, turning it into the equivalent of a slammed door. This was the Ogden Crowley that the public knew best: the rigid, imperial leader who allowed no one to argue with him. The taskmaster who could never be wrong.

The conversation, she knew, was officially over. But she'd never storm out of the room. Only kids did that—and as she had just pointed out to him, she was not a kid. She was used to his temper. She loved him, no matter what.

"Okay," Violet said. "I guess I'll head off to bed. Good night." She stood up. "Don't worry, Dad. You'll find the people who are trying to destroy the Intercept." She didn't want their quarrel to be the note they ended the evening on.

"Yes," he said. But his voice remained cold. It was still the voice of the president of New Earth. Not the voice of her father. "And when we do—they're going to be severely punished." He had made a fist again. He perched it on the arm of his chair.

Violet bent down to kiss his cheek. She had to find some way to bring him back.

"Mom loved rainy nights like these," she said. "Remember?"

A slight but perceptible shudder seemed to run through his body. He closed his eyes. When he opened them again, he was a different man; his face had relaxed. "Yes, I do remember that."

"Hard to believe how long she's been gone."

"She's not."

"Not what?"

"Not gone. She's here. Right here. I see her clearly—every time I look at you, sweetheart."

Violet couldn't speak for a moment. Her father was not a sentimental man. Most people would have called him the least sentimental person they had ever known. But she understood the deep well of feeling that lived inside him.

"I'm not like Mom," she said quietly. "I couldn't do what she did. Medical school, then going down to Old Earth, trying to help the people left there—no way. I'm not that strong."

"You don't know what you are yet. And one day, you're going to make your mark. I'd bet on that." He gave her a tired-looking wave. "Go to bed, sweetheart. Sleep well. The sound of the rain will help. It used to help me, when I was your age."

But that was real rain, Dad, Violet thought. *You still lived on Old Earth, and that was* actual *rain. Rain that came when it came. Not rain that comes from a computer program.*

She wasn't sure why that mattered, but somehow it did.

"Don't stay up too late, Dad." Violet walked to the doorway. She paused under the arch, turning back to him. "Some people have asked me how—how you and Mom ever got together and—I mean, she was—" She gave up. "I never know what to say."

"It's okay, sweetheart. I know why they're curious. They can't figure out why a beautiful, caring, sensitive woman like Lucretia would ever have agreed to share her life with a broken-down old grump like me. Right?"

"No, Dad, I don't think they meant—"

"Don't worry. You can't hurt my feelings, Violet. I used to wonder the same thing myself."

"And?"

"And I'm still wondering."

He smiled. She loved to see his smile. He didn't smile very often, and she missed it.

She missed a lot of things.

Hopeless, Violet thought. She sat up in bed and threw off the covers. Sleep would not be wooed tonight.

The rain had picked up a bit, peppering the dark window with its irregular beat. She reached for her console, tapped the small oval on the screen.

The first page of a journal jumped to life.

Field Notes from Old Earth / Lucretia Crowley M.D.

When Violet turned sixteen, this was her favorite gift. Her mother's journal had been delivered via time delay into her console's memory, along with a small note: *Happy 16th birthday to my beloved daughter.* Lucretia had set it up that way years before. In case anything ever happened to her, her father explained, she still wanted Violet to understand her work and why it mattered.

Violet was now old enough to appreciate the record of Lucretia's medical practice, day by day—up to the day before she had collapsed with the first stage of Missip Fever.

The journal reminded Violet of who her mother really was: someone beloved by her and her father, yes, but also a diligent physician, relentless in her quest to relieve the suffering of Old Earth's beleaguered citizens—even though that commitment had ended up taking her life.

When Violet couldn't sleep, this was her ritual. She would pick a few entries at random and read. Lucretia was gone, but her journal was still here. Violet could almost hear her mother's voice as she read her words, see her radiant face as she talked about her work. The work she described in her journal:

Administered vaccines to five babies in Old Earth Sector 208 today. Set the broken leg of an elderly man who had somehow dragged himself over here from Sector 194. Checked his lungs; emphysema clearly a possibility, but he refused to let me do any further tests. Cursed me while I put the cast on his leg and would not speak or answer questions. Adversity and hopelessness have warped people's souls, even as weapons and constant warfare have warped their bodies.

Violet flipped pages forward with one finger on her console, watching them tick past. She closed her eyes, still flipping. When she opened them again, she would read whatever passage upon which she happened to alight.

She stopped. She looked down at the screen.

This was a portion of her mother's journal she hadn't read before. She took a drink of water from the cup on her bedside table.

A lot of people without any medical training do their best, but it's not enough. Clearly. And these days, frankly, too many of them just want quick payment for switching out Intercept chips so that people can slip into New Earth under a false identity. They don't understand the health risk.

That made Violet scowl. She recalled her mother talking about those kinds of people on Old Earth: greedy, unscrupulous. Preying on the desperate. Pretending to be volunteers offering medical care. Even the ones who had started out kind had evolved into tricky thieves full of false promises. Some claimed they could safely remove the chips from people hoping to sneak into New Earth. Lucretia Crowley had spent a lot of time treating the wounds of the poor souls left to bleed to death after someone had clumsily tried to gouge out a chip for a cash fee. Twice, Violet's mother had had to amputate left arms that had become badly infected after the botched removal of an Intercept chip.

Old Earth is a harsh and terrifying world. The way people treat one another—it's just so unbearably tragic. And the way the land has deteriorated—it's sickening. Reprehensible. What happened to us? How did we let this happen to the Earth we love, to people we should care about?

Reading this now, all these years later, Violet ached for her mother. She could feel the force of her mother's pain and disenchantment, even through the chilly, indifferent medium of the console screen. She wished she could argue with Lucretia's conclusions. She wished she could say to her memory: "No, Mom, you were wrong—the world is not all bad, and people are better now. Kinder. If only you'd lived to see it."

She couldn't say that because it wasn't true. Her mother had been right. The world was bleak and perilous and filled with despair. The only thing that saved it was the Intercept. At least that's what Violet had grown up believing.

Now she picked another page at random. The date was December 8, 2288. Just a week before her mother began showing the terrible symptoms of Missip Fever.

She read.

She blinked.

She read the passage again, to make sure she hadn't misunderstood it.

The words were so surprising to her, so unexpected, that her mind seemed to freeze in place.

She stared at the screen, reading her mother's words over and over again:

I met an extraordinary young man today. He and his brother live on the streets down here in Old Earth, foraging for scraps like everyone else, but there is so much more to them than just the struggle for survival. I could see it right away. It's something in their eyes, especially Kendall's. It's a hunger—but not for food. It's a hunger for knowledge. He and his brother, Danny, asked me to help them.

It was a strange request. I don't understand it. And I don't feel comfortable doing something like this behind Ogden's back.

Still, it only took me a few days to think about it and then to tell them yes. Yes, I'll do it. I understand that if it doesn't work out, the consequences could be dire—for them and for me, too. But I have to try. I have to.

So her mother had known Danny and Kendall Mayhew. And she had done something for them—something that troubled her. Did she know that Kendall was working on the Intercept? She didn't say so in this journal passage.

Each time Lucretia returned from Old Earth, she and Violet's father would sit down and talk about what she'd done down there, and the people she'd helped, the lives she'd saved, and he would say, once again, "Please don't go down there again. Please. Violet and I need you." Violet was there, too, eager to be in her mother's presence again.

At that point Lucretia would give him a slow, sad smile, and she would say, "Darling, please listen. The person you love—the real me— well, *that's* the person who has to keep going down to Old Earth. It's so gray and depressing there, and the people are lost and hopeless and suffering. Diseases are getting out of control. If I don't go to Old Earth from time to time and try to help, if I just stay up here and have a nice, easy life on New Earth with you and Violet—I won't be the person you love. I will be a different person altogether. Do you understand?"

Before Ogden could answer, Lucretia would look over at Violet and add, "I want our girl to see what it's like to care about something so much that you *have* to do it. You just have to. Because I want Violet to be like that, too. I want her to be strong and good. To think for herself. To go against the grain. I want her to work hard for the things she believes in. And to not let anybody stand in her way."

But her mother had never told them about meeting Kendall and Danny Mayhew. They had clearly made a strong impression on her. And whatever it was she had done for them, she was troubled about not telling her husband about it.

What could it have been?

And why hadn't Danny ever told her that he had met her mother?

The Intercept, Violet knew, was eavesdropping on her feelings, just like always. That irritated her. She didn't want her emotion to be picked up, time-stamped, and stowed away. That emotion—a combination of wild surprise and passionate curiosity—was *hers*.

She'd heard about a little trick some people used to hide their real emotions from the Intercept. It only worked for a few seconds at a time. And it only worked now and again. But it was something.

The Intercept only dealt with the most prominent emotion at any given moment. If you were clever, you could sometimes slip another emotion in front of the one you didn't want to get out, and no record would be made of the original feeling—only of the different one you'd willed yourself to have. She'd had friends who did this and swore it worked. She'd never tried it before, but now she did.

She thought about Danny.

She looked down at the crook of her left elbow. A small flash of blue winked under the skin.

Gotcha, she thought.

17

Death in the Rain

The next day Shura came by the lobby of Protocol Hall to meet Violet for lunch. Violet had decided to tell Shura what she'd discovered in her mother's journal about Danny and Kendall.

But as they left the glass-walled monolith and headed for the food kiosks lining the plaza, Violet changed her mind. She still hadn't decided what the journal entries meant. Before she told anyone, she first wanted to do what she always did when she faced a daunting problem: think about it. Her brain, Violet had found when dealing with past challenges, was her best ally.

"Burritos okay?" Shura said.

"Absolutely."

Each kiosk featured a cuisine from a lost culture of Old Earth, a culture that had vanished in the terrible melting pot of global disaster: nations and their distinctive foods slid into one another like objects rolling together on a listing ship. The keen specificity of flavors, the details of preparation, had been lost in the amalgamation. When planning New Earth, Ogden Crowley had hired a cultural historian to research these long-forgotten foods and re-create them here. Thus Violet and her friends often ate tacos or pasta or chow mein, but only knew Mexico, Italy, and China as strange, ancient names in the history lectures on their consoles.

There was a long line in front of the kiosk. By the time they paid for their burritos, Violet had only about fifteen minutes left on her lunch break. Shura found an empty spot along the stone retaining wall that circled the plaza. Other people were perched along the wall, too, eating foods that had not been part of an actual family dinner for well over a century but had found a second life here on New Earth, like animals extinct in the wild that still manage to survive in zoos.

"You've heard, right?" Shura said. "There was another breach. After the one the other night. Just for a few seconds. It's getting pretty scary, right? I mean—who *are* these people?"

"Yeah, I heard." It was all anyone was talking about in Protocol Hall. And everywhere else, for that matter. No wonder her father wasn't sleeping at night.

Lowering her voice, Shura said, "My mom thinks they must have the original source code for the Intercept." She'd also looked carefully around the plaza before speaking, to make sure no one was eavesdropping. "That's the only way they'd be able to get around it. Without the Intercept knowing they're there."

Violet had seen other people do that—give a quick, nervous look around their immediate surroundings. She wondered why. The entity that *was* actually spying on them—and doing it 100 percent of the time—had nothing to do with anyone sitting within earshot. You couldn't lower your voice enough to escape the Intercept. The cleverest safeguards and best evasive maneuvers were irrelevant.

How, then, did the group calling itself the Rebels of Light pull it off?

"Any more threats to your mom?" Violet asked.

Shura nodded. "Yeah." She set down her food. Violet could tell that she'd suddenly lost her taste for it. "She just got back from a trip to

Old Earth to meet with a client," Shura said. "I knew right away that something was wrong. She was—she was *different*. Sort of fidgety. She can't settle down. And I noticed something else, too. She doesn't look up anymore. At the sky."

"Really."

"Yeah. Her head's pretty much always bent down. Looking at the ground. She's sort of sad and upset, I guess, about the people who can't come to New Earth. Who have to stay down there."

"Do you ever wonder what it's like?"

Shura gave her a sideways glance. "I don't have to wonder. My mom tells me all about it. It's awful. That's why she tries to get more immigrants cleared to come up here."

"Still," Violet said. "I'd like to see it for myself. But my dad won't budge." She picked a string of lettuce out of her burrito. She buried it in her napkin. "Danny showed me a picture once of Old Earth. It wasn't from one of the regular drone feeds." She paused again. "It was the place where Kendall died."

Shura's eyes widened in surprise, so Violet quickly added, "He wanted me to know the truth about Old Earth. He thought I didn't understand just how bad it really is down there. He wanted me to *see*."

"So he made you look at—"

"It was after they'd removed the body. For some reason—a reason nobody's ever figured out—Kendall went back to the same run-down neighborhood on Old Earth where they'd grown up. He bought some deckle. And then he OD'ed. He died in an alley, Shura. In the rain. In the cold. Next to a bunch of garbage cans. Kendall Mayhew—the inventor of the Intercept. One of the smartest guys who ever lived.

"You should hear Danny talk about that day," Violet went on. "First he gets quiet, and then it's like something is rising up inside him, this awful guilt. 'Why did I let it happen?' he always says. 'Why wasn't I there? How could I allow him to do that to himself?' Oh, Shura. I try to help him, but there's really nothing I can do."

"It's not his fault," Shura said. "You have to make Danny see that." One of the things that made their friendship so great, Violet had thought for a long time, was this: They took turns being strong. If one of them was distraught, the other one held them together. And then they'd switch.

Right now, it was Shura's turn. "In each of us, there's a different kind of darkness," she said. "And you have to let other people deal with theirs. In their own way. That's what Danny needs to understand. I mean, yeah, sure—Kendall Mayhew was a genius and he changed the world. But maybe he couldn't change his *own* world, you know? He just wasn't able to turn his world into a place that was okay for him. A place he wanted to stay."

Violet nodded. Shura sometimes surprised her with her way of looking at things. But Violet really shouldn't have been surprised. Shura was an artist. Her life was all about looking. And seeing things that most people didn't see.

It was time for Violet to return to Protocol Hall. She said good-bye to Shura and then joined the crowd as it bumped and surged its way back into the building, back to the place where the floor shivered more insistently than it did anywhere else, as if it, too, sensed that a change was coming.

The change might be good. Or it might be bad. But clearly there was no way to stop it.

18

Cats and Rats

Violet was just stepping out of the shower that night when her console went crazy.

It rocked and it buzzed with a hectic variety of strange beeping and whistling sounds. It almost bounced off the blue tile countertop. Violet yanked a T-shirt over her head and hopped into a pair of sweats and moved into her room, settling on her bed cross-legged so she could figure out what was going on. The hair across the back of her neck was still wet from the shower, but she didn't notice.

The screen was fuzzy and gray, with tiny white streamers cascading down from the corners. Violet had never seen anything like it before.

It took her another few seconds to realize what was going on. She had not erased the coordinates Reznik had given her to access the chip-jack. There was a chance—just a small one, but a chance all the same—that Danny's feed would return for a few minutes now and again.

This was it.

Violet felt that funny lurch in her stomach that always seemed

to show up when Danny was involved. She didn't even bother looking at the crook of her left elbow. She knew what she'd see there.

On her console, the fuzziness resolved itself into a view of stark
ugliness. It had to be Old Earth. This was a city, but it wasn't like any
city Violet had ever seen before.

It was a dead place.

A smear of soiled-looking white haze was wrapped across the horizon like a dirty bandage. The wind was blowing, shoving trash
along the filthy, slanted street. It was almost dusk. At this time of
night, Danny had told her, the people on Old Earth tucked themselves
into whatever shelter they could find. Night was a nervous time there.

And then she saw his face.

It was reflected in a mud puddle. Danny had leaned over to look
in it, checking its depth in case he couldn't make it across in one leap.
He moved on, taking the long way around the giant puddle. He ducked
under the sagging remnants of what once had been electrical power
lines but now looked like fraying dead vines.

He stopped again. He took a deep breath. He peered around.

Violet guessed that he needed a minute to reorient himself to Old
Earth, to reacclimate himself to its foul smells and its blunt colors
and the rugged, inhospitable terrain. He'd gotten a little soft after all
that time on New Earth. Even the frequent trips back here couldn't
be like *living* here.

Once, Danny had known every rock in this landscape. Every stick.
Every gully. Every hiding place. When he and his brother were kids,
he'd told Violet, the two of them would jump across the cracks and
gaps in these sidewalks, chasing each other down these torn-up
roads and across the weed-clogged lots, racing through the empty
roofless houses with the falling-away floors and half-gone walls.

Where was he going this time? And the destination, whatever
it was, could not have been the reason for his earlier trips to Old
Earth; Danny would have done it long ago. This was a different mission. A new one.

He turned sideways and slipped into a small crevice between two dilapidated buildings. The gap was hardly big enough to call itself an alley. The space was so narrow, in fact, that Violet wasn't sure how he'd fit himself in there, even after wriggling and drawing in his shoulders. Somehow, though, he managed.

A vaguely rectangular section had been hacked out of the side of one of the buildings. It led to a flight of crooked and crumbling steps. At the bottom was a dented, scraped-up metal door. Garbage had blown onto the steps and stalled in the corners. Near the door was a gray pile of short crisscrossed bones. Rat? Pigeon? Human baby? Something else? Violet couldn't tell. And frankly, she was glad about that.

Danny shoved at the door. It didn't budge.

Now he lifted a booted foot and gave it a flurry of sharp kicks.

Nothing.

More kicks.

Still nothing.

Danny was breathing heavily from exertion. It seemed hopeless; the door was sealed tight. But he wasn't a quitter. Violet knew that just as surely as she knew that *she* wasn't a quitter, either.

He stretched his neck and rolled his shoulders, preparing himself for one last try. He gulped in a deep breath. He aimed a powerful punch of a kick at the dead center of the door.

It popped open like a cork coming out of a bottle.

What waited inside was the most disgusting room Violet had ever seen. The floor was pounded dirt, the ceiling was low, the amount of junk was epic. Water dripped in three of the four corners, a dismal steady rhythm. In the one corner that didn't feature a dirty waterfall, spiders had set up a complicated trapeze of giant webs. Skinny rats scuttled along the narrow twisting passageways between the junk piles, pausing every few feet to rise on their hind legs, sniffing the air.

Danny tried to climb and sidle his way through mountains of

motley stuff—crusted-over computers with shattered screens, over-turned benches, thick coils of wire, old brass fittings, burnt-out plugs, rusty springs, dozens of buckets of mismatched nails, countless piles of oily rags, millions of glittering chips of glass from busted test tubes and beakers. He had to stop every few seconds and move aside ancient vacuum cleaners and splintered chairs and acid-oozing batteries and upended bookshelves and three cracked-in-half chalkboards.

And then, with a lightning flash of insight, Violet realized what this place was.

What it had to be.

This is Kendall's lab. This is where he created the Intercept.

The revelation was half exciting, half terrifying.

She felt goose bumps rising up on her forearms. This was the place.

Danny was still moving. His goal seemed to be the wall at the back of the room. The cinder blocks were in desperate shape, Violet saw; they bore the marks of severe and prolonged water damage. Mold gripped them from corner to corner, a profusion of pale green star-bursts. The wall looked perilously close to collapsing, but it had prob-ably looked that way for a very long time, she thought. It might crumble in the next ten minutes or it might last another millennium; there was no telling which.

Suddenly something jumped and hissed. Danny flinched. Violet did, too, even though she was thousands of miles away, sitting safely on a comfortable bed in a large and beautiful apartment on New Earth.

The cat had leaped down from a rickety tower of old boxes. It landed directly in front of Danny, screaming its own special cat-scream, a thin, high-pitched needle of sound, aggressive and obnox-ious. The ridges of the cat's arched backbone were visible through the patchy, matted gray fur.

For a few seconds Danny didn't move. Animals on Old Earth, he'd once explained to Violet, were notoriously vicious and aggressive. Because they were starving.

Finally, after deploying an intense and malicious yellow-eyed glare, the cat padded away. The flick of its tail seemed to reveal its thinking: A strategic withdrawal now, followed by a patient wait in the corner, would pay dividends later when this tall intruder tripped, fell, found himself trapped, and then died, whereupon the cat would be the pleased recipient of a hot meal.

Danny approached the wall. As a very puzzled Violet watched, he knelt and counted up six blocks from the floor. Then he stood up and counted three blocks to the left.

He tapped the block with two fingers.

Once.

Twice.

Three times.

The block slid out of the wall. It was not really a block at all, Violet saw, but a lined compartment. Nestled in the middle was a small notebook with a red leather cover. There was not a mark on it. The compartment was bone-dry.

Danny lifted the notebook out of the compartment.

The chip-jack's going to fail ANY MINUTE, Violet told herself glumly. She passionately wished it to be otherwise, but she was convinced. That's how her luck had been running lately.

I'm going to lose the image. The signal will fade. And I'll never know—

The signal did not fade.

The signal wasn't the problem. The problem was that she had no idea what he had found.

Danny opened the notebook. He quickly leafed through its pages. When he arrived at the right spot, he stopped. He put his index finger in the middle of the page to keep the notebook from flopping shut again. He read. He was so intensely focused that Violet wasn't even sure he was breathing. Time stopped for him. His world collapsed into the writing on that page.

And she was locked out.

From her vantage point, all she could see were furious scribbles. She wasn't close enough to see anything specific. As to what the letters and numbers *meant,* she did not know. They raced across the page and climbed up both margins, the figures blending in a frantic dance of information.

Violet didn't know why the notebook was so important to him. Or how the notebook was related—if it *was* related—to his earlier visit to Tin Man's prison cell.

Or to his repeated visits—even earlier—to Old Earth.

Danny closed the notebook. He carefully placed it back in the compartment, and then he pushed the block until once again it was flush with the wall. Now the wall looked like an ordinary wall again—if a slimy, mold-crusted, falling-down panel of cinder blocks could be described as ordinary.

Why doesn't he take the notebook with him? Violet asked herself. She answered her own question: *Because he needs to keep it safe. And the safest location for something on New Earth is ... Old Earth.*

She kept waiting for the chip-jack signal to fade, but it didn't. It held steady as Danny left the wet, disheveled lab—or what once had been a lab—in the same manner in which he'd come in, which meant climbing over calamitous mounds of debris and sidestepping puddles of mysterious black goo and platoons of rodent carcasses. Once he was back outside, he yanked the metal door shut behind him, double-checking the tight seal.

He looked around for a few seconds, to make sure no one was watching, and it was at that point—with Danny's gaze sweeping left, right, left, and then right again—that the chip-jack's signal failed.

With a little *fzzzip* sound, Violet's console screen wavered and then went black. The chip-jack was dead. According to Rez, that was it. You sometimes—not always—got that second wind from the device, the one Violet had just experienced. A third wind was unheard of.

She didn't mind. Now she knew exactly what she had to do: go to

Old Earth and find that notebook for herself. She'd do what she had been advising Danny *not* to do for months now—that is, sneak down to Old Earth. She had to uncover the secret contained in those scribbled pages. It could be the key to everything.

The journey would be difficult, and her father would definitely ground her for life if he ever found out—but she was going to do it, anyway.

And to get there, she would have to go through Thirlsome.

The Fall

Thirlsome. The last remaining point of contact between the two worlds.

The name had a kind of magic. And its own peculiar music. When Violet was a little girl and her mother returned from her latest journey to Old Earth, the word *Thirlsome* ignited something deep and thrilling inside her. "And so I went to the docking station on Thirlsome," Lucretia Crowley would say, "and I got into the pod. The same pod I'd ridden in when I came down from New Earth. And I closed the door and then—*whooosh*—off it went, and just a little while later I was right here again with you and Daddy."

Hearing the word *Thirlsome*—then and now—made Violet's stomach do a little tap dance. The syllables stirred up a reminder of everything she wanted in her life: adventure and mystery and maybe a pinch of danger, too. Thirlsome was all about Elsewhere—something beyond the safety and calm and predictability that defined her life, day after day, on New Earth.

Thirlsome.

To Violet, it wasn't just a word. It was the lure of the unknown. It was everything her father tried to protect her from—and chief among those things was Old Earth itself. Thirlsome was the threshold of that distant, forbidden place.

In the present, however, there was a small complication:

How was she going to actually *get* there?

You couldn't just hop in a pod on New Earth and scoot down to Old Earth. No way. Travel was strictly regulated. As hard as it was to go from Old Earth to New Earth—and thousands of would-be immigrants tried, year after year, begging Shura's mother to help them— it was even harder to make the trip down from New Earth to the port of Thirlsome.

People with official business, such as Violet's mother and Anna Lu, were allowed, but only after filing petitions and going through ID checks and submitting to multiple interviews about their intentions.

It would be impossible for a sixteen-year-old girl with no official business on Old Earth to get in a pod on New Earth and somehow make it to Thirlsome.

Impossible, that is, for any *ordinary* sixteen-year-old girl.

But she was Violet Crowley. And she had a plan.

"You know why they picked it, right? Picked Thirlsome for the transport site? It was part of my training. I had to learn all the history junk."

Sara Verity took a long drink of her soda. She was thirsty because she had been talking. And talking. And then talking some more. At the end of every few sentences, she pushed a springy thatch of red curls up and off her forehead; they tended to stray there when Sara became emphatic about a particular point, leaning forward, bobbing her head.

She was *very* emphatic right now, because she was trying to persuade Violet to forget the whole thing. In the middle of her spiel, she had lapsed into the material from her transport logistics handbook. It was her way of buying time, hoping Violet would reconsider. Sara had been talking for quite a long while. She had the dry throat to prove it.

"Okay—why'd they pick it?" Violet said. She didn't really care. She was just being polite to Sara. Because she wanted something from her.

Sara was on pod duty tonight. Violet had showed up and barged in, which technically was against the rules, but pod duty was a lonely business and so Sara didn't mind. The traffic between Old Earth and New Earth was drastically reduced these days, with only a few journeys each month. And those were mostly made by cops or scientists, who never had much to say to the red-haired intern with the shy smile and the plaid bag.

But someone had to be here, twenty-four/seven, and that usually meant an intern. Like Sara.

This was one of those times when Violet didn't mind being the president's daughter. She had been waved past the perimeter checkpoints when the cops recognized her face. Anybody else would have been stopped before they got within a mile of the transport center.

She and Sara sat in the center's lobby, a small room with a black-and-red checkerboard tile floor, white foam walls, and red backless couches that ran along all four walls. When people arrived for transport down to Old Earth, they sat on these couches, waiting for their name to be called by the Pod Officer on duty.

Unless you're Danny, Violet had reminded herself, when she first got here tonight and looked around the lobby. *Then you slip in the back and sneak your way into a pod.*

Part of her was irritated by that. And part of her admired him for it.

"Thirlsome was chosen for the site because of its isolation and its favorable geographical coordinates," Sara droned on. Violet struggled to pay attention. "The Kampura caves on its southern shore of Old Earth matched up ideally with the trajectory of incoming pods from New Earth. In the early 2280s, when thousands of people were being taken up every hour, day after day, month after month, the Kampura caves were overflowing. Vendors set up stalls that sold food and drinks and Old Earth souvenirs. Now, though, since immigration is so tightly controlled, the caves are mostly empty. And so—"

"Only one portal is left. That's what I read," Violet said. She hated to interrupt, but she was getting impatient.

Sara took another drink of her soda. "Right. We've got two up here—they're just behind the heat shield over there—but on Thirlsome, there's only one left. The rest of them were stripped for their metal a long time ago."

Violet was now officially Bored Out of Her Mind.

"Okay," she said. "Listen, Sara, I know this is a huge favor. But like I said, I need to get to Old Earth. Right away."

"Why?"

"It's an errand for my dad." Violet cringed inwardly at the lie, but this was for the greater good. Right? And nobody said no to Ogden Crowley.

Sara was troubled. Her emotions were easy for Violet to read. Her face bunched into a frown. The bunching made the skin around her eyes crinkle, and the crinkling inspired a bundle of wrinkles to jet across her forehead.

"How are you going to find your way around down there?" Sara said. "It's all just a big dirty jumble. Your console's GPS won't work. Even people who've gone down there before have gotten lost."

It was a fair point. Violet had asked herself the same question.

And the answer is—I don't have the faintest clue.

She was scared, but she still wanted to try. Maybe she wanted to try *because* she was scared.

She felt a brief sliver of worry about how the Intercept would classify that when it did its regular eavesdropping on her emotions—as bravado, maybe. Or ego. Or recklessness.

It didn't matter.

A few minutes later, Violet stood in front of the thick pod door. She was nervous. She didn't try to hide it. When she reached up with an index finger and traced the stern march of red capital letters in three lines across the top, her hand trembled:

BY ORDER OF OGDEN CROWLEY
ABSOLUTELY NO UNAUTHORIZED USE
VIOLATORS SUBJECT TO PROSECUTION

"Are you sure about this?" Sara said. "Really sure?"

"Really sure."

"Really *really* sure?"

"They can't trace it back to you, Sara. I can activate it from my console. And I'll erase the console record."

"That's not what I meant." Sara looked a little hurt at the idea that fear and self-interest were at the heart of her concern.

"I know. But it's important. This is my decision," Violet said. "Nobody else should get in any trouble for it." She tapped her console. "I'm ready."

"I know you're ready. But are you *sure*?"

"Sara."

"Okay, okay."

Sara swiped the lock with her ID.

The door to the pod opened with a creak and a scraping sound. After a second's hesitation, Violet stepped inside. The pod smelled a little musty and a little oniony. A lot of people had sweated in here. They sweated because a new world awaited them, and unfamiliar things were scary. Or they sweated because they were going in the wrong direction—back toward Old Earth, which they knew well, and familiar things were sometimes even scarier.

The pod door closed, accompanied by another creak, and then a click and a whoosh and a heavy *cha-THWUNK,* followed by a brief whirring sound. Violet looked out through the inch-high, inch-wide slit. The glass was so dirty she had to rub it with her sleeve to see anything.

She spotted Sara's face, filled with worry.

Violet couldn't give her any last-minute words of reassurance. The pod was soundproof.

She waited. She took a deep breath. It didn't relax her one bit. She took another deep breath. The second one was similarly useless as an anxiety-fighter.

She would have to activate the switch herself. If Sara did it from outside the pod, the signal would be instantly relayed to Protocol Hall. They'd know. They'd check it against the list of authorized trips. They'd discover that it *wasn't* authorized.

And they'd come. They would stop her.

So: If Violet was going to do this, she had to do it on her own. No help. Which was another way of saying: Nobody else would have to take the blame. Only her.

Maybe this is a bad idea, after all. Maybe I'll just bang on the doors and when Sara comes I'll tell her that I've changed my . . .

She thought about Danny. His face flashed before her mind. She pictured the way he looked when he was thinking hard about something, when his dark eyes acquired that faraway glow. Even though he often frowned when he was concentrating so fiercely, it wasn't a grim frown. It was a frown of serious focus. It was one of the reasons she loved him: When he sensed he had a duty to fulfill, he gave it everything he had.

And so she would do that, too. She would discover the secret in that notebook. Even if it meant that she got into terrible trouble, even if she ended up disappointing her father—or maybe even getting suspended, kicked off the team at Protocol Hall as her punishment. Didn't matter. She had to go.

She was going to go.

She flipped the switch.

Suddenly her body began to quake violently. It felt as if someone had grabbed her by the waist and was trying to twist her viciously so that the top half of her body would face in the opposite direction from the bottom half. A furious heat seized her. She was dizzy. She was confused. She didn't know if she was moving up or down or sideways.

She crossed her arms. Closed her eyes. Said a quick prayer.

In less than one one-trillionth of a second the pod was flung aloft like a burning star, a lozenge of light instantly lost amid the silken darkness.

Violet opened her mouth to scream at the drenching shock of it all. She wanted to call it off, to reconsider. *Okay, so I was wrong. I don't care about any lab or any notebook. This really IS a bad idea. I don't want to do this I don't want*

She dropped out of the sky, bound for the swirling darkness below.

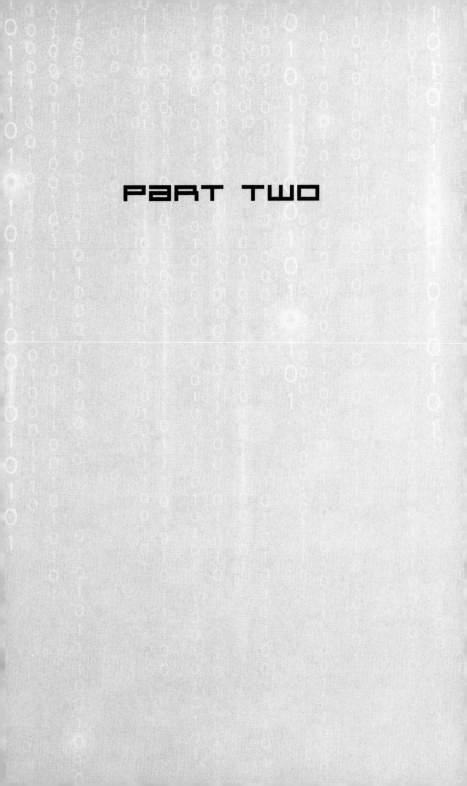

PART TWO

20

Welcome to Old Earth

The gray was amazing. Gray everywhere: the trees, the sky, the ground. A long, steady, soaking rain had knitted a thick curtain of gray. Even her skin looked gray now.

But was her skin really gray? Was that the right word for this color?

Violet stared at her hands. It was as if all the color had leaked out of them, escaping through some hole she wasn't aware of. She turned her hands over and back, over and back. They stayed gray. In fact, the color that had replaced the original shade of her skin was, she now saw, something other than gray. Something lesser. Was it the color of smoke? No, not smoke. That wasn't right, either.

It was a color she'd never seen before. It was a washed-out, fed-up, done-in color that spoke of emptiness and lack.

If she'd been asked to define the color, she would've said: *sadness*. Her skin was the color of sadness.

Violet took a step. She also took a deep breath. Mistake: The smell was like a poke in the nose. It was a disgusting medley of vivid, insinuating odors. Dead things, old things, forgotten things, rotting things—the smells groped and climbed all over one another, spreading out. They twisted and they oozed, growing more intense as she began to move. She took one more step.

And then one more.

She looked at the horizon. It was yet another shade of gray, a gray that was shot through with squiggles of pink. The pink reminded Violet of spongy, undercooked meat.

All at once, she felt a vicious blow to the right side of her head. She cried out. She barely managed to stay upright. Hot blood sluiced through her hair and down her neck. She was instantly woozy. She wanted to scream from the pain.

Someone grabbed her arms, pinning them behind her back.

Struggling to free herself, bucking wildly, flinging her head back and forth despite the dizziness it caused her, Violet saw that she was surrounded by three mean-looking men and two women who looked even meaner. Their faces were inked with grime; their eyes glittered with menace.

The man who stood in front of her had his filthy hands gripped around a long rusty pole as if it were a baseball bat. That's what he had hit her with, she surmised, as he'd rushed from out of nowhere and cracked it hard against the side of her skull.

Violet looked at the wetness on the upper part of the pole and thought, *My blood.* The thought made her shudder, and then it made her even sicker.

She was astonished by the pain. She was also confused by it.

Where's the Intercept? Why hasn't it kicked in? Why aren't these people falling down and screaming, knocked down by a grievous memory? Why isn't the Intercept disabling them?

And then she remembered.

Nobody on New Earth even knows this is happening. Nobody's watching Old Earth. Nobody routinely monitors it. The drone feeds are pretty much ignored by Protocol Hall.

So: no Intercept. She was on her own down here. There was no Reznik, sitting smugly but knowledgeably in front of his computer, punching buttons. No spinning circuits and crackling digital syn-apses set into flickering, instantaneous motion beneath the floor of Protocol Hall, making the floor tremble, a trembling that was so fa-miliar that nobody even reacted anymore. Nobody said, "What's that?" Nobody paid any attention.

Sort of like what was happening now on Old Earth. Sort of like this attack.

Nobody knew.

So this, Violet thought with a wonder that momentarily displaced her panic, *is what life's like without the Intercept as protection. Raw, unpredictable—and really,* really *painful.*

"Check her pockets," growled the man with the pole. His hair was pus-yellow and wild, and it looked like it had been oiled with sweat. "Make sure she doesn't have any weapons." Two of them rammed their dirt-smeared hands down into her trouser pockets. One of the women tried to wrench off her shoes, but didn't have the proper angle and almost fell over when she probed without the right leverage.

With her arms pinned, Violet was helpless to fight back. Her head was throbbing. The pain started at the spot where she'd been hit and radiated out in a red-hot spiral of sheer agony. She was afraid she might faint. The idea terrified her. It would mean she'd be even more helpless in the clutches of these people.

"Please," Violet said. It came out as a desperate gasp. "Please. It hurts." She was crying. She didn't want to cry—she felt weak and silly—but she couldn't help herself. The tears had started up on their own and now they gushed. "Please."

The man with the pole gave her a greasy little smile. Only a few teeth were left in his mouth, and they looked as gray as weathered tree stumps. He laughed. The laugh went on a long time. Too long. The others joined in, but fitfully, as if they weren't sure when he might turn around and use the pole on *them.*

Through the livid haze of her pain, Violet realized something: The man wasn't a man at all. He was a kid. He was younger than she was.

It was the dirt that had fooled her. The dirt on his face was ancient, permanent, baked on, a hard ceramic glaze of filth.

"Please," Violet said, and again it came out as a gasp, because she didn't seem to have enough air in her lungs to do anything except choke and whimper. "Please. Please. I'm from New Earth. I don't mean you any harm. I've never been here before. I'm just looking for—"

The blow to her stomach that interrupted her seemed to come from out of nowhere. It was the rusty pole again. The kid had slammed it into her midsection. The pain made Violet, bending double now, cough and sputter. Bile spun out of her mouth and ended up sprinkling the gray ground.

The kid laughed again. He spread his feet, to give him better balance. He lifted the pole. He wasn't finished yet.

"Welcome to Old Earth," he said in a grizzled voice that made him sound like an old, old man who had done a great many bad things.

21

The Woman in the Red Bandana

The kid was just about to hit her in the head again when something happened.

Violet wasn't sure at first exactly what it was. But as she stood there, waiting for the next blow, she heard a noise that was a cross between a *boing* and a *thwunk,* with a little of pinch of a *kerwhamp* thrown in for good measure.

The kid suddenly got a funny look on his face. His mouth popped open. His expression was a stew of surprise and confusion and pain and a sort of goofy grogginess. Suddenly he toppled forward, almost head-butting Violet as he pitched in her direction.

The moment the kid was down, she understood. Standing directly behind him—or behind where he'd been before he fell face-first on the ground—was a small, almost elfin-looking woman who held a huge cast-iron skillet over her head with two hands.

"I told you to stop!" she yelled. It took Violet a few seconds—she was still dazed from the earlier blows—to realize the woman wasn't talking to her, but to the kid. Or at least to the back of the kid's head. The kid stirred in the dirt. He mumbled something.

The others in the group had all scampered away the moment he went down. Apparently the kid was the leader. Without him, they were directionless and flailing.

"You okay?" the woman asked. She had lowered the skillet by now but still held on to the handle with both hands, just in case.

Violet didn't know how to reply. *Was* she okay? Her body felt like one big pulsing ache. She wanted to throw up. She put a hand to her right ear, and the wetness on her fingertips perplexed her at first, until she realized that it was blood.

"You okay?" the woman repeated. She squinted, giving Violet a peculiar look. "Maybe you oughta come sit down."

That sounded like a very good idea. Violet let herself be led over to a set of broken wooden steps. The steps were attached—barely—to a battered, nearly roofless house whose two burnt-out front windows looked like the empty sockets after the eyes have been gouged out of a corpse. The houses on either side were just shells. One had only a single outside wall left standing; the other had two walls, but a strong wind would've made short work of both.

"That kid's all trouble, all the time," the woman muttered. She sat down next to Violet. "Now, if my boy was here, he'd keep that punk in line. No question. He kept 'em *all* in line."

Violet was still in pain, but it was better now that she was sitting down. She took several deep breaths in a row. She realized she wasn't going to die.

She took a better look at her rescuer. The woman had a thin face that hadn't been washed in quite a long time. Her dark curly hair was partially covered by a soiled red bandana. She had dark eyes and a round chin. The chin was marked by a white scar with a kink at the end, so that it resembled a backward capital *L*.

She was much older than Violet had realized upon first glance. At least thirty-five or forty. Ancient, in other words. The dirt functioned as accidental but highly effective camouflage. Just as it had obscured her assailant's real age, it had also hidden this woman's age, but in reverse. The idea of her rescuer having a son—and one old enough to have once ruled this benighted block—was entirely plau-sible now that Violet had seen her up close.

"Who are you, anyway?" the woman said. "We don't get many people down here from New Earth."

"How'd you know I was from New Earth?"

The woman laughed. It was a big, rich, hearty laugh.

"Oh, honey," the woman said. "Where do I start? To begin with, you're not filthy. You've obviously had a shower recently. You smell good. Soap, am I right? Yeah. Soap." She closed her eyes. A look of ecstasy flitted across her small face. "Mmmmmm. I *love* soap." She opened her eyes. "I haven't smelled soap in—oh, never mind. And your clothes aren't torn. And your fingernails aren't dirty. Do I need to go on?"

Violet didn't answer. She felt silly that she'd even asked.

"So why are you here?" the woman said. "Believe it or not, this is not on most people's lists as a top vacation spot."

She laughed again, and then she kicked at a small pile of garbage at the foot of the steps. Her boots, Violet saw, were just strips of rotting leather held together by fraying string. Her pants and her shirt were filthy. Anywhere that her skin showed—her neck, her hands and wrists—was a place streaked with grime and marked with scratches.

"My name's Violet." The effort to speak made Violet need to cough. She suddenly had to spit, too, and out came a great rubbery gob of phlegm. It didn't seem to faze the woman at all, but it embarrassed Violet.

She had deliberately left off her last name. Ogden Crowley was famous—and not for reasons that made him popular on Old Earth.

"Ever been here before?" the woman asked.

Violet shook her head. "No. First time. I'm looking for something." She didn't want to reveal too much—including her full name—until she knew more about this woman. For all Violet knew, she could be as bad as the kid who'd attacked her. Only smoother and trickier.

By this time the woman had picked up a broken-off tree branch that lay nearby and was tapping it in the dirt. She tapped it three times, paused, then three times again. It seemed to be a nervous habit.

"Okay," she said. "Well, I'm Delia."

"Thanks for saving me, Delia. I think that guy would've killed me."

Delia looked at the spot a few yards away from them, where the kid was still face-down in the dirt. He was certainly breathing; his back rose and fell, and every now and again he snuffled and he twitched. Violet fully expected the woman to dismiss the notion, to say something like: *Oh, no, he's harmless, really—he would've just roughed you up a bit and then let you go.*

Instead, Delia said, suddenly solemn, "You're right. He would have. This is a very dangerous place." She reached over and touched Violet's right shoe. "These? This nice pair of shoes you got here? They're real pretty. They don't have any holes. They look almost new. You've taken good care of them. And that kid out there? He could've sold them in about ten minutes. And with the money, he would've been able to feed his brothers and sisters for a couple of weeks. Maybe a whole month." She rubbed the sleeve of Violet's jacket. Violet was tempted to pull her arm back, out of the woman's reach, but she didn't, because it might seem rude.

"And this?" Delia went on. "This jacket? The others who hang out with the kid—the ones who ran away once I'd smacked him down— well, they would've taken this fancy little jacket of yours and used it as a blanket this winter. It gets really cold down here. Material like this—good and thick and sturdy—it's like gold." She patted Violet's arm and smiled before withdrawing her hand. "And if you'd kept on fighting back, if you'd tried to keep your shoes and your clothes, and if I hadn't shown up, then they would've cut them off of you. Your arms, your feet—they wouldn't care. As long as they got what they wanted. What they needed."

Now Delia reached up and touched the side of Violet's head. Once again, Violet's impulse was to duck and scoot away very quickly, but there was something in Delia's voice—a quality of regretful honesty, Violet wanted to call it—that kept her right where she was.

"And if you had long hair," Delia said, "they would've chopped that off, too. So you're lucky you have short hair. See—you can use hair for a lot of things down here. It's like currency. Good to barter with. You can put it in cracks in the walls to help keep the wind out. Or you can stuff it in a coat or a pair of pants and make a soft pillow. I've even seen some of the older kids take hair and put it inside tin cans when they're making their bombs. It helps to hold the other stuff—the nails, the wire, the razors—in place."

"So they would've killed me for my *hair*?" Violet said. "Or my *shoes*? I can't believe—"

"Yeah. Yeah, they would have. Without a second thought." Delia peered at her. "Where do you think you are, honey?"

"Old Earth."

"Those are just words. That's a label. I mean—where *are* you?"

"I don't under—"

Delia stood up and began pacing in front of the steps. Back and forth. Her quick movement had startled Violet.

"Look, girlie," Delia said. Her voice had gone cold, dropping its gentle, friendly bemusement. "You're in a special place now, okay? All the things you think you know—the books and the music and the poetry and the good manners and the high ideals and all of that— they're *nothing* here. Less than nothing. What matters here is *survival*. What matters here is food. Food for yourself and food for the people you care about. And finding enough warm clothes so that you can get through the winter. And then the winter after that."

Delia sounded angry as she marched back and forth along a very short track, so short that she had to whirl around after three steps and go in the opposite direction. "We see you every now and again, you people from New Earth," she declared. "One or two of you come down, every year or so. Same reason people used to go to zoos, I guess. To gawk. To point. To judge. To feel superior. You come down here and you look at us. Oh, we know what you're thinking when you do that—it's like, 'God, what a bunch of filthy animals. What a bunch of pigs.'"

Violet wanted to interrupt her and say, *No, that's not me, I'm not like that, I'm not staring or judging*—but she couldn't, because that's exactly what she had been doing. She found the filth on Delia's face and hands disgusting. She found Delia's smell—a pervasive stink that was so rank and complex and all-encompassing that it seemed to originate deep in the woman's very cells—to be repulsive.

Delia stopped pacing. She looked at Violet and she nodded. Violet had the unsettling notion that Delia had just read her mind. Or close enough.

"You, too," Delia said. The anger had receded. It was replaced by a soft sadness. Violet realized that she preferred the anger. The sadness was almost unbearable.

"You're like that, too, aren't you?" Delia went on. "You're looking at us and you're wondering why we don't clean up our streets. Or live in decent homes. Or read a book. Or take a bath, right?"

"I don't—"

"Let me ask you something." Delia interrupted her so fast that Violet wondered if the woman had even realized she was speaking. "When you're going out with your friends, what do you do?"

"I'm not sure how to answer the—"

"*What do you do?*" Delia's voice was as sharp as scissor tips. "How do you get ready?"

"Well, I guess I—I guess I take a shower, and then I pick out what I'm going to wear, and then I—"

"Exactly." Delia sounded triumphant. "Exactly. You take a shower. Now, in order to take that shower, what has to happen? There has to be running water, right? And a plumbing system, right? And then clean clothes for you to put on—and they're clean because why?"

"Look, Delia, I don't want to—"

"*Why are your clothes clean?*"

Violet spoke in a slow, chastened voice. "Because somebody washed them."

"Right. Right." Delia flung out her arms. "And what do you see here? Do you see anything like that around here? *Anything?* If we want a drink of water, we wait for it to rain. And even then, the rain tastes like acid. Because it comes from the evaporation of rivers and oceans so full of chemical crap that it stopped being 'water' a long, long time ago. It's something else now. I don't know what it is, but it isn't water. And as for washing our clothes—" She looked down at her dirt-encrusted shirt and she laughed. It was a hard, dark laugh that caused a chill to ripple through Violet. "That's not exactly a priority, okay? Not when our children are dying in front of our eyes. Not when we don't know when—or if—we'll find anything to eat. Not when we're living in houses that are falling down all around us. Or living under trees. Or in caves. Or anywhere we can find where we won't freeze to death."

Delia stopped. She was panting. She seemed exhausted.

"So when you *tourists* from New Earth come down here," Delia said, the bitterness still crackling in her voice, "sometimes I want to grab a big stick or some other kind of weapon—anything that will get your attention—and hold it over you and force you to really look at what we've become. I want you to *see*. We're what you left behind. We're like the trash somebody forgets to clean up when they move on. You wish you could've gotten rid of us, but we stuck. We *survived*. We're hanging on." Delia formed her hands into fists. She shook them in front of her own face. "But sometimes—*sometimes*—I get so mad at you New Earth people and your stuck-up ways and your prejudices—and I want to hurt you. Hurt you *bad*. Every last one of you. I want to hurt you and leave you twisted and bleeding and—"

"But you helped me," Violet interjected. The woman was scaring her now. Her only hope, Violet thought, was to break the trance of Delia's anger. "You saved my life. Just a few minutes ago. Why did you do that? If you hate me so much—why did you do that?"

Delia relaxed her fists. She dropped her hands to her sides. She smiled. It was as if a taut string had finally snapped, and she was restored to herself.

"Oh, that's easy," she said. "You remind me of my little girl. If she had lived, I think she would've looked a lot like you. My baby. My Molly."

Teatime

So what're you looking for?" Delia asked.

She finished winding the cloth around Violet's head, tying it off with a stubby little bow. The bleeding had started up again a few minutes ago, and so Delia had held her by the arm and led her into the bashed-up, broken-down house.

The interior was bare except for one filthy overturned bucket in what must have been—a long, long time ago—the kitchen. That was the seat upon which Delia placed Violet while she checked her own pockets for a piece of fabric with which to wrap the wound.

The kitchen was very cold. From a large ragged hole in the ceiling the leaves constantly drifted down in a silent serenade.

"Are you sure that's clean?" Violet said, eyeing the crusty cloth.

Delia laughed. "I'm sure it's *not* clean. I'll tell you what my great-great-grandmother used to say. 'Beggars can't be choosers.'" She backed away a few steps and turned her head to one side, looking critically at Violet. "That should keep the blood from dripping all over the place." She snickered. "Not that we'd notice the mess in this hellhole, right? Okay—now answer my question. What's down here that you're after? What's on Old Earth that you can't get up there?" Another snicker. "Except for dirt and germs and danger, that is."

Violet touched the makeshift bandage. Her instinct was to trust this woman. But she was still wary. Old Earth was different from anything she'd ever known before. Maybe her instincts weren't valid here.

"Something that somebody lost," Violet answered. "A friend of mine."

"A friend." Repeating the word, Delia gave her a look. The look came with a caption: *Okay, fine. Be that way. I know you don't trust me. I can't force you to.*

"Yeah," Violet said. "Hey, thanks for helping me. Guess I'd better be going."

She stood up. Or tried to, anyway. She felt a sudden gust of dizziness and a swirl of nausea, and her legs went wobbly, and before she knew it, she'd plopped back down on the overturned bucket. She closed her eyes. When she opened them again, Delia was peering at her, slowly nodding.

"You're still woozy from that conk on the head," Delia said. "My advice? Rest for a little while. Then you can go out and resume your search for—oh, that's right. I don't know. Because you won't tell me." She shrugged. "I'm going to make some tea. Interested?"

"Sure." The second she agreed, though, Violet had misgivings. What if the teacup was like the bandage—that is, covered with so many gradations and varieties of grime that the original surface was just a distant memory?

Or what if Delia was plotting to poison her?

She'd have to take her chances. She really needed a cup of tea.

Delia began her task. Violet watched her. To call this kitchen primitive was generous. In the fireplace, something large and awkward and smelly had recently burned. The scorch marks licking the bricks around the opening were a little scary-looking; it would've taken a ginormous animal carcass to jut out that far, and the vision of such a creature being consumed by flames was like something out of a noxious nightmare.

There were no cabinets, no appliances, no table or chairs. No cups or saucers.

As it happened, however, there *was* a cup. Or at least something you could drink out of. Delia knelt down and rummaged through a brown paper sack that was tucked in a corner, hidden under a pile of leaves. She pulled out a tin can with its label missing. From a ratty-looking canteen also stashed in the sack, she filled the can to the halfway point.

"We'll have to share," Delia said.

Violet didn't react out loud, but inside she was thinking: *Um—gross.* But she still wanted some tea.

She watched Delia moving around the kitchen. How, Violet wondered, was this woman ever going to make tea in this empty, forsaken place?

Delia scurried around, gathering up sticks and leaves that had dropped in through the hole in the roof. She dumped three armfuls in the fireplace. Then she turned around and grinned at Violet, wiping her hands on her trousers.

"There's one important thing my boy gave me before they took him away," Delia said. With a flourish, she pulled a small blue box from her pocket. She opened it and plucked out a tiny yellow stick. She scraped the tip of the stick against the side of the box. It took her three tries. At last a tiny but sturdy flame popped up.

"Matches," Delia said, in a delighted voice. She flipped the burning stick into the fireplace. The leaves and other debris quickly caught flame.

Violet had read about matches in Old Earth history. They hadn't been used in hundreds of years, and no one on New Earth had ever actually seen one, but her father had told her stories about them. When he was a boy, his parents built a fire every night. Outside, in the open, in a small ring of rocks. They used matches to light the flame. The fire kept the wild animals away, he explained to Violet.

Delia went back to the sack. Out came a small tea bag. Violet could tell by looking at it—it was limp and wrinkled and almost colorless, and the string had long ago disappeared—that it had been used many, many times. Next Delia retrieved a long branch propped in the corner. At the threshold of the fireplace, she set down the tin can, using the branch to push it into the fire.

"Won't be long now," Delia said.

"There's nowhere for you to sit."

"Sure there is." She walked closer to Violet and plopped down on the floor.

Violet had never seen someone this old—Delia had two kids, according to what she'd said—behave quite this way, with a sort of free-spirited jauntiness. Violet had assumed all old people were alike: reserved, dignified. Just like the ones she knew. But then again, she reminded herself, she'd never been to Old Earth before. People were different here. They had to be, in order to survive.

She looked at Delia, cross-legged on the dirty wooden floor. From here, Violet could plainly see the crook of her left arm. It was home to an exceedingly ugly wound, a red, puckered, angry-looking space that looked as if something had exploded beneath the skin, and then the heaving flesh had been flash-frozen.

"Your Intercept chip," Violet said. "Did something go wrong with the insertion?"

Delia pulled her sleeve down over the damaged skin. It was the first self-conscious gesture Violet had seen her make.

"Nope," Delia said. "The *insertions* always go really, really smooth." Her sarcastic tone descended into bitterness. "It's not putting it *in* that gets you, right? It's trying to take it *out*."

Violet was shocked. "Trying to take it—? That's illegal."

Delia laughed darkly. "Yeah. And what're they gonna do about it? How're they gonna punish me? Ship me off to Old Earth? Oh, right— I'm already *here*."

Violet shook her head. She felt silly. But she wanted to hear what had happened to Delia's arm. "So what messed it up like that?"

"I tried to get rid of the chip. Used a rusty spoon. Bad infection. Not one of my better ideas." She chuckled as if it were a joke. "Looks like a suicide attempt by somebody with really bad eyesight— somebody who tried to slit a wrist but missed."

"That's not funny." Violet knew that she sounded prissy. She couldn't help herself. "I've read that infections from botched chip re- movals can kill you."

"They can. And it *is* funny. It's all funny, Violet, because if it's not funny, it's tragic—and you know what? I've had all the tragedy I can stand." Delia unfolded her legs. She stood up. She was a lot more lim- ber than any old person Violet had ever met. "Gotta check on our tea," Delia said. She used the long branch to fish the can out of the fireplace. She stuck in her index finger. "A few more minutes." Back went the tin can into the fireplace, which by now was producing more smoke than flame.

"You must've needed medical care," Violet said. "Antibiotics, at the very least."

"Yeah." Delia sat back down again.

"So where'd you get it?"

"What are you—the police?"

"Just asking."

"Unauthorized removal of a chip is a serious offense," Delia de- clared. "If your New Earth pals happened to get wind of it, they'd take it out on us. And they'd try to get the doctor, too, most likely. There'd be raids and roundups and—oh, God. Don't get me started." Her voice went from brusque to bemused: "There was this doctor, okay? Best person I've ever known. If I thought that the people on New Earth were anything like *her*—well, I'd be changing my opinion about a few things. Fast. She used to come down here all the time. You couldn't miss her. She had this long red hair. And she'd help anybody who needed it. No questions asked."

While Delia spoke, Violet was getting a funny tingling sensation in the pit of her stomach. It wasn't a bad feeling. It was excitement and anticipation.

The woman who'd helped Delia had to be her mother. Had to be.

"What happened to her?" Violet said. She spoke softly and carefully, trying to keep the emotion out of her voice. She didn't want Delia to know anything about her. Not until she was sure it was safe.

Delia frowned. "We don't know. About six years ago, she just stopped coming. It didn't make sense. Before that, *nothing* got in her way. She'd march into the very worst sections of the very worst towns. Never hesitated. And she'd take the hardest cases—people who were dying of Missip Fever or slab gun wounds or radiation poisoning. She'd do whatever she could. If she couldn't save somebody's life, if it was already too late for that, she'd make her final hours as peaceful as possible. So it can't be that she got frightened. That wouldn't happen. She was the bravest person I ever knew. And she cared. I *know* she did. I felt it, whenever she was around me. When she changed the bandages on my arm, she'd ask me about my children. About my life. She cared, all right."

Violet let a minute go by. She was positive now that Delia was describing her mother.

"What was her name?" Violet asked.

Delia shook her head. "We never knew. Down here, names don't matter much. Most of us just called her 'Doc.' She seemed okay with that." She shrugged. "You could tell when she was close. When she'd come back down from New Earth, I mean. There was a feeling in the air. A sort of lightness. A little bit of hope."

The Intercept still had a total-access pass to her mind, Violet knew. Just because no one was monitoring the feed didn't mean that the Intercept wasn't doing its job, sparking and whirring, grabbing her emotions and sending them back to the machinery beneath Protocol Hall. But she *hated* the idea that it was picking up her feelings right now—feelings of awe, of pride and gratitude that her mother had saved Delia, of sadness that her mother was gone forever. The Intercept was picking up her emotions the way somebody shopped in a grocery store: grabbing things and flipping them in the cart.

It couldn't be helped, though. Violet couldn't stop the pride that bubbled up inside her. Let the Intercept have it. She didn't care.

She started to say something to Delia, to tell her that she had a pretty good idea who their mysterious benefactor had been. To tell her what had happened to Lucretia Crowley.

And why Lucretia Crowley had never returned to Old Earth.

But before Violet could speak, Delia said, "And you know what? I think Doc's coming back. I really do. I can sort of feel it inside me. It's like this special knowledge that is part of my body now, like an arm or a leg." She lowered her head. When she lifted it again, there was a light in her eyes that Violet hadn't seen before. "That's all that keeps me going sometimes—the certainty that Doc's going to show up again one day," Delia said. "I'll turn around and—*yes*. Yes, there she'll be. Carrying her little black bag. Telling us to hang in there. Smiling, like she always does. And asking us how she can help."

Violet fell asleep.

How in the world—she would ask herself this later, when she thought back on the strangeness of this day—had she fallen asleep while sitting on an upside-down bucket in the middle of a freezing kitchen?

But she had. Head sunk down on her chest, hands dangling, she must have drifted off after a few sips of the completely tasteless tea. The beating she'd taken surely was responsible; she was exhausted, and her head and her stomach throbbed rhythmically, like mean matching metronomes. She was desperate for a short break from consciousness.

She woke up. Her head jerked sharply. The motion nearly rocked her right off the bucket.

"Whoa. Hold on there," Delia said from across the room. "Don't hurt yourself." She was standing by a window—or what was left of it—staring out at Old Earth. Six of the eight panes were gone, replaced by cardboard with badly taped edges. The other two panes were intact. And they were just at eye level, enabling her to have a view. Having a view—and not just a view of cardboard, blocking the real one—was a tiny miracle in a place from which most of the miracles had flown long ago.

"What are you looking at?" Violet said.

"If you were from here," Delia answered, moving back toward Violet, "you wouldn't ask that. Because the answer is 'nothing.' The answer will always be 'nothing.' The scenery won't change. It can't change. This is Old Earth, remember?"

Violet stood up. She felt marginally better. At least she wasn't tempted to throw up or fall to the floor in a gelatinous ooze of fatigue. Her head even felt relatively okay.

She took a step. She took another. So far, so good.

She considered, once more, telling Delia that the woman who had done so much good here on Old Earth was her mother, and about what had happened to her. But she stopped herself. If the expectation of Lucretia's return one day was what kept Delia going, then Violet didn't want to take that away from her. No matter what the truth was.

"I'm heading out," Violet said. "I've got to be back at the portal in an hour. Doesn't leave me much time for what I have to find. Thanks for the first aid. And the tea. And the nap."

Delia looked concerned. "You're going to have to be a lot more careful, okay? Keep an eye on your surroundings. If somebody starts coming at you, go in the other direction. How fast can you run?"

"Fast." Violet wasn't bragging. She was stating a fact.

Delia's face changed. It softened. "The way you said that—it sounded so much like the way my little girl would've said it. She *loved* to run. And she was very proud of being fast. 'I'm fast as lightning, Mama,' she used to tell me. 'You just watch.'" Delia swallowed hard. "I never thought I'd lose both of them, you know? But that's what it's like down here. You can't count on having a tomorrow."

By this time, Violet thought, she'd earned the right to ask. After all, she hadn't even complained about the terrible tea.

"What happened to your kids?"

"Molly died of Missip Fever." Delia's voice sounded strained, as if just saying those words had put a stressful burden on it. "My son Tommy's in prison."

"I'm sorry."

"Not your fault." She shrugged. A sharpness came into her face. A meanness. "Or maybe it *is* your fault, come to think of it. You're from New Earth. And that's what started this whole stupid mess in the first place. It's what forced Tommy to do what he did. Old Earth, New Earth—what was wrong with just the plain old *Earth*? I'm old enough to remember the time before. And it wasn't perfect, God knows—in fact it was pretty miserable with all the wars, all the pollution, and all the death—but you know what? We were all in it together. And look at us now. Is this really better? Is it?"

Violet didn't answer. She knew that the arguments over the wisdom of the split had been intense, and that they had raged for years. It wasn't likely that a few words from her were going to change Delia's mind. Not even if she pointed out that New Earth worked—that it was clean and safe. Nothing like this place, with its blasted streets and blown-down buildings, its dust and its danger.

You have no idea, Violet wanted to say to Delia in a pointed, deliberate tone. *You don't have a clue. If you ever came to New Earth, you'd see. You'd* know. *And then you wouldn't be so angry about—*

It was no use. Delia would never get to New Earth. With only a few exceptions, the gates for immigrants were closed and locked. Danny and Kendall had made it in—but that was a special case. Kendall had something that New Earth wanted.

Violet's head was clear now. And she didn't want to argue. So she knew it was time to leave.

She thanked Delia one more time, and then she went back down the broken steps and out into the windy, barren street. She looked around. The kids who'd attacked her were gone; the only reminder of their presence was the jumbled imprint in the dirt where the ringleader had fallen and thrashed around a bit. Right now, she thought, he surely had a major headache. Worse than hers.

Good.

She shivered. The sky was going from gray to black, like someone whose bad mood is escalating into a lethal rage. Something brooded over this world, something sinister. Violet's shivering increased. It wasn't really cold, but it felt cold, anyway. It was as if even the idea of warmth had run away from this world as fast as it could go.

She heard a ferociously loud bang.

She turned quickly, trying to spot the source of the noise. She thought her heart might sprint right out of her chest.

And then she saw it: a dilapidated gate, farther up the road. The fence itself was long gone. The wind had pushed the gate so that it flapped against the crumbling post, creating the bang. *And scaring me silly,* Violet thought. She trembled a bit from the shock. Then she pictured Danny's face, and she wasn't so afraid anymore.

She didn't know how she was going to find Kendall's lab. She didn't have a map. All she had was a sketchy memory of the landmarks she'd seen while following Danny with the chip-jack. Her quest was completely illogical.

But that was the thing about love: It wasn't even on speaking terms with logic.

The Notebook

Violet walked along a bleak stretch of dirt road. She wondered what this land had been like Before: before the Water Wars and the Mineral Wars.

Before the land was scorched by bombs. Before the trees died and the crops shriveled in the fields. Before the ice caps melted and flooded the coastlines.

Before the world was divided in two. Before New Earth. Before the Intercept.

Even inanimate things had a Before and an After, Violet realized. Even a road. Even an ordinary, everyday road like this one.

The road took her to the edge of a city. She wondered what city it was and then she realized it didn't matter. Why would its name matter? She was surrounded by the hunched ruins of once-proud buildings. People slunk past her, but unlike the welcoming committee outside Delia's house, these people had no interest in her. They didn't even make eye contact. Some of them mumbled, but they weren't talking to her; they seemed to be talking to themselves. *This is what people look like,* Violet thought, *when all the hope is taken away from them. This is what's left.* They pulled their rags tighter around their frail torsos and dipped their heads and kept going. They were hurrying somewhere, or they were hurrying nowhere. Once again, it didn't matter.

She tried to remember the particulars of Danny's journey so that she could follow it: the turns he had taken, the route he had followed, the angle of the horizon she had seen through his eyes, which would let her know she was going in the right direction.

As she walked the gray and garbage-filled streets, passing through battered neighborhood after battered neighborhood, feeling sadder with every step, she wondered: Would she ever be able to confess to him that she had used a chip-jack to spy on him? Was it the kind of thing you could ever forgive someone for? Even if it was for a good cause?

And then there it was: the alley.

The steps.

The door.

She did not hesitate, even though she was still sore. She flung herself at it shoulder-first, hitting the spot that Danny had hit, too, when he slammed against it. The door popped open, just as it had for him. Inside, the room was just as she remembered it—dark, crowded, clotted with a massive amount of junk that was packed tight in every direction. But there was a difference. Before, she had only been *looking* it.

Now she was *living* it.

The smell was the knock-you-over kind, worse than anything she'd smelled outside. The outside smells of Old Earth were foul, but the foulness was constantly on the move, quickly dissipated by the constant, constant wind. Here, the smell was like a green blobby toad squatting right in the middle of the path: It did not move. It was a permanent feature of the place. The lab had been locked up for years, except for Danny's recent visit, with no ventilation. The deadness of the dead things behind the walls and under the piles and piles of junk had only gotten deader. The stink had only gotten stinkier.

Violet stood still for a few moments, trying not to keel over from the rich, insinuating odors. She tried her best not to breathe too deeply. Gradually, she was able to adjust her lungs to the rancid reality; she acclimated herself to the incredibly hideous stench.

She remembered Danny telling her that for the first few years after he and Kendall left for New Earth, people had broken in, escaping from the cold. They stole what they needed to survive. They stored the junk they'd scavenged. When he returned, Danny said, he saw the results: a once-amazing place had become just another hiding place, just another port in the never-ending storm of Old Earth. He wasn't too upset by that, however; people needed to live. They did what they had to do. A lab was only four walls and a floor and a bunch of stuff. A lab didn't breathe. A lab didn't hope. *People come first,* Danny told her. *People are more important than computers or equipment. I'm glad they used this place to save themselves, even though I hate seeing what it's become.*

Violet moved forward. She had to shove an old sewing machine and a bicycle wheel out of the way in order to do so.

She kept going. Now she had to turn sideways, because the only trail through the stacked-up stuff was skinnier than she was. And she was pretty skinny.

She had to get to the cinder-block wall in the back. That was where the notebook was.

As she scooted and ducked and crawled and twisted and climbed, she glimpsed, now and then, the bones of the lab, the things that lay at the bottom of all the junk that had taken over the place during the years of neglect. She saw wires and shattered test tubes. She saw long workbenches—resting on their sides now, or upside down, with pieces hacked out that had been used as firewood—and she saw microscopes and monitors. The microscopes had been stripped of their knobs and the monitors were all smashed. But they were there—the ghosts of a working lab, a lab where Kendall had created the Intercept.

I'm in Kendall's lab. The place where Danny spent a lot of time when he was a kid. Where—despite everything that was happening all around the two brothers, despite the danger and the chaos—Danny was happy, because he was with his last surviving family member.

The thought was exhilarating. And deeply sad, too. She didn't bother looking into the crook of her left elbow, checking for the flash; she didn't care what the Intercept thought about this moment. It was hers. It belonged to her, and her alone.

At last she made it to the wall.

She hesitated before touching it, because it was green and slimy and disgusting. But this was why she had come here. *A little slime never killed anybody, right?*

Well, maybe it had. She imagined the billions of germs that were probably gyrating in the spongy ick, ready to latch on and tunnel under her skin and infiltrate her bloodstream and . . .

Violet swallowed hard. *Get a grip, girl.* She counted six blocks up from the floor. Three blocks to the left.

She tapped on the block three times, using two fingers, just as Danny had.

The block slowly opened.

She reached inside. Her heart was pounding hard and fast. *If I have a heart attack, I bet that mean cat eats me in, like, five minutes or less.* She didn't have a heart attack. Her hand shook as she touched the red leather cover, but her heart kept on beating, just as it was supposed to.

She opened the notebook. On the inside cover, she saw the name scrawled with a pencil:

Kendall Mayhew

With a deep breath, she began turning the pages. Faster and faster and faster. She was searching for whatever it was that had made

Danny come back to the lab. Searching for whatever secret was hidden in his brother's notebook.

Surely this was a journal, like the one her mother had kept. Violet expected long entries detailing Kendall's thoughts and feelings.

The first few pages were filled with numbers, symbols, equations.

The next batch of pages was filled with . . . the same thing: numbers, symbols, equations. Squiggly lines and formulas. Fractions and graphs and parabolas.

The next was filled with . . . the same thing.

And the next.

And the next and then all the pages after that, too.

She flipped through the notebook, growing increasingly frustrated. Every page was the same. Different, but the same. This was a workbook, not a personal record. And it was meaningless to her.

The Intercept was already a reality. Why would Danny need the notebook? He wouldn't be able to understand the soaring, complicated mathematics and crazy-brilliant formulas any more than she could.

Violet put the notebook back in the compartment. She slid the block into the wall. Danny would never know she had been here.

Disappointment washed over her like a cold shower.

Damn, damn, damn.

She looked around. Maybe there was something to be gained from the trip, after all. Maybe, if she dug through some of this mess, she could find a clue. Maybe Kendall had left something else behind that would explain—

Her console beeped. It was Shura's ringtone. Violet hadn't expected her console to work this far from New Earth. Kendall's lab must be one of the few pockets of Old Earth with a strong signal.

"Hey," Violet said.

She kept it on audio. Only Sara Verity knew where she was, and Sara could say she'd been lied to about Violet's purpose for going to

Old Earth. Which was true. Violet didn't want anybody else to get into trouble if she was discovered. She'd answer for her own actions.

Shura's voice was peppered with desperation. "Violet," she said, choking back tears. "I need you. *Right now.*"

First Attack

What's wrong?"

Shura's words came in a panicked gush. "It's my mom. She was attacked when she was leaving her office. She got away—but she's in the hospital. She's hurt really bad. She might even—" She stopped, uttering a sob. "That's where I am right now. My dad's in the room with her. They haven't let me in yet."

The words shocked Violet. "Did they arrest anybody?"

"No. But Violet—how could this happen? Why didn't the Intercept stop it?"

Violet didn't know what to say. She was wondering the same thing.

"Can you come?" Shura said. "Can you be with me here? In case—" She broke off her sentence. "They don't know if my mom's going to—" She broke off that one, too.

Violet was torn, but only for an instant. Yes, she eagerly wanted more time to look around the lab. Maybe she could find something to shed light on the notebook. Maybe she could figure it out. She was smart, after all. Not Kendall-smart, but smart. She was good at codes and puzzles, especially after working with Rez and getting pointers from him.

But Shura was her best friend. And Shura needed her.

"I'm coming," Violet said. She signed off and tapped her console, notifying Sara that she would be returning very soon. Kendall's lab could wait. She was going back.

How, Violet wondered as she raced to the pod, would the Intercept label her current emotion? It was a mix of love—she loved her friend—and loyalty and protectiveness, and other things as well. And there was a rising anger at whoever had hurt Anna Lu. Plus a profound curiosity: What did the markings in Kendall's notebook mean? Who had cracked the code of the Intercept—and what did they want?

"My God, Violet—you look *awful*."

Shura stared at her.

"Rough day," Violet said.

"You look like *you* should be admitted, too. Those bruises—" Shura reached out toward the nastiest one on the side of Violet's face, but before she could get there, Violet gathered her up in a hug. Violet was still the world's worst hugger, but if there was ever a moment when that didn't matter, it was now.

They broke apart awkwardly.

"Tell me what's going on," Violet said. "Your mom—is she—"

"My dad came out a few minutes ago to talk to me. She's stable. That's all they're telling him. She's still unconscious."

They stood in a long, brightly lit corridor. People in green smocks hurried past them from time to time, speaking into consoles or consulting notes on tablets. Everyone seemed preoccupied. *That's a good thing*, Violet told herself. *They're focused on getting patients well. Patients like Shura's mom.*

She didn't like to think about sick moms. Even though she was forced to now, because that's why she was here.

"So what did they want?" Violet said. "The people who did this to her, I mean."

"We don't know," Shura said. "My dad told me *how* it happened, but not why. Nobody knows the 'why' yet."

They stood close to each other, talking in soft voices. *Something about being in a hospital makes you want to keep your voice low,* Violet thought. *It's like if you whisper, if you don't make a fuss, maybe you'll go back to sleep and realize the whole thing is a bad dream.*

It wasn't a bad dream.

Shura looked more traumatized than Violet had ever seen her. Her friend's pale complexion had faded to an even paler shade, which Violet had not thought possible. The red rings around her eyes testified to the fact that Shura had been crying for quite a long time. Her small shoulders were drawn forward, as if she was trying to ward off an attack—the emotional kind as well as the physical kind. Her hands—the part of her that Violet most admired, because they were the transfer point between the visions in Shura's mind and what showed up on the canvas—were constantly in motion, opening and closing, opening and closing.

"So my mom was meeting with one of her clients," Shura said. Her agitation increased as she told the story. "And the client got a call. My mom could hear the voice on the other end. Something important was about to happen. Something big. It was related to the Rebels of Light. As soon as the client left, my mom called my dad and told him about it. She was really shaken up. Her client had gotten nasty, my mom said. A real bully. He wanted her to come with him to some kind of meeting. She said no. He got even more upset. He called her a traitor.

"She was getting ready to come home when it happened. Somebody jumped her. Right outside her office. They tried to drag her away. She fought back. And they—they hit her in the head and then they—" Shura faltered. Violet put a hand on her friend's shoulder. She felt clumsy doing that, but it was better than nothing. Violet wished once again that she was better at the whole hugging-and-comforting thing.

"Anyway," Shura said, after a deep breath, "the attackers must've been scared off by the guy who found my mom and called for help. Thank God he came along. Otherwise—" Shura shivered. She was thinking the unthinkable. Violet knew that because she was thinking it, too. She had to get her best friend's mind off what might have happened. It was just too terrifying to contemplate.

"Could the police trace the call?" she asked her. "The call the client got in your mom's office?"

"They used burner consoles. Untraceable." Shura's voice was bleak. "I just don't understand. Why didn't the Intercept stop them? It doesn't make any sense. I guess it must be true—they've found a way around it."

Violet had too many things on her mind. Her brain, she decided, was like an overstuffed closet. If she tugged on even one small object, the rest of the contents would collapse on her head and smother her. She wouldn't be found for weeks.

She looked across the living room at her father. He sat in his armchair with his eyes closed. He wasn't sleeping. He was thinking. When his thoughts were especially deep and significant, he went into a sort of trance of heavy thinking. Violet had watched him do that ever since she was a little girl.

The living room was dense with complicated shadows. Once again, her father had not turned on any lights. Dusk on New Earth was a muted one tonight, its colors more charcoal than ruby.

She had just arrived home from the hospital. Shura's mother had not yet regained consciousness.

"How is Anna Lu?" Ogden said.

He still didn't open his eyes. She'd had entire conversations with her father when his eyes were closed.

"No change."

"I sent the standard memo of consolation and concern to Edgar

Lu on his console. I'd appreciate it if you could add my personal re-
grets as well."

"Sure, Dad."

Violet wanted to tell him about her trip to Old Earth. She wanted
to tell him about the notebook and the mystery and all the rest of it,
too. She had the same impulse that she'd had the other night, when
she almost told him about her feelings for Danny. She didn't like keeping secrets from her father.

But sometimes, secrets were necessary. She had learned that.

She looked over at her father. Eyes still shut. She knew how hard
he was working these days, trying to uncover the identities of the
Rebels of Light, fighting the threat to the Intercept. His face showed
worry and fatigue, but there was still a rocklike harshness to it, a
layer of steel under the layer of flesh.

Violet knew what people said about Ogden Crowley. Some considered him cruel, even barbaric, in the way he ran New Earth. She
didn't care. She knew him better than any of them did.

They never saw him the way he was right now: so weary from his
work on behalf of New Earth that he could barely move or speak.

Violet arranged herself on the couch. She was grateful for the
darkness and for his habit of closing his eyes; both had kept her father
from seeing the deep bruises on the side of her head. She'd finally
gotten the bleeding to stop. She still had a headache that reverberated
throughout her entire body, like somebody was using her for a gong,
and she didn't especially want to picture the giant bruise that she
knew was blooming across her stomach. But she was feeling so much
better than she'd felt in Delia's kitchen that it seemed like progress.

"I've been wondering, Dad. What did Mom think about the Intercept?"

No answer.

"Dad?"

"Why would you ask me that?" His voice didn't sound the same
anymore. It wasn't cordial. It was barely even nice.

Violet was too surprised at the sudden change to answer. The question had arisen naturally in her mind as she thought about her mother's journal, and about the revelation that she had known Kendall. Her mother had died too soon to see the system fully operational—but if she knew Kendall, she must've known what he was working on, and why.

"I asked you a question," her father snapped. "I would like an answer. And I would like it *now*." His eyes were wide open, but there was no chance he would spot her bruises. He was focused too intently on the topic.

Of all the directions Violet had speculated the conversation might go, this was not a scenario she had considered: an angry Odgen Crowley. A demanding and insistent Ogden Crowley. This was the side of her father that *other* people had to deal with. Not her.

"I just—I was just thinking about it," Violet said. "No reason."

Even in the semidarkness, she could see his shoulders slump as he fell back against the chair. As quickly as it had come, his anger dissipated.

"Forgive me," he murmured. "I shouldn't have snapped at you. It's just that—well, a long, long time ago, the Intercept prompted a major argument between your mother and me. The system was barely a gleam in Kendall Mayhew's eye back then—it was just a bunch of lights and wires and bad smells in that filthy lab of his, down on Old Earth. But she hated the very *idea* of it. She told me that pursuing it for New Earth was morally wrong."

"I didn't know. I'm sorry."

"She was going to leave me, Violet." The statement came out with simple starkness. "She told me that if I continued down that road, checking in with Kendall Mayhew while he worked on it, and planning on mass installation up here in New Earth—she would leave. And she would take you with her.

"But it didn't really matter, in the end. Because she died. So I suppose you could say she *did* leave me, after all. She left both of us."

Anguish in his voice now. "Whether or not I'd ever brought the Intercept to New Earth."

For a few seconds Violet was quiet. The information had startled her. She realized that she needed to say something to her father—something reassuring, something supportive. She could figure out what she felt about all this later. Right now he was in distress. And he was still her dad, no matter what.

She rose from the couch and moved in his direction.

She never got there.

Second Attack

moment after Violet stood up, the front door exploded.

That's what it sounded like to her as it sprang open with a violent shattering of wood, a screaming wrench of hinges. She would've sworn that a bomb had been detonated within a foot of where she stood, turning the world upside down.

With a roar, a swarming horde of masked intruders in heavy boots rushed in, half running, half marching. They wore black helmets, black tunics, black trousers. They must have knocked down the door with the butts of their slab guns; those guns were still held aloft in black-gloved hands, ready to strike and smash and crush, as they surged forward.

Violet's first thought—*This can't be happening*—was quickly replaced by another one: *What happened to the bodyguards?* Bodyguards were posted outside the president's door twenty-four/seven.

There was no door anymore. She looked out into the hall. Four bodyguards lay in a heap.

"Get down! Get down! I said *GET DOWN!*"

One of the intruders was yelling at her. He grabbed Violet's shoulder and shoved her onto her knees, and then gave another hard push, forcing her to lie flat on the floor, facedown and helpless. She was still weak from her ordeal on New Earth—otherwise she would have fought back harder. She felt pathetic and stupid and very, very frightened.

"Dad!" Violet cried out. "Dad, I—" Something small and round jammed against the base of her skull. That something, she realized, was the snout of a slab gun.

"Shut up," the angry voice commanded. "And stay down."

She heard her father's agitated voice, climbing above the other voices: "Violet, do what they say, do exactly what they tell you to do, don't taken any chan—" And then came a horrifying thud and her father's voice was cut off.

"Get him," someone yelled, and Violet lifted her head an inch off the floor, just high enough to watch three of the intruders grab Ogden Crowley and wrench him out of his chair. The side of his face was red from the blow he'd just taken, the blow that had stopped his sentence, but still he tried to fight them off, his arms flailing, his body bucking and writhing, trying to free himself. But even his one good leg was useless. He was an old man, and no match for them.

"Violet," he gasped as they dragged him from the living room by his arms and legs. Before they cleared the door he'd turned his attention back to his kidnappers, exclaiming, "Leave her alone! Leave my daughter alone! Don't you *touch* her—not a hair on her head—*Do you hear me?*—Don't you—"

Violet tried to get up, but the muzzle was pushed even harder against her skull. Her head was buzzing and throbbing. Waves of pain started at her temples and radiated throughout her body in endless concentric rings, a fierce and fiery ache.

She didn't know if a minute went by, or an hour, or several days. She didn't know if time even had meaning anymore in the universe. At some point the slab gun was removed from the back of her head, but she didn't know when. Her life was an agonizing dazzle of the terrible Now.

She had let strangers take her father. She had let them pick him up like a sack of garbage and hustle him away, where anything could happen to him. She would never, ever forgive herself for that.

Just before they flung a hood over her head, Violet took a quick look around the ruined living room. On the white wall behind the couch, in slashing black letters that looked like cuts inflicted on tender skin, were the words they had scrawled: REBELS OF LIGHT.

Why hadn't someone at Protocol Hall stopped this attack? Why hadn't the kidnappers been incapacitated by a private emotion that tunneled into the deepest parts of their brains and brought them to their knees?

Where was the Intercept?

26

Into the Darkness

Shut it down. Now."

The room was black. The voice that filled it had a machine-like quality, a strange, cold force born of filament and steel, not flesh and blood. Was it computer-generated? Violet didn't think so. Her best guess was that it was someone she knew. Someone who was trying to disguise her or his voice. Someone who was trying to sound sinister.

They wanted to intimidate her and her dad. They wanted to frighten them.

Good luck with that, Violet thought. It might work with her—okay, it already had—but not with him. Nobody intimidated Ogden Crowley. They would find that out. *Oh, yeah.*

The voice spoke again:

"Shut down the Intercept."

Her father laughed. Just one short sharp bark, but it made Violet very proud of him.

She was sitting in a chair. Her wrists and ankles were tied. They had made the knots fairly loose, as if they didn't want to hurt her too badly, but she still couldn't escape. And she had the worst headache of her life. Even worse than the one she'd suffered through on Old Earth.

From somewhere close beside her in the dark, she heard her father's breathing, the raspy, clotted rhythm she knew so well. After the laugh, he had gone silent.

Their captors had swept them out of their apartment and into some sort of vehicle. The hoods over their heads prevented them from knowing where they were going. Violet had listened intently during the ride, straining to pick up on any clues about their captors' identities, and she assumed her father had, too—but the kidnappers said nothing. She tried to remember the turns the vehicle made, and the number of stops, and the probable direction in which they were heading, but at some point, she lost track. She must have passed out. When she awoke, she was in the dark room.

"Shut it down," the voice said once again.

"This is getting a bit tiring," Ogden said. "Can't you think of something else to say?"

Violet understood her father's plan. He was being argumentative on purpose, buying time while he tried to figure out a few things. The most important thing he was trying to figure out, she knew, was why the Intercept hadn't been triggered at the moment they were taken. There was nowhere on New Earth where its reach did not extend.

So it was true: They had found a way to get around it. To thwart its power. Violet was mystified. Her father would be more than merely mystified: He would be livid. He'd been absolutely sure that the system was foolproof. Kendall Mayhew had guaranteed it. There *was* no way around it. And yet this group—these faceless criminals, dressed all in black—had found one. They had discovered a loophole.

"Shut it down and we will release you," the voice declared.

"Go to hell," Ogden replied. His tone shifted. "Violet, are you there? Are you okay, sweetheart?"

"I'm fine," she said. She wasn't fine—she was about as far from fine as it was possible to be, and she tried to keep her voice from shaking—but she didn't want him to worry about her. If he could be brave, then she could be brave, too.

Her father was completely under the control of whoever had kidnapped them—and yet he didn't back down. He only had one good leg, and he was an old man, and he was weak—but he was standing up to them.

"You'd better start cooperating, Crowley."

"Release us," her father declared. "This instant. I *demand* that you let us go."

"You're not in a position to demand anything. You're not in charge here."

"I'm the president of New Earth," Ogden shot back. "And when I get out of this place, every single one of you is going to be arrested. I'll see to that. And I'll also make sure that you serve your time in an Old Earth prison. Do you know about those? Do you know what you're in for? You'll be locked away in a cell carved into the side of a mountain. You'll *rot* there." Her father's tone revealed his complete satisfaction with that idea.

"Shut it down."

"This is pointless," Ogden went on. "You can't win. You're going to be caught and punished. I don't know who you are, but I'll find out. You might as well just give up now before you—"

He stopped.

"Give up now," her father said, picking up his sentence where he had left off, "before you face severe consequences and—"

He stopped again.

Something was wrong. Violet heard him moving restlessly within his bonds, shifting his position in the chair. He coughed. His breath was even raspier than usual, as if he was having trouble getting enough air into his lungs.

"Dad?" she said. "Dad, are you all right?"

"Violet," he said. His voice had lost its bravado. It was small now, and filled with agitation. "I see . . . I see *colors*. Red and green and blue. It's not . . . it's not what I thought it would . . ." His words trailed off. When he spoke next, he sounded frightened and lost: "Violet, *help me*."

She fought against the ropes that held her, frantically squirming and pulling. "Leave him alone!" she cried out. "Stop hurting him."

The words of their captor came out calmly and evenly. "We're not doing anything to your father that he hasn't done to others. This, you see, is what is commonly known as payback." He uttered a low chuckle. Somehow it sounded more menacing to Violet than a threat or a curse. "And we've decided," the voice went on, "that you get to watch."

A screen was thrust in Violet's face. It was held steady in front of her eyes by two hands sheathed in black gloves. Another pair of gloved hands held her head in place, so that she couldn't look away. She was forced to watch everything that happened on the screen, every image, every nuance, and to hear the sounds.

It took Violet another few seconds to realize what she was seeing.

They had somehow initiated her father's Intercept feed. An intense emotional memory was sweeping into his brain. And he was powerless to stop it.

Twenty-five years ago:

Ogden Crowley is disgusted. It's supposed to be a political rally, but nobody showed up, because the guy who was supposed to do the promotional work plainly didn't. So nobody knows about his speech.

So nobody's here.

He sits in the front row of the small basement theater. The "curtain" is an old drape, scavenged from an abandoned house. The rickety, mismatched chairs are little more than sticks. The rows and rows of empty seats? A total embarrassment. It isn't supposed to be like this.

He clutches his stupid notes. Almost crushes them in his twisted, gnarled hands. The plan was for him to be introduced to the raucous cheers of an enthusiastic audience and make his way up onto the stage as best he can—he *will not* use a cane, no matter how many people tell him he ought to—and then he'll deliver a fantastically effective speech about his idea:

A new Earth.

And afterward, if they've caught the fever, too, the fever of his colossal idea, somebody might just start a chant: *Crowley, Crowley, Crowley.* Because if they listen to him, if they follow his logic, they'll want to join him. They'll see that he's right.

But the place is empty. He's angry and he's disappointed. The next time he sees that guy—the guy who took his money and said he'd get the word out and deliver a big crowd—he's going to take a swing at him. Ogden might not have a right leg, but he's got a right hook. A mean one.

"Are you Ogden Crowley?"

He's just risen from his seat and is about to storm out—as best a man with a bad leg can do, anyway, on the storming-out front—when he hears the voice. A woman's voice.

He turns around.

The red hair. That's what he notices first. How could he not? It's a soft wavy maze of hair, a complex arrangement of curls. But she's not vain about it. He can tell. In fact, she flips it carelessly over her shoulders, as if she's a little tired of it, and really intends to have it cut as soon as she gets the time.

She is not a frivolous person. Somehow he can tell that, too.

"Yeah," he says warily, because he's aloof with everybody. His shattered leg has made him this way. "That's me."

"I came to hear your speech."

"There's not going to be any speech." He lets his bitterness show in his voice. "Nobody's here, in case you haven't noticed."

"*I'm* here."

And so, because he's so intrigued with and inspired by her, he stands in the dingy basement and he gives his speech. He gives it in front of all those empty rows. He doesn't care. She's sitting there. She listens intently as he describes the world and where it has gone wrong. He talks about the Water Wars, and the First and the Second Mineral Wars, and how everything will end unless they act *now*. They must build it *now*.

He doesn't hold back. He raises his voice and he swings his arms over his head. He is passionate. He is scolding. They are running out of time. They have to escape this world. And build a new one.

At the end, she claps for him. She has been listening fiercely. He loves that. He thinks he loves *her*, too. Already.

"So," he says. "You agree with me, yes? We need to build a new Earth?"

She laughs. "Absolutely not!" she says, shaking her head. "We need to stay right here and deal with our problems—not peel off the top layer of people and go somewhere else and start over. I think you're one hundred percent wrong!"

Now he knows for sure that he loves her. He relishes a good argument, and he appreciates people who speak their minds.

Just as they are about to climb the steps back to the first floor, she kisses him.

She kisses him

She kisses him

She kisses him

Violet could sense the agony of what her father was feeling: He could not turn away from that memory. He felt the kiss. He *feels* that kiss.

He couldn't *not* feel it. It was there, waiting for him, no matter what he did. And it was excruciating, it was unbearable—because each time he feels that kiss, he is reminded anew that *she is gone forever.*

She's not coming back.

He will never see her again, his beautiful Lucretia.

The truth of that is like a burn. Like a scalding, forever burn. Each time the kiss blooms in his memory, he is stung and branded and shredded all over again.

Violet knew what he was feeling because she had felt something very similar during her Intercept experience.

The pain spiraled through him. It was worse than the agony in his leg—far, far worse.

For some people, Violet now knew, the Intercept plucked out the worst, most painful memory from their archive and deployed it back into their brain.

For others, the Intercept plucked out the *best* memory—the happiest time, a time that would never, ever return—and deployed *it* back into their brain. That was a far worse torture.

Because it was wonderful. And because it was gone.

Her father was sobbing. Ogden Crowley, president of New Earth, the most powerful man on two worlds, was sobbing. Sobbing like a little boy.

Violet knew he couldn't help himself. If his mind turned one way—he feels that kiss. If his mind turned another way—he still feels the kiss. The kiss that will never come again. It is lost for all eternity, just as Lucretia is lost. His wife, his soul mate, is lost. He is alone. Utterly, crushingly alone.

His sobs were louder now. Violet couldn't see him in the dark room, but she could imagine the tears on his face, wetting his chin and then his collar. Dampening his shirtfront.

"Please," he said, in a gasping, croaking voice. "Please. Please. No more."

If they would just stop cramming the images into his brain, he could recover his emotional poise. If only they would show some mercy and . . .

"Stop the feed," Ogden cried out.

"No," the man said. "Not until you agree to dismantle the Intercept. Permanently."

"Please," he said. He was begging them. He wasn't strong anymore. "Please."

Violet could feel the intensity of her father's anguish, a searing, impossibly intense pain that pummeled him. A pain that, unless she could figure out what to do, was going to kill him.

The hood was abruptly slipped back over her head. Violet was so surprised that she had no time to call out her father's name. She was being carried—carried away from her father, away from any chance she would have to help him—from one dark room into another dark room, and then another one after that.

"No! No!" Violet yelled. Her words were muffled through the material of the hood. "*No, no, no!* I want to stay with him! Please!"

There was no response. There was only the swaying rhythm of the chair's movement through space and time, as they separated her from her father. Would she ever see him again? Violet had no idea. Even forming the question caused a sickening terror to rise up in her heart.

At last they stopped. The chair was quickly lowered to the ground.

Violet heard the snick of hinges as a door opened. The air changed; she was outside now. Cool wind reached her cheeks through the hood. She was shoved into the side door of the vehicle that had brought them here—wherever "here" was.

More time passed. Violet was too disoriented to get a sense of distance or direction. When the vehicle braked hard, she was thrown up against the back of the front seat. She wanted to cry out from the pain in her shoulder, but she wouldn't give them the satisfaction of knowing they'd hurt her.

No way, she thought. *I'm tougher than all of you put together. And I'll be back for you. You just wait.*

Next thing she knew, she was hauled out and thrown down. Someone yanked off her hood. She landed on her side.

She struggled to stand. The vehicle had roared away; she heard
it take the corner at a high rate of speed, its tires shrieking and its
engine shifting into another gear.

Violet looked around, exhausted and confused. She thought she
might throw up. Her body ached. Her head was spinning. She didn't
know where she was. All she knew was that it was still night.

And her father was still a prisoner.

27

The Sensenbrenner-Cooley Code Derivative v. the Pforzheimer Equivalent

Each workstation in Protocol Hall was supposed to hold two people. Three at the outside.

Right now this particular one contained five people—Violet, Danny, Reznik, Shura, and Chief Callahan—and the word *overstuffed* would not have been an inaccurate description. Adding to their sense of being crammed into a tiny lidless box was the fact that they were not a quiet, orderly group of five people. They were an active, agitated, excessively bossy group of five people, five people who constantly interrupted one another with questions and suggestions and proposals and counterproposals, and very nearly poked one another in the eye when they pointed at the computer screen, and shouted and then apologized and shouted again.

They were five people desperately determined to track down the whereabouts of Ogden Crowley. And then further determined to figure out why the Intercept—which seemed to be working fine everywhere else on New Earth—had suffered an inexplicable blackout at the crucial moment when the president was seized from his home.

"Try the Pforzheimer Equivalent," Violet suggested to Reznik. He was the only one sitting down. The others were hovering behind his chair, barely able to contain themselves. Reznik had taken point on the computer work, running through a series of tests to make sure the Intercept was back online, functioning properly. And to see if it could provide any help in locating Ogden Crowley.

"Already did it," he said.

"And the Brady-Selden Curve analysis?"

Reznik twisted around in his seat and gave Violet a scathing look. She interpreted it easily: *Are you serious?*

"Did it," he said. Violet could tell that he was trying not to be insulted by her last several suggestions for ways to test the Intercept— suggestions that were basic, obvious, and that he'd performed right at the outset, to no avail, and which she knew full well he'd already tried, because she had, after all, been standing right here watching him do so.

He didn't snap at her, though, the way he ordinarily would have. Violet knew why. Because he felt sorry for her. Anybody who got a good look at her would feel sorry for her.

She hadn't gone home yet to shower or change her clothes. Hence she was a mess. Her clothes were ripped. Her hair was a nightmare. And her face, courtesy of all the bruises, looked like one of the rags Shura used to clean her brushes—a lurid, splotchy combination of red and yellow and purple.

After being abandoned on that dark street, Violet had walked for over an hour until a car went by. She flagged it down and used the driver's console to call Shura. Shura arrived in minutes in a police car driven by Chief Callahan.

As soon as Violet had answered their questions about the ordeal, she had a question of her own, for Shura: "How's your mom?" The answer was reassuring: Anna Lu had regained consciousness. She had no memory of the assault, but it looked as if she would recover.

And now they were all here, huddled in the workstation at Protocol Hall, in search of President Crowley—and answers.

"How about the Sensenbrenner-Cooley Code Derivative?" Violet said. She was nervous, and she was speaking so fast that she didn't put enough space between her words and that was why it sounded like she'd said "*sensenbrennercooleycodederivative,*" which did not make sense. But Rez, she knew, could understand and he was the only one she cared about right now. "That way," she added, "you could use the vector coordinates from the—"

"Violet. Hey—Violet," Reznik interjected. In contrast to her agitated speech, he spoke slowly and carefully. Violet realized that he was trying to settle her down. "I've done all those things. You know I have."

She did. She did know that. Reznik was very smart, and he knew computers backward and forward, inside and out. He'd taught her most of what she knew about the Intercept. But Violet was frantic right now, and so worried about her father that she thought she might jump right out of her skin. Giving orders to Reznik—trying to come up with something he'd forgotten or overlooked, some new angle, some way to get a clue about where they'd taken her father—was her only outlet right now for the tension she felt. And the fear.

Violet took a deep breath, trying to center herself. She looked around. She could only turn her head, not her body, because the last time she'd tried to move her position she had ended up stepping on Shura's toe and elbowing Callahan in the ribs. But she needed a quick break from staring at Reznik's screen, so she shifted her gaze to the large farm of cubicles that surrounded them.

A general alarm had been issued throughout New Earth about the kidnapping, and most people were huddled in their homes, but those who worked in this facility were still on the job. They had to be. No matter what, the Intercept had to keep functioning. No one could imagine life—orderly life—without it.

Callahan was growing impatient. "I've got twelve divisions out searching for President Crowley and for the criminals who took him. My guys are turning New Earth upside down. Tell me why this computer crap matters so much."

"This 'computer crap,' as you put it," Reznik said, sounding testy and resentful at having to interrupt his mental calculations to speak to a lesser mind, "is the key to everything." He turned to Violet. "Let's go over this again. Put in the descriptors for everything you remember about what happened tonight. Heavy on the details. I can run another keyword program and see if we get any matches for previous incidents."

He leaned to one side. Violet bent over and started typing on his keyboard.

While she did that, Callahan touched Danny's sleeve. "This is highly irregular. I want to make sure you understand that. Your friendship with Violet means you should recuse yourself from the investigation. But frankly, I need you." She narrowed her eyes. "And I'm still angry about your repeated trips to Old Earth. Disobeying direct orders. None of that has been forgotten. Are we clear?"

"Clear, ma'am," Danny said. "Right now, I'm just trying to help find Violet's dad."

Violet, of course, was listening to this conversation, as was everyone else in the small cubicle. Eavesdropping was a given. And under any other circumstances, the moment might have been awkward: hearing a boss reprimanding an employee. But such was the nature of the emergency that nobody squirmed, nobody coughed, nobody pretended to find something fascinating to look at so that they wouldn't have to look at Danny or the chief.

"Okay," Violet said. She stood up straight again, relinquishing the keyboard to Reznik. "That's it. Everything I can remember."

He nodded. He punched some keys, frowned, and punched a few more keys. Orange symbols kinked across his screen.

They waited.

"I'm glad they let you go," Shura said. "But I don't really get why they did."

Violet shrugged. "Best guess? It's Dad they wanted. Not me. I was just a liability. One more problem to deal with. They probably didn't even know I'd be home last night. Just an accident."

She took a moment to glance at Danny, wondering what was going on in his mind. She didn't believe he had anything to do with her father's kidnapping—but he knew more than he was saying.

He knew what was written in that red notebook.

Moments later Reznik sighed a deep, frustrated sigh. He swept a hand toward the computer. The symbols had stopped moving. They were quiet now. They'd done their job, revealed all that they were capable of revealing. Which was not enough.

"Nothing," he said. "Or least nothing we didn't know before."

"The earlier vandalism perpetrated by the Rebels," Callahan said. "Surely you can cross-check the police reports against—"

"Did it," Reznik snapped.

"How about checking the frequency of the deployment of the Intercept for the past twenty-four hours?" Danny said. "Maybe it'll show if someone on the inside tried to interfere with the—"

"Did it."

"Or," Shura said, "you could test the—"

"Did it. Did it. *I did it all.*" Reznik was annoyed. He had been annoyed for a while, to be sure, but only Violet knew that, because she had worked with him for so long. He was fairly good at hiding his annoyance. Now, though, he was letting it show. These people did not appreciate the fact that he was doing his best—and that there was nothing *they* might think of that he hadn't already thought of.

There had been times in the past when Violet disliked his arrogance, but tonight, she realized that she counted on Reznik's arrogance. His expertise and his arrogance were sort of the same thing. She felt a surge of affection for him, an appreciation, and that was followed shortly by sadness because she would never feel about him the way he felt about her.

The only person she felt *that* way about was Danny.

She glanced over at him. Danny was frowning, and his face had its shut-down, closed-for-business look that he got when he was thinking hard.

The workstation had grown quiet. No one moved. Violet vastly preferred the way it had been before—a too-loud, too-close, uncomfortable but oddly consoling circus of strong personalities and competing opinions, a free-for-all of concerned people doing their best—to this ominous and depressing calm.

"Okay," Danny said, breaking the silence. "It looks like we're not going to be able to track down the kidnappers with the usual police methods. They're just not working."

Violet looked at Callahan. The chief had stiffened a bit when Danny made his point, but there was no arguing with it.

"And that being the case," Danny went on, "I think we need to review what we already know. So that we can come at this from another angle."

"What do you mean?" Shura said.

"Well, we've been trying to figure out where they took Violet's dad. Maybe we should be focusing on *why* they took him."

"That's easy," Reznik said. "They hate the Intercept."

"Yeah," Callahan added. "They want it to be dismantled."

"Fine," Danny said. "But why? Why do they want that?"

Reznik shrugged. "I've skimmed a few of their manifestos on the Internet. The most important one is called *The Dark Intercept*. It's long and it's actually pretty well-reasoned. They say the whole concept is barbaric. And wrong. They believe people's emotions ought to be private—not government property. They shouldn't be used against us. The manifesto brings up a lot of past stuff, like the American Revolutionary War back on Old Earth. It says that the Intercept ought to be called 'the Dark Intercept' because the system is based on fear. On the darkest parts of human beings. Not the good, positive stuff."

"We've tried to infiltrate them," Callahan said, cutting into his story. "Get someone on the inside. Nothing works."

"Because they're too smart?" Shura asked.

"Because they're too *small*," Callahan answered. "It's a very, very tiny faction. They don't let in a lot of new members, as a security measure. So it's been impossible to embed a spy. They all know each other too well."

"There has to be a way," Reznik said. "A way to figure out their identities. Which will help us find out where they've taken Violet's dad."

Silence reigned over the cubicle once more.

Violet snapped her fingers. The sound wasn't loud, but it was so sudden that Reznik flinched.

"Hey," she said. She turned quickly to Shura. "Some of your mom's clients—they're against the Intercept, right?"

Shura nodded. "Yeah. That's why I think they're the ones threatening her. Because they oppose it. Not all of them—just a few. They may even be the ones who attacked her. They wanted her to join them. Work with them. Get something for them during her trips to Old Earth. I don't know what it was—my parents never discussed it when I could hear—but my mom wouldn't do it."

Violet looked at Reznik. He had caught on to her line of inquiry, and now he resembled a kitten who'd just been scratched in his favorite spot.

Callahan, too, was nodding. "I think I see what you're getting at, Violet," she said. "One of Anna Lu's clients might have some information about the Rebels."

"Okay," Shura said. "I'll call her at the hospital. She's doing so much better now. I can get the names of immigrants. The ones who asked for help." She gave Callahan a sideways glance. "But if you don't mind, I'm going to tell her that this is about finding President Crowley. Not about helping the police. She's not a fan."

Callahan shrugged. "Not many people are. Until they need us."

Marvel Breckinridge. Roger Rodale. Piers Ostrum.

Those were the names that Anna Lu supplied.

By the time Shura clicked off her console call, Reznik had already pulled up the files of Breckinridge, Rodale, and Ostrum. He started to type in another command, but hesitated. He dropped his hands into his lap.

"Chief Callahan," he said. He voice was oddly stilted.

"Yeah?" she said.

"Requesting your permission under the Emergency Police Surveillance Act to access the Intercept files of three civilians for whom we have no current evidence that they have committed—or are about to commit—a criminal act."

Violet understood. Accessing an Intercept file with no crime actively under way was a serious offense. Even in these circumstances, when they were working as fast as they possibly could to find and free her father, Reznik needed to follow the rules.

Ogden Crowley would understand, too, Violet knew. Because he'd written them.

A police supervisor could override the directive. Callahan, who didn't like formalities, gave Reznik a frown and an impatient wave. "Yeah, yeah, whatever—of *course*," she declared. "Just do it. Go on. Figure out which one's got the best motive to join up with the Rebels— who hates New Earth and all it stands for."

Reznik nodded. His hands returned to the keyboard. With a speed that always impressed Violet—he had a great feel for his computer, an intuitive understanding, as if he and his computer were twins separated at birth who'd been reunited during Reznik's Intercept training—he pulled up the first image, an image drawn from Rodale's memory file and reconstituted by the Intercept:

The ID photo showed that Rodale was a heavy-faced, middle-aged man who had immigrated from Old Earth last year. In his feed, a much younger Rodale watches an elderly aunt die. The shriveled old woman lies upon a narrow bed. She is barely able to draw breath in and out. Rodale's sobs are copious and loud. At one point he lifts his head and cries out, "Why, God? Why are you taking her?"

Reznik flipped a switch. The image disappeared.

"No motive," Reznik explained over his shoulder to the four people hunched around him. "He might hate the Intercept, but it has nothing to do with New Earth. She died of natural causes."

Next he pulled up Ostrum's feed. The ID photo showed a bald, spindly, shifty-looking man, and when the Intercept unleashed the images of Ostrum's most excruciating emotional pain, Callahan snickered.

Ostrum sits at a table with three other bald, spindly, shifty-looking men, each of whom has a sloppy pile of poker chips and a shiny fan of playing cards spread in front of him. It is clear that Ostrum has just lost a great deal of money. The others look sly and elated.

"Just imagine," said Callahan, her voice flecked with sarcasm, "having to live with the memory of the worst poker hand of your life. Kind of amazing the poor bum hasn't killed himself by now. Okay, next."

Now Breckinridge's feed arrived on the screen, fresh from its slot in the woman's Intercept file, where it had been waiting since it was first collected. Before he punched the key to roll the feed, Reznik gave them the woman's background. "Thirty-two years old," he said. "Allowed entry to New Earth six months ago on a hardship visa. Anna Lu helped her get settled in Franklinton."

According to her ID photo Breckinridge was large and stolid, with a mass of crinkly brown hair and an unpleasant facial expression, a sort of pinched scowl. With a couple of keystrokes, Reznik accessed her Intercept file:

Breckinridge is arguing with a cop. This is Old Earth. You can tell by the withered trees, the gray, low-hanging sky, and the face of the cop, etched deeply with vertical lines. The color has leeched out of that face, just as it eventually will drain away from virtually everything on Old Earth, leaving only husks and rinds.

Marvel Breckinridge is howling. She is shrieking. She repeatedly thrusts something at the cop—a small bundle wrapped in cloth, about the size of a loaf of bread—but he refuses to take it. His hands, both of them, stay fixed on his slab gun. He looks young and uncertain.

Her crying is louder now. She keeps trying to hand him the bundle. He still won't take it. He stands there, blinking and stiff. The woman begins to sway. She says, "Please. She's sick. My baby's so sick—if you could just take her to New Earth. Please. The doctors there—they can help her. They can save her. I don't need to go. I'll stay here. But just take my baby—please, please."

The cop finally speaks: "I can't, lady. There are rules. Unless you have immigration papers, I'm not allowed to—"

The woman cuts him off with a shriek: "YOU HAVE TO TAKE MY BABY! PLEASE, OH, PLEASE!"

The cop says, "I'm just here to insert Intercept chips, lady. That's all. I can't come back with a baby. Much less a sick one. My supervisor, Officer Stark, would suspend me."

She tries again to make him accept the bundle. In the confusion, she drops the bundle into the dirt. The cop quickly kneels down to check on the child. He unwraps the cloth. He discovers a ghastly, rotting corpse. The child has been dead for months. Missip Fever, it seems, judging by the faint orange color on the last intact scrap of skin.

"Take her," the woman begs. "Take her to a New Earth doctor. They can fix her there. They can do anything on New Earth. I *know* they can make her well. If only they will try. If my baby dies now, it's their fault. It's the fault of New Earth."

The five people in the cubicle were silent as Reznik clicked out of the feed. For half a second, before the wriggling orange algorithms returned, the screen was blank.

Callahan was the first to speak. "I think we have a winner," she said grimly.

Little Girl Lost

It was very late now—well past midnight—but they found Marvel Breckinridge sitting at the dinette in her small apartment. The place was a plain white box, with one tiny plant on the windowsill.

"I brought that plant up from Old Earth," she said proudly, in an eerie singsong voice. The plant was not thriving. Its fallen leaves made a sad little circle around the pot.

Callahan's team had punched in the front door and then moved quickly into the kitchen. Violet was right behind them. The chief had agreed to let her come along.

Between cupped hands Breckinridge held a picture of a baby, a pretty, blond-haired child with blue eyes and a sweet smile.

The woman didn't stir, even when all those pairs of heavy boots crashed in.

They jammed around her, firearms at the ready. Callahan led the way. She had to say Breckinridge's name three times before the woman looked up at them.

"Yes?" she said. There were cops on all sides of her, ready for her to make a move. She didn't seem at all flustered by their presence. Perhaps she wasn't even aware of it.

Callahan stood across the table.

"We know you work with the Rebels of Light," the chief declared. "And we need to know where they're holding Ogden Crowley."

Breckinridge smiled. She seemed to be addressing Callahan but she wouldn't make eye contact. "I don't have the slightest idea what you're talking about."

Callahan hitched a thumb into her gun belt. "Don't do this, lady. Don't force our hand. We know you've been helping them. Give us a location."

"All I can say, Officer, is that I believe you've made a mistake." The whimsical smile again.

When Callahan was angry, she had the kind of voice that didn't need a bullhorn. "Tell us where the Rebels are."

Breckinridge continued to smile. She still held the picture in her hands.

"We have the Intercept," Callahan added. "And your friends aren't here to help you. We realize that the Rebels have found some way to get around it—but they're not here now. This is your last chance to cooperate." She gestured toward the picture. "You know what we can do."

For the first time, a look of concern crossed Breckinridge's face.

"You wouldn't," she said. Her eyes widened as they finally met up with Callahan's. "You wouldn't."

"I most certainly would." Callahan touched her console. "Reznik," she said, "we're ready over here. Deploy the Intercept."

Back in Protocol Hall, Violet knew, Reznik was feeding Marvel Breckinridge's coordinates into the Intercept. She synced her console to the same coordinates.

The feed was horrific to watch.

In seconds, Breckinridge began to spasm. Her body shook. Drool flooded her chin. Her eyes grew wild and then they rolled back in her head so that only the whites were showing.

In her mind, her baby is propped up in the bed. There are no pillows, so her mother has used old coats, bags, rags, wadded-up paper—anything to help the child stay upright. For some reason, being upright helps with the pain.

The child's skin is orange. A terrible color. The color of death.

The baby cries. She cries silently. Her mother realizes that she's crying not so much for what is happening to her now, but for what will never happen at all. Her child will not get any older. She will never grow up. She will always be this age. She will always be propped up in a makeshift bed in a sad little house in a decaying city under a sullen gray sky in a forgotten world.

And then, before her mother has a chance to say one more word to her, *just one tiny word,* she is gone. The child's head slumps to the side. Her body relaxes and starts to tilt. Her mother screams and cries.

The image repeats itself, only stronger this time.

Her baby is propped up in the bed. There are no pillows, so her mother has used old coats, bags, rags, wadded-up paper—anything to help the child stay upright. For some reason, being upright helps with the pain.

The child's skin is orange.

The mother is living the memory of her daughter's death all over again. The Intercept owns this moment now, and will continue to deploy it, sending it back into the mother's brain repeatedly.

She will keep living the pain all over again, and over and over again after that, and over and over and . . .

"No," Breckinridge cried. "No, no." She finally managed to stop her hands from shaking. "Not again. I can't stand it. Tell them to stop. Please."

"Location," Callahan said coldly.

Breckinridge rattled off an address in Mendeleev Crossing. Callahan nodded. "If you're lying," she said, her voice as taut as her face, "it'll be worse next time. I won't shut it down so quickly. You'll suffer more. I promise you that." She touched her console. "Reznik, stop the intervention for now. But keep the coordinates handy, okay?"

If Callahan had had the time, she could have gotten more information out of this woman. Violet was absolutely sure of that. She might very well have found out how the Rebels were thwarting the Intercept. At the very least, she could have found out what it was that the Rebels sought down on Old Earth, and sought so desperately that they had threatened Anna Lu's life to get it.

But first they had to find Ogden Crowley. Who knew what the Rebels were doing to him at this very moment? His will might be strong, but his body wasn't. He was not a young man.

Callahan looked down at Breckinridge. The picture of the child had slipped out of the woman's grasp. It rested on the tabletop. Callahan had no sympathy for traitors. She wanted to twist the knife one more time. She wanted to make this traitor pay—even beyond the prison sentence Breckinridge would receive for conspiring against the Intercept.

"Cute kid," Callahan said. "Shame about what happened to her. Oh well." She signaled to Violet that they were ready to go. It was time to find Ogden Crowley and save New Earth.

29

Last Rebel Standing

They approached the dark, run-down building with slab guns drawn and nerves on high alert. The streets were deserted, swept clean of people by Callahan's order. There was a stillness in the night air; the slight trembling of the ground beneath their feet seemed more pronounced than ever, as if the Intercept wanted to remind them of its central position in this story. In all the stories.

"Here?" Garrison said, keeping her voice low. She was the chief's top lieutenant and she seemed incredulous as she beheld the shabby storefront wedged between two skyscrapers. It was a runt, hiding out amid giants. "In *this* dump? This is where the Rebels meet?"

"I guess you'd prefer a sign out front, right?" Callahan shot back. "Something like, 'Rebels Meeting Here Tonight. Bring a Friend and a Dish to Share.'"

Violet snickered, which caused Garrison to give her a prolonged scowl. *Fine,* Violet thought. *I don't like you and you don't like me. So it's mutual. Let's move on.* Allison Garrison had short blond hair and hard green eyes that unnerved Violet; she had heard Danny describe her as the kind of cop who secretly enjoyed watching people suffer.

She and Garrison had clashed during the ride here in the chief's car. Violet wanted to join the raid, but Garrison argued that she was a liability. Callahan sided with Violet, pointing out that they might need her to identify her captors.

"This is definitely it," Danny said. He had called Reznik on his console and requested a heat-signature check on the address. Sure enough, there was evidence of multiple people inside.

Garrison motioned to her team. They divided into two units and surrounded the building on both sides. Callahan and Danny would make the initial entry from the front, with another unit right behind them. A fourth unit had already taken up positions in the rear. A sharpshooter unit was stationed across the street.

The Rebels could very well be waiting just inside the door, with slab guns ready.

"On my signal," Callahan said. "Violet, stay back. If something happens to you, I don't want to be the one to tell your father."

"Good to know you care, Chief," Violet muttered back. She felt like an honorary cop tonight, and figured she might as well sound like one, heavy on the sarcasm.

Callahan and Danny crouched side by side under the blackened window. They double-checked their weapons.

Callahan gave a silent three-count with her fingers—*one, two, THREE*—and then she and Danny sprang up and shouldered their way through the door.

The sizzle and crack of a slab gun discharge came at them with a desperate fury. Danny and Callahan rushed in low and fast, eluding the initial barrage. The inside was dark, but every few seconds, a red tracer of slab gun fire illuminated the space. It was a square room with nothing in it—except for the shooter, a black-hooded figure down on one knee, holding his slab gun with both hands and firing indiscriminately.

Danny flew at the shooter, knocking him sideways. They rolled over and over and over, the shooter clawing at Danny's face, kicking at him. Danny was stronger, however, and he pinned the man's arms.

Callahan quickly lit a series of flares. By the light of them she found the shooter's weapon, jarred loose during the skirmish. She secured it. The unit that entered right behind them was spreading out in front of a door that led to yet another room.

"Shields up," Callahan reminded her colleagues. She turned to Danny, who was just rising, tying the shooter's hands behind his back. "Stay here with the prisoner."

Danny nodded. He ripped off the squirming man's black mask— and discovered that this wasn't a man at all. It was a young woman. Her face was twisted with hate, her mouth a thin line of pure defiance.

Another barrage of cracks and whooshing sounds and small explosions ripped through the building as the officers were met by more slab gun fire. From her position across the street Violet watched the action by the light of the flares. She heard shouts and screams. She heard Callahan yelling, "There he is!" And she heard a snarling mess of other voices.

It was over quickly. One by one, the Rebels were led out by the officers, hands tied behind their backs, masks ripped off. Violet watched as five went by. There had to be more of them, right? Of course there were. They just weren't here in this building.

She waited. In another few seconds Ogden Crowley himself emerged from the back room. He was flanked by two police officers who were trying their best to assist him. Her father kept pulling away from them, angry and prideful. He wanted to walk on his own, even though his damaged leg made it difficult. He looked wretched. His face had aged a hundred years in just the past few hours, or so it seemed to Violet. The wrinkles had multiplied. The crevices cut deeper. The skin under his eyes was dark and loose. He was bent over, his back curved like a shepherd's hook. He didn't acknowledge Danny as he lurched past him, muttering, spent.

Violet rushed up to her father and embraced him.

What had they done *to him?*

And then she realized that her father's state wasn't the result of anything the Rebels had inflicted. Only one thing could make a person look like that: the Intercept. A memory selected by the Intercept and reinserted into his brain—and then repeated, until he did their bidding. They had used Ogden Crowley's own mind against him.

Violet led her father over to the medical team that waited in the street. She wanted to go back inside with Danny; she wanted to see this place where the Rebels had plotted against New Earth.

"Where's Callahan?" she asked him.

"Still inside," Danny answered. "She told me she was going after the leader."

And then they heard it—a strangled cry, a cry of shock and agony. They ran toward the sound.

In the room at the very back, its corners lit by the police flares, stood Michelle Callahan. With one hand, she clutched the arm of the last Rebel left. With the other, she held the mask she'd just pulled off.

She stared into the hard, dark face of her husband, Paul Stark.

After and Before

It should have been excruciating.

It should have been unbearable.

It should have been tearing him to pieces—this reminder of all that he had lost. It should have been agonizing. He should have been howling and screaming.

Instead, Paul Stark looked a little bored. He folded his hands on the small table. Then he unfolded them. Folded them again. He glanced up at the wall clock. Scratched his left cheek.

Violet, watching from behind the glass partition, could see Stark's Intercept feed on her console—she'd asked Reznik to patch her in—and that's why she was so stunned by his nonchalance. It didn't make sense.

The Intercept was inundating his brain with a memory of what he had been. Not what he was now, trapped in a HoverUp, but the self he had been four years ago, just before a pulse from a slab gun had changed his life forever:

Striding through the world on his own two feet. Bold. Strong. Resolute.

Violet knew what he was *supposed* to be feeling as the image of this pivot-point in his destiny was thrust into his brain. He was supposed to be in the grip of an immense, razor-edged sadness as it jammed its way through his body, cutting him, slicing him, leaving him in emotional tatters. He was supposed to be bereft. Inconsolable.

And yet he . . . *wasn't.*

It was just past six in the morning, an hour after the rescue of Ogden Crowley in the raid of Rebel headquarters. Violet had helped her father settle in at home, and then she had come right back to the station. Her curiosity wouldn't let her stay away. She had to know: How did the Rebels resist the Intercept?

She had stationed herself in the observation terrace that overlooked the interrogation room.

Stark sat calmly in his chair. This was the largest and coldest and grimmest of the ten interrogation rooms in the Hawking police station. He winked at the cop who stood across the room. He smiled. *Bring it on,* his smile said, more eloquently than any words could have done.

That cop was Allison Garrison.

"Can you double-check his coordinates?" Garrison said into her console. "Nothing happening here."

"The coordinates are correct." Reznik's voice crackled through the speaker with its usual crisp arrogance. Violet recognized that tone. She'd heard it directed at herself many times. *Of course* the coordinates were right. He'd done them himself, and Steve Reznik didn't make mistakes. "But I'll check, sure. Whatever floats your boat." That was another phrase Reznik had picked up during his readings of manuscripts from the twentieth century. He'd figured out its meaning from context. "Ready to go again?" Garrison said into her console.

"Ready" came Reznik's reply.

Garrison looked over at Stark. The smile was still on his face; if anything, it had gotten bigger. More carefree. The faint *whish-whoosh* of his HoverUp had a jaunty sound to it now, not a mechanical one.

Stark took a nonchalant look at the inside of his left elbow. He saw the tiny blue spark.

Four years ago:

Once again, his mind is filled with the image of the second before a photon-pulse from a slab gun splinters his spine. He sees the scene, as if a film is being projected in front of his eyes: He falls to the pavement. The lower half of his body is a smear of dissolving skin and mutilated muscle.

He'll never walk again.

He'll never be able to stand up on his own.

He laughed.

"We'll shut it down if you cooperate," Garrison said. "Are you ready to talk?"

"Ready to *talk,* Lieutenant? No, I don't think so," Stark said amiably. "But I'll tell you what I *am* ready to do. I'm ready to have some breakfast. Any chance of getting a couple of eggs over easy and maybe some hash browns?"

Callahan, stiff-backed, blank-eyed, was seated behind the desk in her office down the hall from the interrogation rooms. The desk was a throwback, an old-fashioned wooden one, wide and chipped but solid, a souvenir from Old Earth. She had told Violet a few minutes ago that the desk made her feel grounded—which was an indispensable attribute right now, because her world had officially been shattered.

Violet liked the desk, too. It was the kind of object she rarely saw on New Earth. It clearly had a history, a past. From her seat across from the chief, she leaned forward and ran her palm across the craggy surface.

"We picked out this desk together, Paul and I," Callahan continued. She didn't look at Violet as she spoke. Instead her gaze was aimed at some distant point that, it seemed to Violet, no one but she could see. "Right after we were married. We brought it with us to New Earth. Wasn't easy. Your father put a strict limit on physical possessions you could bring." Her eyes had a faraway cast to them. "We had to leave behind so many things. I'm glad to have the desk—something from our old life."

Violet nodded. She didn't know what to say.

Callahan had asked her to be here, to keep her company while Garrison finished up the interrogations. She had finally given up on Stark—for the time being. She'd make another run at him later, Garrison said. Maybe another Rebel would crack first, spill some information, and they would have some leverage to use against Stark.

Keep me company.

That was the exact phrase the chief had used. Pretty strange, Violet thought, coming from a woman as tough and self-reliant as Michelle Callahan.

But then again, not so strange when you realized the extent of her husband's betrayal. Stark was a traitor. A conspirator.

What's it like, Violet asked herself, *to suddenly realize that someone you love is a stranger?*

"We had a little slogan," Callahan said. "A thing we shared."

"What was that?"

"It was something we said to each other. 'Once a cop, always a cop.' Because we knew what we were. We had the same values. We had the same reactions. The same black-or-white, right-or-wrong way of viewing the world. And even though Paul didn't wear his blue tunic anymore, I still thought he was—I would've sworn that he'd never abandon—" The chief faltered. "I was sure he was still a cop at heart."

Except that he's not, Violet thought. *He couldn't be. He's a person his own wife barely recognizes.*

As they were leading Stark out of the Rebel headquarters, he'd held his head high. Even though his hands were shackled behind his back, he moved with pride and purpose. His HoverUp made its familiar *whish-whoosh* sound. Violet had tried to catch his eye. Could this be the same man who'd eaten tomato basil soup across the table from her a few days ago?

Stark ignored her. But he did pause before his wife.

"Why are you doing this, Paul? Why?" she had asked him.

"That's not the question, Michelle. The question is—why aren't you doing it, too?"

Violet had had no idea what he meant by that. She still didn't.

There was a knock at the door.

"Chief? Sorry to bother you."

It was Garrison, and her face indicated she was not here to deliver good news. "I've finished the other interrogations. Time to go back to Stark. As you know, his Intercept feed had no impact."

"Not surprising," Callahan said. "The Rebels have found a way to get around it."

"Yes. But I have an idea."

The chief shrugged. "You'll have to run it past someone else. I'm not supervising this case. I can't. Not with such a close personal tie to the prisoner."

"Understood. But you're my mentor, Chief. Ever since I joined the force. I'm just asking for your opinion—not your approval."

Callahan nodded curtly. "Okay. Go on."

Garrison stepped into the office. She'd been hesitating on the threshold. She glanced dismissively at Violet before continuing. "Well," she said, "from a quick preliminary assessment, it looks like the Rebels may only be able to resist the Intercept for short periods of time. They can stop its effects and do what they want to do. And then the shielding—or whatever it is—breaks down and they're as susceptible as anybody else to the Intercept's power."

"That may be the case, yes."

"So let's wait a bit," Garrison went on. "Leave Stark sitting there in the interrogation room. He's been a cop. He knows how it usually works—we go in full strength, right away, and try to wear the suspect down. I bet he's counting on that. But maybe that's playing right into his hands. He's *expecting* us to do that. And then—just when we're ready to give up—*that's* when he'll actually be at his most vulnerable. When whatever method he's using to keep the Intercept at bay is at its weakest."

"So we stop."

"For a period of time, yes."

"We do nothing."

"Right. We do nothing."

"Seems like a long shot."

Garrison's tense expression relaxed just a bit. "With all due respect, Chief, I wouldn't call it a long shot. I'd call it our *only* shot."

Violet dipped a small corner of the cloth into the liquid. She had carried a bowl of cool water to her father's chair. She used the cloth to dab at his forehead. Once, twice, on each temple. He flinched at each touch. He was not a man who enjoyed such visible proof of his frailties.

He had refused to lie down on the couch, as Violet had advised. Instead he sat in his armchair.

She would return to the station when Stark's interrogation resumed, but for now, Violet needed to make sure her father was resting. Clearly the night's turmoil had taken a toll on him. His skin was sallow and clammy, and he was so weak that he did not so much sit down in his armchair as stagger into it.

"I wish you'd let me call a doctor, Dad," Violet said. "Just for a quick check. You've been through hell."

Ogden shook his head emphatically. Violet had to wait until he'd finished before she could try another dab with the cloth.

"Nonsense," he declared.

It was morning now, and the apartment's glass walls let in the abundant light. In the streets below, another day on New Earth had begun. When Violet had returned home that morning she had found her father gazing out these windows, watching the sunlight awaken this bright dream of a world.

After the longest night, there was always a next day. That's what her father had taught her. Morning was the essence of New Earth. A new hope.

Ogden took a deep breath. Violet saw him grip the armrests with his scarred hands, readjusting himself in his chair.

"I'd been through interventions before, you know," he said. "I felt it was only fair that I test the system. But those times, the Intercept retrieved more predictable moments, such as the deaths of my parents. The moment I was told that my leg was useless. Moments that you would expect it to fetch.

"But to tell you the truth, Violet, it had never occurred to me—until last night—that the Intercept might select a *happy* moment. A moment so golden, so joyful, so perfect, that the fact it would never return could hurt me far worse than a horrific one." He settled his hands on his lap. "The Intercept has moved a step ahead. It understands things I've only just come to realize. Happiness—happiness that has passed, never to return—can be as painful as sadness."

Violet was struck by an unsettling thought. The Intercept didn't simply respond to what people like her and Rez told it to do anymore. It seemed to know more about human emotions than human beings did. It wasn't just thinking.

It was thinking ahead.

Twenty minutes later, Violet's console alerted her to a call. Reznik's face materialized on her screen.

"Glad to hear you're okay," he said. "And your dad, too."

"Thanks. Hey, I've got a lot to do, and so if that's the only reason you called, then I need to—"

"Wait. Wait, Violet. There's something I have to tell you."

"What is it?"

"It's *big*," he said. He was talking faster now. He sounded nervous. "I had to hang out here all night, in case they needed me, and I passed the time doing a retroactive analysis of weight distribution in portal fields and I found this anomaly that could only mean that—listen, I need to tell you in person. Can you come over to Protocol Hall? I can't leave—I'm on call all day. For the cops."

Violet looked over at her father. He had fallen asleep. Deeply this time. Restfully. Which meant she could return to the police station to watch Garrison take another run at Stark.

"I'll get there as soon as I can," she said. "No promises."

She could tell by his silence that Reznik wasn't pleased at the delay. Reznik always seemed to want more from her than she could give.

"Okay. Guess that'll have to do," he finally said. "Oh, and Violet—whatever you do—don't bring Danny, okay?"

"What's this got to do with him?"

"Just make sure you come by yourself."

The Kiss

Allison Garrison walked back into the interrogation room. She nodded toward the observational terrace. She wasn't saying hello to Violet—like *that* would ever happen—but rather acknowledging Violet's presence and offering the silent but unmistakable opinion that she was nothing but a nuisance.

Got my eyes on you, girl. That was how Violet interpreted Garrison's nod. And that green-eyed stare of hers.

This time, Violet wasn't alone in the small room. Callahan stood beside her.

Why would Callahan want to be here? Violet asked herself.

"Maybe this will help me understand," Callahan murmured, as if Violet had spoken out loud. "How could Paul do this? How could he have undermined my work—which was his work, too, until his accident—by leading the Rebels?"

Stark sat in the same seat he'd been sitting in before, yet he looked very different now. He was weary, Violet surmised, from a long day spent in a cold gray space. But it was more than that, too.

His eyes had lost their glitter. They didn't follow Garrison's movements as she crossed the room to stand in front of him. They stayed fixed on a spot on the wall. There was a layer of sweat across his forehead. His hands trembled.

"Are you ready to talk?" Garrison said.

Stark didn't answer. That, too, marked a change. Before, he'd been happy to reply with a joke or a wisecrack.

"How do you withstand the Intercept?"

Garrison had asked him the very same question many, many times, but that was before. Eight hours before. "How, Stark? You and your friends—how do you do it? You know we have to find out. We can't allow a loophole like this to exist. So tell us. And we'll make sure you end up in a nice warm prison instead of a cold, filthy one."

Stark licked his lips. Still no reply.

"One last chance," Garrison said. "What's the secret?"

Stark was slumped in his seat. His skin looked haggard and yellow. Even the *whish-whoosh* of his HoverUp sounded fainter now, less sure of itself, as if the machine that held him up somehow echoed his unraveling.

"Okay," Garrison said. "You know the drill. I'm going to call for the Intercept." She tapped her console. "Protocol Hall? Are you there?"

Stark's face suddenly contorted with anxiety. He still didn't speak, but his body began to tremble.

Garrison tapped her console again. "Let her rip."

Prodded by a series of keystrokes on a computer in a workstation in Protocol Hall, the Intercept jumped into action, plunging deep into Paul Stark's file to choose his most profound memory. It was different from the one it had chosen for him earlier, because emotions were always changing, second by second, with some emotions growing more intense as others faded.

The Intercept force-fed that memory back into his brain.

This time, there was nothing to block the reception, nothing to stop the feeling from flooding his senses—and sending him headfirst into the most dangerous place of all:

The past.

Violet hated to admit it, but it looked as if Garrison's hunch had been right. Whatever Stark and the Rebels used to keep the Intercept from affecting them, it had a limited shelf life. It was wearing off. And leaving Stark vulnerable.

Stark writhed and twisted in his seat. He jerked his head from side to side, trying to escape—but there was no escape from his own memory-induced emotions.

"Please," he called out. "Stop this. I'm begging you—I'll do anything—I'll do—"

"Tell me how you beat the Intercept," Garrison said, cutting him off.

"I can't. *I can't.*" His voice rose into a sob. "We've worked too hard—people have died helping us—I can't betray—"

"Don't go there, Stark. Don't talk about betrayal. You and your friends are trying to destroy New Earth."

Stark lurched forward. He was gripping the tabletop, trying to stop himself from vibrating right out of his chair from his shaking.

Violet tuned her console to the Intercept feed—the record of what was being inflicted on him. Surely it was resurrecting the day he was shot, the moment he realized he would never walk again. Surely it was slamming those images back into his brain. Surely he was being forced to relive the horrific moment when his body melted and congealed from the pulse of a slab gun.

Callahan leaned over to watch, too.

And that was not what they saw.

A long narrow room.

A room lined with gray lockers. This is Old Earth.

A woman in a crisp blue tunic walks smartly up that corridor.

Wait, Violet thought. *That's—Callahan. Yes. It's Michelle Callahan.*

A man is looking in a mirror. He's handsome, but in a rugged, off-hand way. His body is muscular, his arms strong. His hands look as if they could rip out every one of these lockers, just for sport.

He grins.

It's Paul Stark. He's in the locker room of Precinct 12, and the mirror is on the inside of his locker door. He slams it shut.

"So," he says. "Want to, like, get a cup of coffee sometime?"

They've been flirting with each other for months, ever since they joined the force. Talking, laughing, making sure to linger just a little bit longer than necessary when they happen to brush past each other in the corridor after roll call.

"Sure," she replies.

And then he takes her in his arms and he kisses her. It's not a casual kiss. It's a serious kiss. A kiss that makes a promise. A kiss that she looks as if she's feeling all the way down to her toes and then right back up again.

"Tell me," she murmurs, when he finally lets her go, although she doesn't want him to, "that it will always feel exactly like this."

"Yes," he says. "Always."

Paul Stark was facedown on the floor, quivering and sobbing. He tried to rise but he couldn't. He didn't have the strength to direct the HoverUp to lift him.

It's tearing him apart, Violet thought. *This memory of a time that can't return. A memory that pierces and sears not because it's horrendous and ugly—but because it's beautiful.*

And gone forever.

It seemed more like torture than interrogation. She looked up from her console to see how Callahan was enduring the scene.

No Callahan.

What the—

Violet's eyes dropped to the interrogation room below. There was the chief, standing face-to-face with a startled-looking Garrison. She had slipped out while Violet watched the feed.

"Stop this," Callahan declared. "Shut it down. Stop this *now*."

Garrison might have been shocked, but she stood her ground. "I can't do that, Chief," she said. "I think he's just about ready to talk."

"I told you to shut it down. That's a direct order."

Garrison stared at her. Her expression was puzzled, but it was also defiant.

"This isn't your case, Chief," she said calmly. "You had to step down on this one, remember? You have no authority here."

Callahan ripped her slab gun from its holster. She aimed it at Garrison, who backed away from her, hands raised.

"Chief," Garrison said, her voice rising in agitation. "What are you doing?"

"Turn it off." Callahan tightened her grip on the weapon. "Don't test me, Allison. Please. You'll regret it. I don't want you to end up like—" She inclined her head toward the suffering man on the floor. "—like Paul." Now she looked up at the terrace. "Don't get involved in this, Violet. I don't want to hurt you, either."

Garrison had made her decision. She tapped her console. "Shut down the feed. Now."

In a few seconds, Stark's breathing returned to normal.

"Paul," Callahan said. "Can you stand up?"

"I can stand up," he declared.

"Then let's go." She handed him his backpack, which Garrison had confiscated when the questioning began.

He glided forward, talking as he maneuvered the HoverUp. "Make sure you get a drink of water, Michelle. We may be on the road awhile." He pulled a water container from his backpack. "Here."

They were halfway out the door—Callahan had to back out, in order to keep the gun aimed at Garrison—when her lieutenant spoke.

"Why, Chief? Why are you doing this?"

Callahan let a few seconds pass before she answered. "They're right. The Intercept *is* torture. Our emotions are nobody's business but our own, Allison. Nobody should be able to use them to control us."

Garrison's expression didn't soften. "This—what you just saw— is what the Intercept is *supposed* to do. You know that. You're just confused. You're distraught. This is the price we pay for New Earth. For an orderly, well-run world. We don't want New Earth to turn into Old Earth."

Stark touched Callahan's arm. "We have to leave. Now."

Garrison's voice was brusque with certainty. "We'll find you, Chief. You'll never get away with this. There's nowhere for you to go. You can't hide from the Intercept. You *know* that." She tried one more tack. "If you haven't done anything wrong, you have nothing to fear."

"It's not about fear," Callahan said, as she and Stark hurried through the automatic door side by side. "It's about love."

The Revelation

Reznik was always happiest when he was working at his computer. His computer was like a broken-off puzzle piece of himself with which he was being constantly and joyfully reunited, making the picture whole again.

Coming up behind his seat in the workstation they shared, Violet realized that anew. She'd known it for a long time—as long as she'd known him, in fact—but each time she approached him in Protocol Hall from his blind side, it came back to her: the solid certainty that no human being would ever satisfy Steve Reznik's soul in quite the same way his computer did.

"Hey," Violet said.

"Hey." He didn't turn around. She didn't expect him to. That was pure Rez.

"So you heard about Chief Callahan joining the Rebels."

"Another workstation's handling that. They'll find them in a flash. Guaranteed. No matter what's happened, we've still got to trust the Intercept." He still hadn't taken his eyes off the screen.

Violet wondered how much sleep he'd gotten over the past twenty-four hours. She knew how much *she'd* had—roughly zero. Reznik usually averaged far less than she did. She halfway wondered if there was such a thing as negative sleep: if, after a while, the sleep you lost doubled back around and was recycled as *actual* sleep.

If anybody could make that scheme work, Violet thought, Rez could.

"What's up?" she said. "And can we do this, like, fast? I've got to get back home to my dad. He's pretty upset about Chief Callahan. He trusted her."

At the sound of the word *trusted*, Reznik frowned.

"I have something to tell you, Violet."

"What's going on?"

He punched a flurry of numbers on his keyboard. Turned a dial. Instantly his screen was alive with bright green figures that wiggled at different speeds.

"Look," he said solemnly, pointing to the wild dance of symbols. She looked.

"I'm sorry, but I don't know what I'm supposed to be seeing."

"Look." His voice was more emphatic now. He swept a hand toward the screen. "These are the calculations. They're not refutable, Violet. It's math. The numbers *have* to be correct, do you understand? There is no other plausible interpretation."

Now he was making her mad. She wasn't scared anymore. She was annoyed. This was a busy time for her, for everyone. She had to take care of her father. There were Rebels still loose on New Earth. She hadn't seen Danny in hours. She needed to—

"Violet, I don't know how to tell you this, but—" He faltered.

"We're friends, Steve. You know that. You can say anything to me and it'll be okay."

He swallowed. She watched his Adam's apple rise and settle.

"Not this," he said.

"Try me."

He pulled his hands away from the keyboard. When Violet recalled this moment later, she would speculate that he didn't want to be touching his computer when he told her what he had to tell her. It was as if he wanted to be fully human for this moment. Not half-man, half-computer. He wanted to be human—for her.

"Violet," he said. "I'll explain in a minute how I know—it was an accident, I swear, I wasn't looking, I wasn't out to get him—but I know for sure now."

"Know *what*?"

Reznik's next words changed Violet's life forever.

"The guy we think is Danny isn't Danny. The real Danny Mayhew died on Old Earth a year and a half ago."

PART THREE

Flicker

If only, Violet thought.

If only there was a way to see the Intercept in action. If only she could watch as it snatched up her emotion and flung it into her file.

That way, she would know what she was feeling. She could just read the label. Because otherwise, she had no idea.

Would the Intercept call it shock? Or anger? Or betrayal so sharp and awful that it felt like another punch in the stomach with a rusty pole?

Or all of the above?

And how about disbelief—that was there, too, wasn't it, in the array of her emotional responses to Reznik's news?

Violet sat in the workstation and tried to figure out what she was feeling. There were thousands of other people in Protocol Hall. The soft drifting buzz of conversation lapped all around them, a steady, constant wash of noise, noise that joined up with the muted vibration of the Intercept spreading out beneath the floor.

She felt sick. Hey, *that* was a feeling—nausea. Maybe she did know what she was feeling, after all. She was feeling like she wanted to throw up.

"Violet?" Reznik said. "Are you okay?"

Of COURSE I'm not okay—you just told me that the guy I'm in love with is some kind of fraud or imposter or whatever. How "okay" do you think it's possible to be, under the circumstances?

"Yeah." She kept her voice steady. Or tried to. "So your theory is based on what?"

"The numbers. And it's not a theory. It's fact."

"Just tell me how you got there, Rez."

"Okay, okay. Here goes." He scooted his chair closer to the screen. "You know about biometric records, right? And how meticulously they have to be kept on New Earth?"

"Yeah." In a lifeless, mechanical voice, Violet recited what every kid learned in New Earth schools: "The weight of New Earth has to be constantly and minutely calibrated in order to leverage the stress on the hybrid materials. Each individual has a unique body mass signature. That signature and its accompanying DNA are recorded in the Living Tissue Database. Fluctuations are noted and instantaneously accounted for."

"Right. Right. So when somebody's born, or somebody dies, or somebody so much as eats a piece of pie, the total weight of New Earth is recalculated instantly and recorded. If need be, weight is added or subtracted. These recalibrations take place at least a hundred million times a second." Reznik took a breath. Then he plunged forward. "I was tooling around the databases last night, because I had to hang out and see if the cops needed me—well, needed my computer. I was bored, and so I went over all the weight differentials for the past few years. It's like watching the world happen—birth and death and growth and surgeries and everything—from a long way off. Sometimes there's a significant change from second to second, but usually it's tiny. Just a flicker."

"A flicker."

"Yeah. And so I noticed this flicker that occurred on a day about eighteen months ago. The total weight on New Earth was reduced by the tiniest bit. So I thought, 'Hmmm. Wonder what that's about?' And just to pass the time, I cross-checked the percentage of the change against the weight tables. Turned out that the unique weight and DNA signature of Danny Mayhew—the real Danny Mayhew, because you can't fool those sensors—left New Earth at 3:03:01 on June 14, 2293, bound for Old Earth. The signature disappeared from the Living Tissue Database at 3:23.07. And never reappeared."

"Meaning that Danny died." Violet said the words with no emotion, as if she was verifying the time and temperature.

"Yeah. Meaning that Danny died."

They were silent for a moment. The noise level in Protocol Hall had risen as the afternoon shift change approached. Violet was glad about that. She wanted noise all around her. The noise was helping to cushion her shock. It was as if somebody had wrapped her in a thick blanket.

She touched Reznik's arm. She was pretty sure she had never touched him before.

"There's no chance of a mistake," she said. "It couldn't just be that Danny left New Earth and didn't show up on the monitors anymore."

"No." Reznik didn't bristle at the fact that she was challenging him on his computer skills—the heart and soul of how he saw himself. Normally, he would have snapped the "No." Not now. "The Living Tissue Database records all unique cellular activity on Old and New Earth. If Danny was alive—anywhere—the Database would tell us." He wanted her to know that he had considered all the possibilities, too. All the angles. "Somebody might be able to fool the cops," he added. "And somebody might be able to fool the immigration service. But you can't fool the DNA sensors. You can't fool the Living Tissue Database." A pause. "He's dead, Violet. He doesn't exist anymore."

"So why didn't anybody find this out before?"

"Because nobody was looking. Why would they?"

Why would they? He was right, as usual. You generally only look for what you already think you might find. And you generally only find what you are already looking for.

"Are you okay?" Reznik said. "I know it's got to be pretty awful to find out that—"

"I'm fine."

She wasn't fine. She was devastated. She thought her head might explode. But she had to hold it together for a little while longer. She couldn't let go. She couldn't give in.

"Listen, Violet—I'm here for you," he said. "If you want to talk, I mean. Or process. Or whatever."

"What?" she said. She'd forgotten Reznik was even present. Her mind felt as if somebody had lit a fire in the center of it, and the flame was swiftly destroying everything she thought she understood about the world.

Violet had been so relieved when they found her father, and when she saw he was unharmed. *It's just about over,* she had thought. *Everything is going to be okay again. We're safe.*

Yes, some of the Rebels were still out there, but Callahan would come to her senses and then she and Danny would track them down. The cops would force Stark to reveal the Rebels' secret—the method they had devised for thwarting the Intercept. Everything would get back to normal on New Earth, with the Intercept keeping the peace.

That's what she thought.

And now, she had just found out that somebody she loved was . . . somebody else.

So who *was* he? And why had he lied to her all this time? What was he hiding?

Confrontation

She found him at home in his apartment. She didn't call first, so there was no guarantee that he'd be there—but somehow she knew he would.

He's been waiting for this, she thought with fierce certainty, the moment the door opened and she saw his face. *Dreading it. He's been waiting for weeks. Months. He's been waiting for this moment since we first met. Waiting for the day I discover the truth about him.*

It was just a hunch, but it felt right to her.

He seemed to understand instantly what had happened, without her having to say it out loud. He looked at her face and he said: "So you know. I'm not me."

He stood to one side and she swept past him into his living room. There was fury in her steps, but it was a well-controlled fury. She had gone from confusion to disbelief to sorrow to anger and back again to confusion—and she wasn't finished yet. She wasn't even *close* to being finished yet. There were too many emotions still out there, waiting to descend on her.

The Intercept has quite a job on its hands right now, Violet thought. Labeling her current feelings, cataloging them, would be a challenge. They were flying by much too fast. Her emotions were crazy, spinning things.

She stopped in the middle of the small room. She whirled around to face him.

"Who *are* you?" she demanded. "Who *are* you? And do *not* say that you can't tell me. Do *not* say that."

"Want to sit down?"

"No. I don't want to sit down. I want to know who the hell you are. And what happened to the real Danny."

"He died."

She already knew the real Danny was dead—that was what had tipped off Reznik that something was not as it seemed to be—but hearing the words spoken that way, bluntly, forthrightly, was unbelievably painful to Violet.

Two words. *He died.* Two simple words, expressing a reality of which she was already aware—but Violet was staggered by them, all the same. She couldn't show it, but she was. She felt a little light-headed.

He died. Danny. Her Danny.

No. *Not* "her Danny." It was more complicated than that. This man, the one standing in front of her, looking earnest and concerned—*he* was the man she knew by the name "Danny Mayhew." So whoever had died was . . . *who*?

What was she grieving? A name? This man *looked* like Danny— but he wasn't, according to what Rez had discovered.

Now she felt even more light-headed. Her arms and her legs seemed to be weightless. Her anger had backed off, and its retreat made her realize how much she'd been relying on its heaviness to anchor her, to keep her feet on the ground. Now that it was gone—well, she might begin drifting up and up and up, tethered to nothing.

Fainting was *not* an option. So Violet gave herself a quick internal pep talk. *Come on, girl. Be strong.* She wished she'd taken a moment on her way over here to call Shura and tell her what was going on. Shura was another kind of anchor. The best-friend anchor. Without a best friend, you could fly off the face of the world. Any world.

"I *know* Danny died," Violet snapped at him. "That's how Reznik found out who you *aren't*." She spoke in short, choppy bursts of outrage. "Did you kill Danny? Take over his identity? Is that what happened?"

"Did I—" The man formerly known as Danny shook his head. "Come on. You don't believe that."

"I don't know *what* I believe right now, okay?"

"I can explain all this."

She glared at him. "Oh, I'll just bet you can. The question is—will it be the truth? Or just another lie?"

He started to say something. She put up her hand to make him stop. There were tears in her eyes now. She'd willed herself not to cry. But here they were, anyway—tears, and lots of them.

"I love you," Violet said. She said it not with tenderness but with frustration. "I mean—I love *Danny*," she corrected herself. This was not how she had dreamed it would be, the first time she told him she loved him. This was not the scenario. This was a confusing, overwhelming mess.

With the heels of her hands, she wiped roughly at her eyes. She wanted to get rid of these stupid tears. "Pretty lame, right? Loving somebody when he's not even who he says he is. God, what an *idiot* I am. What a—"

"I love you too, Violet."

He caught her totally by surprise. She felt a soft flutter in her stomach. For a second or so, she couldn't breathe. Her cheeks were suddenly warm.

He followed up his words by gently pulling her close and holding her. Without thinking, she let herself be held for a few golden seconds—and then reality returned.

She broke free. Now she was more upset than ever.

"How *dare* you!" she exclaimed. She backed up a few steps. "You're mocking me, right? I waited and waited *all those months* for you to say something—I thought you were feeling it, too, but you never said anything. You let me just—just wait and hope and *yearn* and—and NOW? *Now* you say this to me? *Now* you say you love me? When it doesn't matter? When I don't even know who the hell you are? What kind of monster *are* you, anyway?"

He looked stricken by her outburst. "I mean it," he said quietly. "I do love you. I always have. But until I could tell you the truth about myself—there was no way I could ever consider a deeper relationship with you. No way. Until the moment I could admit who I really was, I couldn't—"

"Then for God's sake," Violet said, interrupting him and doing it with so much heat and passion that she barely recognized her own voice, "who *are* you?"

"I'm Kendall."

Before she could fully absorb the meaning of what he had just told her, his console chirped. He checked the text.

He grimaced. He was wearing his Cop Face now: eyes hooded, mouth a straight line. He spoke to her in a series of bullet points. "We've got a situation. I have to go. They've found Callahan and Stark. They're cornered." His voice softened. "I know there's a ton more we need to talk about and so—could you wait here until I get back? We can talk all night, if we have to. We can—"

"I'm coming with you."

"Violet, this is police business. I can't let you do that."

Even through the haze of her shock and incomprehension, she wouldn't put up with his bossiness. "You don't have to 'let' me do anything. I do what I please," she declared. "And I've been involved in this from the beginning. I'm sure as hell not going to start sitting it out now."

He tried one more time as he strapped on the belt for his slab gun. "You could get hurt."

The look she gave him was a combination of mild contempt and not-so-mild sadness. "Really," she said. "*Really*. So I could get hurt, could I? Listen. With what I just found out, I've been hurt about as badly as it's possible to *be* hurt. No matter what happens—it can't be any worse than what I've already suffered. So come on."

"Okay. One thing, though. Let's put off dealing with this—with who I really am—until this is all over. Out there, I'm still Danny Mayhew, the cop. Because that's what they need right now—a cop. Not a scientist."

35

On the Run

They're heading to the transport site," Garrison said.

She had set up a staging area along Riemann Ridge. It was a hasty hodgepodge of portable tables and telescopes and weapons caches. All around her, cops checked and double-checked the photon-pulse charges in their slab guns, then slid the slab guns into their holsters.

There was tension in the air—but there were other things in the air, too. Violet noticed them right away: Intensity. Expectation. Alertness. New Earth cops didn't have a lot to do these days, except to clean up after the Intercept had done its job. *We're glorified janitors,* Callahan once had complained to Ogden Crowley, when Violet was listening.

And now they had a chance for some real action. No one would have admitted it, because Callahan's betrayal was so astonishing and the mood was supposed to be grim, but Violet could feel the excitement. It moved in the air like an electrical current.

She and the man she'd known as Danny had arrived a few minutes ago. Garrison frowned when she spotted Violet, and turned her eyes immediately to Danny. One of her eyebrows was raised. He shrugged.

Violet saw the raised eyebrow, too. She addressed Garrison directly. "I'm not leaving," she said.

"Fine," Garrison replied. "But you stay out of our way. Or I'll have you removed."

I'd like to see you try, Violet thought. Out loud, she said, "Copy that."

Below them was the dense forest that spread out between L'Engletown and Higgsville, a tightly woven thicket of green and brown. The designers of New Earth had decided to put something magnificent here. Clear streams curved around tall stands of pine trees. Woods opened out upon lush meadows like louvered shutters revealing a new day. A fairy-tale quality suffused this place, and that was no accident: The designers had consulted the illustrations in several books of Old Earth fairy tales when they put it together.

"How do you know the transport site is their destination?" Danny asked.

Garrison tapped her console. "Take a look."

He leaned in. Violet did, too. The Intercept feed provided a perfect view of Callahan and Stark, deep in the dark furled heart of the forest.

The fugitives had paused to rest alongside a small, fast-flowing creek. The chief was kneeling down to dip her cap in the water; her tunic was torn and streaked with dirt, and somewhere along the way, she had lost a boot. Sticks and leaves were caught in her hair. Stark looked even worse: He was stretched out on the ground, eyes closed, resting his head on a small rock. He was clearly fading, and so was his HoverUp. Violet could tell from the sound of the machine that its batteries were running perilously low; the engine had switched to the auxiliary power reserves.

"I don't get it," Violet said. "If the Intercept has known where they were all along, why can't we just do an intervention?"

"The signal keeps getting jammed," Garrison answered. "We don't know why. We'll have it for a while—as you can see on my console—

and then it goes out again. It's okay for surveillance, but the signal's not nearly strong enough for an intervention. We'll let them get a little closer to the transport site and then move in. We're being cautious. We don't want anybody to get hurt. And Callahan still has her weapon."

She turned up the volume. Callahan was talking to her husband. Her voice was gentler than Violet had ever heard it be.

"We've got to make it to the transport site. If we can reach it, we can get away. We'll hop in a pod and go back to Old Earth. Hide out and rest. Figure out how to contact the Rebels who escaped the roundup. Then we'll slip back to New Earth—and try again to destroy the Intercept."

Stark opened his eyes and tried to lift his head, but gave up. "I know you don't want to hear this, Michelle, but I'm not sure I can survive the trip back to Old Earth."

"Shut up."

He smiled at her. "You're a bully. A hard-ass."

"You bet I am. That's why they made me chief."

He smiled again, but the effort was almost too much for him.

"But seriously," Stark said. "If I can't make it, I want you to go on. It doesn't matter what happens to me. One individual is irrelevant. What *does* matter is getting rid of the Intercept."

"I know that now."

"I'm glad. I hated having to keep the secret about leading the Rebels. It tore me up inside. I never wanted to have any secrets from you. I never will again."

"You did what you had to do, Paul. Before today, I'm not sure I would have understood. But now I do. I always thought the Intercept was a pretty good idea. Keeps people in line. Cuts down on collateral damage when we have to go after a bad guy."

"But the price is just too high. Safety's a good thing—but it's not the *only* thing. It's not even the most important thing." His voice trailed off a bit. He was very, very tired. He had to rouse himself to go on. "And now your career's over," he said. His voice was thinner still. "I'm so sorry, Michelle. I know how much you loved the chief's job."

"I did. But I had no choice. What they were doing to you—" She shuddered. "It was wrong. I love you, Paul. My place is with you."

"Yes," he murmured. "Yes."

"Are you warm enough?"

He murmured another "Yes." She settled next to him, and she looked up at the sky that stretched over New Earth like a cathedral dome.

"Remember, Paul? Remember the night, right after we were married, when we went to that beach? That rocky one on Old Earth? We tried to name the stars. Remember? The planet was in terrible shape. All anybody talked about was the rumor about a new civilization. A new Earth. It sounded so far-fetched." Her voice sounded wistful. "And now here we are." She looked over at him. "Paul? Are you asleep yet, my love?"

"Not quite. I'm only going to rest for a bit. I'm pretty tired."

"I know. It's okay. Take as long as you need." Callahan sat up. The woods were very close. The occasional noises—a frog plopping into the creek, spring peepers and their chanting—were computer-generated. There had not yet been time to introduce the smaller species on New Earth.

"Paul," Callahan said. "We'll be okay, right? Even if they try to use the Intercept to track us down? And get us to surrender?"

"We'll be fine." He laughed softly. "That'll be the least of our worries, honey."

"How do you mean?"

"Well, why do you think we're still free? Why haven't they hit us with an intervention?"

"I don't know. Why?"

"Because I made us both immune to the Intercept." Pride had restored a bit of his strength. "We know how to do that. It really works.

It's only effective for short periods of time now, but we're increasing the duration. Bit by bit. We started out with just a few minutes. We're up to several hours now. We'll get there." He yawned a long, slow, languid yawn. "One of the Rebels discovered it by accident. And it was just what we needed."

"How does it work?"

"Deckle," he said.

"Deckle? What do you mean?"

"If you take it in small doses, it blocks the effects of the Intercept. I don't know the brain chemistry behind it—so I don't know why it does that. I don't think *anybody* knows why it does. Even Kendall Mayhew himself didn't know why—and he *invented* the Intercept."

"But it's an illegal drug. Even if it does block the Intercept, doesn't it have bad effects? Doesn't it impair your judgment?"

"Nope. Turns out deckle is harmless. Somebody down on Old Earth started all those rumors about it a few years ago because they wanted to sell it as a narcotic and make some money. But it's not. Not even close. It's as mild as aspirin."

"So that's how you do it," Callahan said. "That's how you block the Intercept."

"Yes. I gave us both a dose when we left the station. The water, remember?"

"I remember." A thoughtful look had moved into Callahan's features. "And the material you wanted Anna Lu to smuggle in for you was—"

"Deckle. It's hard to find up here. So we have to use immigrants to get it for us. Or whoever we can find. I didn't enjoy having to rough up Anna Lu—but helping us was the right thing to do. She should've figured that out on her own."

Callahan was silent.

She touched her console.

The moment Violet saw the gesture—Callahan pressing two fingers to her communication device—a cold dread rushed through her body.

No.

No, it can't be.

Giant floodlights suddenly drenched the area in harsh illumination. The heavy sound of a helicopter rotor blade throbbed overhead. As Violet watched on her monitor, the displaced air shoved the pine trees violently to one side and churned up the water in the stream.

From a bullhorn came shouted words:

"Paul Stark, you are hereby under arrest for kidnapping, conspiracy, and escaping from police custody. You will surrender immediately."

Stark struggled to his feet. It took him a long time, because his power-starved HoverUp had slowed down to less than a quarter of its usual speed. Confused, he turned to his wife, anguish in his face.

"How did they find—"

And then the realization dawned. No charges had been read out against her. *He* was the target. Not her.

He had betrayed the Rebels' secret.

And she had betrayed him.

Violet remembered the moment in Callahan's office when Garrison suggested that they break off the questioning. And then she had gone home to take care of her father. That must have been when they planned this, the two of them: the chief and her loyal lieutenant.

Violet's attention returned to the feed. Callahan was talking to her husband.

"I'm sorry, Paul," she said. "But I had to find out how you were getting around the Intercept. Public safety was at stake."

"So you staged the whole thing." He was angry, and he tried to slap away the hands of the officers who had just swooped in with their shackles. They subdued him easily. "So it was a *show*. Watching me suffer," he went on, bitterness rising in his voice. "Pretending to care about me. Rushing in and holding Garrison at gunpoint. Escaping with me. It was fiction. You two set it all up."

"Yeah. I'm sorry, but—yeah."

They led him toward the helicopter. He twitched his shoulders. He wanted to speak to her again. The officers looked at Callahan; she nodded, and they let him turn. His voice wasn't bitter anymore. It was suffused with sorrow.

"You have no idea what you've done, Michelle."

"The Intercept keeps us safe," she said. "We need it."

"There's more to life than safety."

"Like what?"

"Freedom."

She motioned impatiently to her officers. "Take him away."

But he still wasn't quite finished. He called out to her, "Why? Why did you do this?"

"You know why. Once a cop, always a cop."

The Story

And now it was time for Violet to learn the truth.

She was back in his living room, sitting on the couch. They were side by side, but they weren't touching. She would not let him touch her. She didn't know who he was.

He had said he was "Kendall"—but what did that mean?

"Ten years ago," he began, "my brother, Danny, and I were orphans on Old Earth. Our parents were dead. Killed on the streets. We were on our own. If it hadn't been for Danny, I wouldn't have survived, either. He protected me. He was bigger and stronger and faster. He got us our food. Got us a place to live. Kept the predators away.

"All I wanted to do was work in my lab. He'd rigged up this amazing lab for me. Down there, down in that place where most people didn't have a crust of bread or a warm blanket, my brother, Danny, made me a lab." There was awe in his voice. "So that's what I did. I worked. And after a lot of time and a lot of very hard work, I came up with what you know as the Intercept."

He took a deep breath. When Violet didn't say anything, he went on.

"Word got out over the years, of course, about this weird new thing I was inventing. One person told another, who told another, who told another. The news even made it up to New Earth. And that was why your father came down to Old Earth and visited my lab that day. I hadn't perfected it yet. I was still years away. But I was getting there. And when it was finished, I was sure that it would—it would take all the pain away."

"What are you talking about?" Violet said. "The Intercept is for law enforcement."

"No." He shook his head. "No," he said firmly. "It was about taking away the pain of emotion. *That's* what it was for. *That's* why I created it." He seemed to be searching for a way to make her understand. "Every time I thought about my mom and dad, I got this blinding panic. The grief just paralyzed me. I couldn't move. I couldn't think. I could barely speak. So I thought, What if there's a way to take the emotion—the one that's tormenting me—and escape from it for a while? Turn it into a form of energy? And then put it back in my brain, once I had learned to handle it? Once I was stronger? And if I could do *that,* then maybe I could also find a way to make the positive emotions stick around. The happy memories. The ones that didn't haunt me. The ones that felt good. So that emotions wouldn't—wouldn't rip me apart, which is what they were doing. *That* was my motivation. I didn't want to control anybody." He smiled ruefully. "I just wanted to get a good night's sleep."

"So you're blaming this on my dad," Violet said quickly. She was even angrier now. "You're saying the Intercept was a good idea until *he* came along and misused it. Weaponized it."

"That is *not* what I'm saying." He seemed exasperated. He looked around the room, as if searching for the words to make it clearer. "Look, Violet, I had no problem with how your father used my invention. It got Danny and me out of Old Earth. And it got me a beautiful new lab up here. I just want you to know that the Intercept was created to relieve pain—not to cause more of it for anybody. Or to control anyone. That was *never* my idea."

"Fine," she said. She needed to hear more. "Whatever. So let's skip ahead to the part where you switch identities. The part where the big lie begins."

He winced at the word *lie,* but he nodded and went on. "Once people realized the full import of what I was working on, I started getting threats. Every day. People didn't like the idea that some computer program could mess with their heads, okay? There was a good chance I'd be attacked. So Danny suggested that we switch. Nobody knew us yet. Not as individuals—just as these two crazy brothers with a wacky lab. We were totally unknown. If we traded identities, and if somebody came after Kendall Mayhew, the skinny little inventor of the Intercept, they'd suddenly be facing this big, tough, strong guy. This guy who could take care of himself. Not some puny geek."

She stared at his arm, which was wiry but very hard and muscular.

"I didn't look like this back then," he said, in response to her stare. "I've been a cop for two years now. I had to train."

She considered this. She made a circular motion with her index finger. *Go on.*

"You know how the Intercept works," he said. "The chips use signals from your brain—so they're an absolute form of ID. You can't fool them. So the only way we could pull it off was with the help of your mother."

Violet was quiet for a few seconds. "My mother."

"Yeah. We'd seen her working on Old Earth. Taking care of people. So we asked her to switch our chips. We explained about the Intercept. She hesitated, of course. But then she did it. She performed the surgery. And she did such a neat, careful job that no one on New Earth had any idea about what we'd done."

"But my father visited you in your lab. He met the person he thought was Kendall."

"I was always wearing goggles. And Danny wasn't in the lab that day."

Violet stood up. She walked over to the window. It was a small one, with a curtain that didn't fit quite right, and the view was ordinary: a parking lot. Beyond that, silver streets. Yet she stood there and looked out a long time, saying nothing.

When she turned back around and spoke to him, her voice had lost a bit of its brittle edge.

"She must have liked you," she said. "A lot. My mother wouldn't have done that—wouldn't have broken the law—unless she liked you. And trusted you. And thought it was the right thing to do."

"She did. All those things—she did."

"Okay," Violet said. She needed to change the subject. Thinking too much about her mother was distracting. It made her feel soft inside. And vulnerable. She needed to stay focused. "How did Danny die?"

He nodded solemnly. He would have to talk about this, as difficult as it might be.

"I always knew there was a flaw with the Intercept. Certain people seemed to be immune," he said. "So I'd done some experiments to try to fix it. I recorded my notes about those experiments in a red notebook—the same notebook I'd used as I invented the Intercept, jotting down all the steps in the formula. I kept it hidden in my lab back on Old Earth. I had to hide it because if anybody else got hold of it, they would know how to get around the Intercept.

"But once we got here, I realized it was crucial that I fix the flaw. Because somebody was bound to exploit it. So I worked secretly in my lab up here, late at night, after my shift." He relaxed just a bit. His voice shed some of its intensity. "It's funny—here I was, working as a cop all day when I wanted to be in the lab, and there was Danny, desperate to be a cop but stuck in a lab all day. Just because we switched our identities didn't mean we were able to switch our passions."

He shook his head and went on. The smile vanished. "Anyway, I discovered that a substance called deckle—sold as a street drug—was responsible. The main chemical in it somehow blocked the Intercept. Created some kind of temporary shield. I needed to do a lot more tests. But I couldn't tell anyone about any of this. The implications were just too monumental. It threatened everything that New Earth had become—safe and serene. So I had to keep sneaking to Old Earth to get deckle for my experiments." He paused. "Danny wanted to help. He volunteered to take it, so that I could record the results. Make himself a sort of human guinea pig. I said no."

"He sneaked down to Old Earth on his own, didn't he?"

That sounded like the person she had known as Danny. The real one. The one who wanted to be a cop because he liked helping people.

"Yeah," he said. "And one night—a night when I didn't know he'd gone down there again—somebody sold him a different drug. They were desperate for the money, and they just sold him whatever they had. And it was a much, much stronger substance. A deadly one. Danny didn't know what he was taking. So my brother died in an alley on Old Earth. He died alone. He died trying to help me."

Violet heard his voice break. She went over to the couch. She stood close to him. She began stroking the back of his head. He put his arms around her waist. And he cried silently for his lost brother.

For Danny.

She didn't know how much time passed. This wasn't about time. When he had recovered, she put her hands on both sides of his head, gently tilting it up so that he was looking at her. She pushed a lock of dark hair from his forehead.

"When Rez and I rescued you," she said, "in that alley. You were searching for deckle?"

"Yes—but really I was searching for *answers*. I wanted to ask Tin Man if he knew who sold Danny the tainted drug. I didn't get a chance to, though. You and Rez intervened—and I'm damned lucky you did. Who knew he had a slab gun?" He shuddered. She felt that shudder and held his head closer to her body. It had been a close call. "I visited Tin Man in prison," he said.

"Really." She considered telling him about the chip-jack. Was now the time? No. It would shift the balance of guilt back in her direction. After all, she had spied on him.

"Yeah," he said. "Another one of my unauthorized trips."

"Did he tell you who sold to Danny?"

"He didn't know. But he confirmed what I thought about deckle—that it's harmless. What he *didn't* know—what only a few people know—is that it blocks the Intercept." He shrugged. "Tin Man's not a bad guy. I had to treat him like one, because I was in a hurry that day. But he's like everybody else on Old Earth—just trying to take care of the people he loves."

"That's true of New Earth, too," Violet said. His sentence about taking care of loved ones had revealed something to her—not about him, but about her. "You know what? I need to go home now," she said. "To my dad." And she added one more thing, so that he would know she was on her way to forgiving him. "See you soon, Kendall."

Ogden Crowley stood in his library. Massive bookshelves climbed from floor to ceiling on three sides of the room, the volumes spread across the shelves in a magnificent array of antiquated communication technology. This was his one indulgence: Old Earth books. He did his official work digitally, of course, but when it came to his personal reading, he preferred books. Real books. Not words on a lighted screen.

He had just taken down one of his favorites—*The Complete Poetical Works of Robert Browning*. It was bound in dark brown leather. The title was stamped in gold leaf. Even through the thick, twisted scars on his hands, Ogden could feel the pebbly sumptuousness of the leather, a texture he loved.

Night had fallen, and the pools of light from the table lamps looked like large gold coins arranged across the carpet.

"Violet," he said. There was a deep pleasure in his voice, prompted by the sight of her. "So glad you're home."

"Hey, Dad. How are you feeling?"

"Better. The sleep was good."

"Can we talk for a minute?"

"Of course. But first you have to listen to something."

"Sure, Dad."

He put the thick book under one arm. Violet helped him get to his chair in the living room. She pulled over the ottoman so that she could sit in front of him while they talked.

"Browning is one of my favorite poets," he said. "He lived such a long, long time ago, back when there was still hope for the earth. Back when people believed in progress." He opened the book and read aloud:

But the best is when I glide from out them,
Cross a step or two of dubious twilight,
Come out on the other side, the novel
Silent silver lights and darks undreamed of,
Where I hush and bless myself with silence.

"That's beautiful, Dad," Violet said. "The part about 'darks undreamed of'—that reminds me of the Intercept."

"Yes," he said. He closed the book but left it balanced on his knee, so that he could touch the rich leather binding. "Yes."

And then it was Violet's turn. She told her father the story. She told him about Kendall and Danny Mayhew, and about what Lucretia Crowley had done for them.

At first he seemed too shocked to speak. Then, in a faltering, faraway voice, he asked her to repeat some of the details. She did.

"Lucretia switched their Intercept chips?" Ogden said. As chief executive, he had lobbied hard to make that a criminal offense. The penalty was life in prison.

His wife had risked that for two strangers on Old Earth?

"All I know, Dad," Violet said, "is that Mom thought it was worth it. Whatever price she had to pay. She wanted Kendall and Danny to get to New Earth. She wanted them to be here. Here in this golden place—this place that *you* built, Dad. Not with your hands, but with your mind. With your emotions. Your passion."

Violet didn't know how she knew all that, but she did. She knew it with as much certainty as she'd ever known anything. She could sense her mother's presence right now, in this very room. It was as if her mother was speaking to her. Telling her what to say to her father, to make him understand.

"Emotions aren't bad things, Dad," Violet said. She was feeling her way from sentence to sentence, guided by her mother's spirit. "They're powerful, yes. And they can hurt. But they can heal, too. And people can *create* things with them. Look at what you've created here—a whole new world. New Earth. A place where people don't have to live in fear. Where they can live in peace. And love their families. And dream." She paused, listening for her mother's essence, waiting for the words to enable her to go on. "I think that's what Mom was trying to tell us. Emotions aren't things we should try to control. They can be messy and scary and overwhelming, but in the end—you have to let people feel what they feel. And be who they are. Because the only reason anybody ever tries to control somebody else's emotions is because they're afraid.

"And that's not you. You're not afraid, Dad. I *know* you're not. Mom wasn't afraid, and you're not afraid. And I'm not afraid anymore, either."

Her father had gone silent again. Violet looked over at him. She could not read his face.

When he did speak, it was in a thin, choked-sounding whisper.

"I was wrong. Wrong to bring the Intercept here. To have it installed. To use people's emotions against them. Your mother didn't want it. She *knew*. Somehow, even before I did it, she knew it wasn't right." He drew up his damaged right hand into a fist and placed the fist on his book. This time, though, the fist didn't look menacing. It looked like he was sealing in the words. "I should have listened to her. But I didn't. I was too stubborn. Even though I loved her—I didn't listen." He relaxed his hand again. "I think I was afraid of looking weak to her. Afraid that if I took her advice and walked away from the project, she might lose respect for me. Even though it was what she wanted."

Violet was aware of a great wave of love for her father. She'd never fully appreciated how vulnerable he must have felt around her mother, with his bad leg and his unsightly hands. She knew how much her parents loved each other—she had always felt it when they were together—but she'd never considered that her dad might have had to struggle to feel worthy of Lucretia.

"It's not too late," Violet suddenly said. She didn't know she was going to say that until she did.

"What do you mean?"

"You can always shut off the Intercept. Close it down."

He seemed stunned by her proposal. "I couldn't just—"

"Why not?"

Before he could answer, Violet's console chimed. It was the special ring she and Shura used for emergencies, so Violet knew she had to take the call.

When Violet touched the screen, Shura's agitated voice filled the room. "I'm over at Protocol Hall with Rez," she said, "and I'm uploading a feed to your console right now. You and your dad *have* to see what's going on."

"Where?" Violet said.

"Just outside the forest. The cops tracked down the rest of the Rebels. They've got them cornered. Okay—here comes the feed. Somebody's got to stop this. It's going to be a slaughter."

37

The Last Stand

The cops had arranged themselves across a long low hill at the edge of the trees, shields and slab guns at the ready. They formed an intimidating-looking blue line. At one end of it stood Chief Callahan. She had raised her right arm; she was ready to give the signal to attack.

The Rebels were far fewer in number. They'd been chased out of their hiding place in the woods and now made a ragtag line of their own, on a hill just across from the cops. They had no shields and no slab guns. But they did not run.

"You have one minute to surrender," Callahan called out to the Rebels. "After that, we're authorized to shoot to kill."

Several of the cops looked uneasy at that. Shoot to kill? That didn't sound like their orders.

From his seat in his living room, Ogden Crowley was fuming. As they watched the feed, Violet could feel his anger escalating.

"She has *no such authorization,*" he declared.

Her father snatched up his own console from the coffee table. He punched in a code.

"Jefferson," he said. Violet recognized the name of one of her father's top aides. "What the hell is she doing?"

"Unknown, sir." Jefferson's voice through the console sounded perplexed. "She's not answering our messages. She brought her husband back into custody an hour ago and then she ordered an armed unit to join her at the forest. I think this is some kind of vengeance, sir. If I had to guess."

Ogden clicked off the call. He moved his jaw. Violet could tell he was weighing his options.

"Callahan thinks she's doing the right thing," Violet said. "She wants to keep New Earth safe. Destroy the Rebels who threaten it. This is her duty."

Her father didn't seem too interested in the chief's motives.

"Only one way to stop her," he said grimly. He punched another code into his console. "Reznik, initiate the Intercept for Michelle Callahan. Immediately."

Ogden looked over at Violet.

"Might be the last time I use the damned thing," he explained. "Might as well go out with a bang."

Violet had another thought: While he was in an order-giving mood, maybe the timing was right.

"There's one more thing you might want to do," she said. "When this is all over, I mean."

"What's that?"

"Let everybody in. All the people on Old Earth—just announce that you're bringing every last one of them up here, Dad. Build a bunch of new pods. Reopen all the old portals."

"That would be a very hard thing to do," he said. "We'd have to absorb all of those people, all at once—the logistics would be daunting. All the vetting. And we'd have to reconfigure every last—"

"Come on, Dad. You're telling me that the same brilliant minds that built New Earth couldn't tweak things a bit to accommodate a few hundred thousand extra people? How about all that space between Franklinton and Mendeleev Crossing—didn't you tell me those sectors were deliberately left empty to absorb future population growth?"

"Yes. That's right. But we don't know what we'd be getting, Violet. The people on Old Earth—some of them are criminals. Thugs."

"Sure. There will definitely be a mix of good and bad people—just like here on New Earth. That's the risk, Dad. And you've never minded taking a risk."

His face told her that he was seriously considering her proposal.

It's a start, Violet thought. *I've planted the seed. And that's enough for now.* Morning would be here soon, bringing a new day. She'd be able to persuade him. She was sure of it.

They returned their attention to Ogden's console and the vivid scene it revealed: High on a hill overlooking the rugged green glory of the forest, the two sides tensed for battle.

In the right-hand corner of the screen, however, another scene was being unveiled: Michelle Callahan's Intercept feed. The one weapon that, no matter how tough she was, no matter how determined, would take her down.

Deep below the floor of Protocol Hall, the Intercept purred and ticked, reaching deep into a file marked CALLAHAN, M. M., Citizen No. 71184-17-WA-GHY21.5, selecting a memory and ramming it home.

Four years ago:

She's on the streets of Old Earth. She and Paul are assigned to a dangerous neighborhood today. A wretched place, swarming with desperate people.

There. Over there: that man.

Paul gives chase, his boots smacking the torn pavement with a rhythmic crispness. He's an excellent runner, fast and tireless.

The man turns. Whips out a slab gun.

No. No. No.

Paul lies on the pavement, writhing. The lower half of his body looks like a puddle of dirty bathwater. His life is leaking away.

"Paul," she says. She's kneeling beside him. "Paul—"

"Let me go," he whispers. "Please."

"I can't. I need you." Frantic, she starts to unhook the emergency equipment hanging from her belt—the respirator, the cardiac monitor. Her fingers fumble at first but they get the job done.

"No," he murmurs. "I don't want to live like this."

She is too busy to talk as she sets up the devices that will keep him alive until the medics arrive.

"Please," he says. "Let me go. Just let me go."

She won't look in his eyes. She knows what she will see there. He wants to die. He doesn't want to live with half his body gone. That's not Paul Stark.

"Please," he says. Begging now. She ignores him and keeps working.

In a few minutes it is too late. The medics are here, and now the lifesaving efforts are serious and prolonged and professional. No more chance that he can just slip away with no fuss—which was his wish, his one desire.

She is selfish. She knows it. His terrible, terrible request has revealed that to her. She cannot forgive him for revealing to her what she really is: weak and unreliable. A coward. She loves him but she hates him, too, for what her love for him has done to her. Love is like a mirror. It shows us who we are.

Michelle Callahan dropped to her knees. The slab gun slid from her grasp. She thrust her face into her hands, weeping with such fervor that she could barely breathe, her shoulders heaving, her body convulsing with the pain of relentless memory.

When her slab gun hit the ground, the cop nearest to her snatched it up and then signaled to the rest of the unit to holster their weapons and wait for new orders.

Ogden Crowley looked up from his console. Violet read the pain in his eyes. She knew how much he liked Callahan and respected her. Tonight he had been forced to witness her fall. First, he had thought she was a traitor to New Earth; now he knew she was simply a frightened woman who had lost her way. A traitor to herself.

Violet put a hand on her father's shoulder. There was nothing she could say that would make him feel better about what had unfolded on his screen; all she could do was remind him—silently, by the weight of her hand on his shoulder—that she was here, by his side. She would always be here, no matter where she was.

He reached up and placed a hand on top of Violet's hand.

Her hand was small and smooth; his was large and scarred, the skin on it riven with craters. Yet in that moment the differences did not matter. Father and daughter were fused by their sorrow.

Violet had a final task to perform before she went to bed. She called Shura on her console. A question had occurred to her.

"Why were you at Protocol Hall tonight?" Violet asked. "What made you go over there in the first place?"

She sat cross-legged on her bed as she had done so many other nights, when she and Shura talked. Outside her window, Violet could see the quarter-moon rising over New Earth. It looked like an orange slice. Its glow was reassuring.

"I needed to talk to Rez," Shura said.

"To Rez."

"Yeah."

Violet waited. There had to be more. She and Shura were best friends. She knew when Shura was holding back.

"Okay," Shura finally said. "I had to ask him."

"About what?"

"About something that's been bothering me ever since you and your father were kidnapped." Shura sounded as if she was half afraid to go on.

"Tell me," Violet said. She was mystified. She pictured Rez's face, always eager and hopeful when they arrived at their cubicle each afternoon, as if he'd decided that today was the day—the day she'd realize that they ought to be together.

"Well," Shura said, "when the Rebels grabbed you guys and took you back to their headquarters, they did an Intercept on your dad, right?"

"Right. It was hard to watch."

"Yeah. So how'd they do that?"

"What do you mean?"

"The Rebels don't control the Intercept. The government does. Out of Protocol Hall. How would they have initiated the Intercept?"

"I don't know."

"It's bad news, Violet. It's really bad news." Shura paused. "It was Rez."

Violet had been certain she couldn't be shocked any more. She had been shocked so profoundly by the revelation about Danny and Kendall that she was beyond the reach of all last-minute epiphanies, dark discoveries, and suddenly revealed secrets. Or so she thought.

"Rez?"

"It was just a hunch, but when I confronted him, he admitted it," Shura said. "They sent him a signal that night and he activated your father's Intercept file."

Violet let the information sink in. "But I don't understand. Why would he do that? Rez is my *friend*. And he doesn't take sides. He doesn't care about politics."

"You're right," Shura said. "All he cares about is code. And you. He loves you, Violet. You know that. And you also know that you don't feel the same way about him. So he got mad. Finally, he just sort of—sort of *snapped*, I guess. He's been waiting around, ever since you guys started working together. Waiting for you to fall in love with him like you fell in love with Danny. The hopelessness finally got to him. And then he felt like a fool. So he decided to help out the Rebels just once—to get back at you. It wasn't political. It was personal. Later, when things got out of hand, he regretted it and tried to make things right again."

Violet was still knocked sideways by the news. "So he did the wrong thing," she said, her words coming slowly. "But it ended up being—sort of—the *right* thing, because it helped the Rebels. But it was the *wrong* thing, because it put my father through a terrible ordeal."

"Now my head hurts," Shura said.

"Why didn't the Intercept pick up on Rez's feelings? And stop him?"

"He saw his own codes streaming in. And he overrode them. He's not proud of himself, believe me."

"What's going to happen to him?"

"He just sent a confession to your dad's console. He wants to take his punishment, whatever it is."

Violet sighed. "Here's Rez—this brilliant, *brilliant* guy. This guy who can program a computer upside down with his eyes closed and suffering from a bad case of the flu. And what brings him down? What makes him do something like that?"

"Feelings."

"Yeah. Feelings. They can be a real pain in the ass sometimes, right?"

Shura gave her a weak smile. "Right."

"One more thing. Can you do me a big favor?"

"Name it."

Violet made her request. Shura agreed. And then Violet signed off, because she needed her sleep. She had an appointment to keep. She'd had a conversation with her father about something that haunted her, and received his blessing. Tomorrow afternoon she and Kendall were meeting at the transport site.

The Search

They did not find her right away.

It took them several days on Old Earth to locate her. She had left the house in which she'd nursed Violet's wounds. There was no sign of her in the streets surrounding that house, either. Among the people they came across—kids, mainly, with scared eyes and mangy skin—few would talk to them. But the ones who did, and who seemed to know Delia because they reacted to her name when Violet said it, just pointed to the horizon and murmured, *Away.*

Away.

She had gone away.

"Which could mean she's dead," Violet said glumly. She and Kendall stood in the kitchen of what had once been Delia's house. They had just searched the place for the second time, hoping for a clue—anything would do—that would tell them where she had gone.

"I don't think so," Kendall said.

"Why not?"

"If she was dead, they'd say so. The people down here aren't big on euphemisms."

Violet shrugged and moved around the kitchen. She looked up.

The hole had gotten even bigger. Soon the entire roof would collapse, and the house would sift and sink and become one with the dirt, which was, Violet said as she rummaged through the few items scattered on the floor, the fate of all things on any world, old or new.

"Cheery thought," Kendall said.

"You know what? I kind of liked you better as Danny. He wasn't so sarcastic."

They had swiftly gotten to the point where they could tease each other. They had been through too much, too fast, to be formal and shy; they had fought battles together and suffered losses together, and this was the result: a fast-acting friendship based on honesty and necessity.

Could it ever be more? Could she, that is, ever come to love Kendall the way she had loved Danny?

A silly question, in one way, because Kendall *was* Danny. But in another way it wasn't silly at all. Because Kendall and Danny were not the same person. Violet had been in love with someone she thought of as Danny Mayhew. Transferring that to someone named Kendall—even though he was the same person—would take time. Maybe years. And maybe, after all those years, it still might not happen.

"Hey," he said. "What's this?" He pulled something small and pale and wrinkled from a sack he'd dragged out of the corner.

Violet looked. She laughed.

"It's the tea bag," she said.

"*The* tea bag?"

"Yeah. There's just the one." Violet scratched her cheek. "I wonder if that's a good sign or a bad sign—leaving the tea bag. Does it mean she's never coming back, so anybody's welcome to it—or does it mean she *is* coming back, so hands off?"

Kendall shrugged. "I'm not really up on my tea-bag symbolism, so I'll leave that to you." He moved closer to the scabby, peeling wall. He touched it with his fingertips, spreading his fingers and arching his hand. It was as if he was grounding himself, reorienting himself—not to this particular house, but to Old Earth itself.

"So what'll we do?" Violet said. "Go back home or keep looking for her?"

He dropped his hand and turned to look at her. "The Violet I know," he replied, "is not a quitter."

"Damn straight."

And so off they went.

They traveled mainly by day but sometimes by night, too. The moon was muted here on Old Earth, not nearly so bright as it was on New Earth. *Although maybe I'm just imagining that,* Violet thought. *I think it ought to be true and so when I see it, I make it true.* She remembered the term for that from her probability class: *confirmation bias.*

When they came across yet another dead lake or burnt-out field or stinking animal carcass in the road, she felt a deep sadness at a world left to rot this way. And then it would strike her: Someday, she might be able to feel whatever she wanted to feel. The Intercept would not be gathering up her emotions and then sliding them into virtual folders with her name stenciled on the side.

She would be free.

Less safe, maybe, but more free.

Kendall told her stories as they walked along. He talked about the games he and Danny would play when they were kids, simple games that required only sticks and rocks, and how, despite the hunger, and the sickness, and the terrible cold that swept down from the mountains and fingered its way into every crack in the wall of whatever shabby, run-down house they found themselves in when winter came, they had fun. They had hope. Because they had each other.

Violet loved to hear the stories. She laughed at some of them, and others made her want to cry. But mostly she just enjoyed being with

Kendall, traveling side by side with him on their shared mission to track down Delia.

And then, on the morning of the fifth day, they found her.

It was Violet's idea to search near the prison. Delia had one child left, and Violet speculated that if she had decided to leave her home, she would want to be near him. Even though visitors were prohibited, and even though she was separated from her son by thousands of tons of rock—she'd be here. As close as she could get.

At the base of the mountain was a small trading post. The economy of Old Earth was primitive, makeshift, mostly based on barter, but a few stores did manage to say in business. On the rare occasion when prisoners were released on probation, this was their first stop; Violet figured that after years of doing without simple pleasures, they probably walked up and down the aisles with a glassy-eyed awe, touching the most mundane items—sticks of gum, pencils—as if they were religious relics.

She spotted Delia right away. The small woman was standing behind the front counter, arms crossed, keeping an eye out for shoplifters. The red bandana was as soiled as ever. The scar on her chin looked even whiter against the pale yellow of her skin. Violet assumed there was a skillet—Delia's weapon of choice—hidden under the counter to deal with troublemakers.

She saw Violet and let out a whoop, waving her closer.

"So you're back," Delia said. "Vacation spot like this—folks just can't stay away."

Violet introduced her to Kendall. Then she got down to business.

"I had two reasons for wanting to find you," Violet said. "First, I need to tell you something about the woman you call Doc. She was my mother. And I'm very sorry to say that she passed away six years ago. I should have told you before. When I was down here. I just didn't want to spoil—Well, anyway."

Delia looked down at the dirt floor. Then back up at Violet. Her mood had shifted into another register, a more somber one. "Your mother," she said quietly, "was a fine person."

Violet nodded. She took a deep breath and moved on. "The second thing is—I want you to come to New Earth. To live. We'll arrange it. Get you a place to live. A job."

Delia shook her head. "I can't leave. My son's here. In prison. He doesn't know I'm here, but—I wanted to be, anyway."

"As a matter of fact," Violet said, "he's been pardoned by the chief executive of New Earth."

Flustered, Delia put her small hands flat on the countertop, spread out wide. "But why? Why would the head guy of New Earth do that? And how would *you* know he did that?"

"Trust me," Violet said. "It's a done deal. Look—you may or may not want to come to New Earth right now. Or ever. Make up your mind whenever you like. No rush. But your son is being released. I wanted to give you a couple of things for saving my life."

"I didn't save your—" Delia grinned. "Well, yeah, I guess I kinda did."

"Right. So I'm offering you—and Tommy, too, if he's interested—the one thing that everybody wants."

"And what's that?"

"A fresh start."

Delia let it sink in. "Yeah," she said, obviously pleased. "Oh, and—not to be greedy, but you said 'a couple of things.' More good news coming my way?"

Violet gestured to Kendall. He pulled a long thin tube from his book bag. The tube had been brought down from New Earth a day ago by Jefferson, her father's chief assistant. He had tracked them down and delivered it.

Kendall shook out the tightly wound canvas and unrolled it on the counter. He kept it from springing back shut again by anchoring a palm in two opposite corners.

It was a portrait of a tiny young girl of perhaps five years old, racing along a dirt road barefoot. Her light blue dress was little more than a rag. Her blond hair flew out behind her. She was quick and strong. She was smiling, despite the grimness of her surroundings. She was having the time of her life.

Because of the painting, she would be running this way forever.

In the corner was the signature *Shura Lu,* and below that, *2294.*

Delia stared. She wiped away a tear with the back of her hand.

"My little girl—how did you know—you never met Molly—you didn't—" Delia's voice cracked with emotion. She couldn't go on.

"I saw her once," Violet said. She didn't want to tell her about Tommy's Intercept feed, the means by which she had seen Molly in the last few seconds of the child's life, a time of such suffering. "I described her to a friend. She's an artist."

It was true, Violet thought. No matter what profession Shura chose, she was an artist. And always would be.

Sunrise over New Earth

On a scintillatingly crisp and golden morning two weeks later, Violet and Kendall stood in the center of the ground floor of Protocol Hall. Glass-sided cubicles rose all around them, like a symmetrical forest of center-cut diamonds. But the cubicles were empty now. The building was deserted.

Kendall held a sleek black briefcase in his right hand. In his left, he held a small round detonator.

He slipped the detonator into his pocket.

They knew what they had to do. They would do it not only because they had made a pledge to Violet's father. They knew in their hearts it was right:

Wipe out the Intercept.

Ogden Crowley had ordered the destruction of Protocol Hall—and, more important, of what lay below it. The evacuation had been completed two days ago. This place had always been noisy and crowded and filled with a kind of buoyant, youthful energy; it had seemed the very embodiment of the vigor of New Earth.

No more. In fact, because of what Violet and Kendall would do here today, this entire sector of Hawking was deserted. It had been deserted for a week.

Kendall looked up. He had to tilt his head back a long, long way for his gaze to scale all those translucent stories. Violet saw what he was doing and she looked up, too. This had been her workplace, a second home.

She looked down. She could feel, under her feet, that restless shimmy. She knew that Kendall felt it, too. In a way it was sad, Violet thought; the Intercept believed it was still on the job. It didn't realize that no one was monitoring the feeds anymore. No one was requesting it to intervene in perilous situations. Nor did it know that it had been disconnected from the chips. The Intercept thought it was collecting and sorting, collecting and sorting, collecting and sorting, just like always.

The machine also didn't know that its time could now be measured in minutes, not millennia. Kendall had built it to last forever—or for as long as there were humans in residence in the universe, flawed beings who were ruled by their emotions.

And now the Intercept had to die.

The drastic move had been debated for days, with opinions expressed eloquently and forcefully on both sides. The Intercept already was effectively shut down. The drones no longer downloaded their daily surveillance records into its main circuits. Yet the Intercept continued to run, just as farm animals, even after being decapitated, would prance around the barnyard. Ogden Crowley had provided the analogy. He'd been raised on Old Earth. He had seen a real farm.

So why not just let the Intercept run on harmlessly? Why destroy it?

Because as long as it exists, Ogden had said, *it's a potential threat. The technology might be revived one day by an unscrupulous person.*

His argument won the day: The Intercept would be destroyed.

Violet checked the time on her console. She nodded at Kendall. He opened the briefcase. He dumped out the contents. Loose sheets of scribbled-on paper, ripped out of the red notebook, swished to the marble floor in a series of scalloped arcs, the way falling leaves did. These were his original notes for the Intercept, the key technical specifications—the pattern of the connections, the ingredients for the biochemical parts, the code. The precious code. He had never stored this information in a computer. They were his handwritten notes. As long as he kept them out of a computer, he could control them. No danger of their ever being disseminated without his approval.

That also meant, however, that once they were gone—they were gone. There would be no way to retrieve them. With a computer, even a deleted file could sometimes be recovered. Without a computer, it was a different story. Once sheets of paper were destroyed, they were destroyed forever. There was no hope.

But that was a *good* thing, right? When it came to the Intercept? Because it had wrought such havoc. And yet . . .

Kendall snapped the briefcase shut. He flung it aside. It hit the floor with a smack and then skidded a few feet.

He and Violet exchanged a brief, fraught glance. And then they walked away. The matter was settled. They would leave the papers here, in the middle of the floor, which meant that when Kendall initiated the detonation and then stood on the plaza in front of Protocol Hall—at a safe distance, one they had calculated and recalculated—and as, two minutes later, this entire structure collapsed in a heap of smashed glass and pureed steel beams and computer components flash-welded into hot gray blobs, the specifications would go, too.

The Intercept would disappear forever.

And Kendall wouldn't have any notes from which to rebuild it. Not that he *wanted* to rebuild it. No. Never. It had all been decided.

Violet waited for the glass doors to open so that they could leave. Excitement stirred in her. She looked down at the inside crook of her left elbow: Nothing. No tiny blue flash. The system was shut down. No signals would ever again pass from her to the Intercept, or from the Intercept back to her.

A small part of her missed that flash. A bigger part of her didn't.

Kendall was right beside her. As he crossed the threshold, he felt in his pocket for the detonator. He pressed the small red button in the center of it, setting the trigger.

Now he and Violet began to walk faster. Then they began to jog. The countdown had begun. They had ninety seconds to get to that safe distance before the blast happened.

Running now, her legs rising and falling in rhythm, Violet had a vision of the lab, the one back on Old Earth. She had an image of Kendall working feverishly in that lab: intense, disheveled, in love with code but basically scared of emotions because emotions were things you couldn't control. His parents were dead. His world was dying. He had no idea what to do—except to get out in front of those emotions, to wrangle them, gather them, be in charge of them. Somehow.

And so he had built the Intercept. He had made it out of science and magic and fear and love and awe. It was ... *himself.*

Without being totally aware of what she was doing, operating on pure passionate instinct, Violet stopped abruptly. Kendall, too, stopped. They knew their thoughts had synced up. They looked at each other. They asked the question silently:

Who's faster?

"I am," Violet said. Kendall didn't argue. He knew it was true.

She ran back toward Protocol Hall, tearing across the flagstone plaza, taking the steps three at a time. Her body felt light and strong. She had less than a minute now. She ran to the spot from which she and Kendall, just seconds ago, had leaned back their heads and marveled at the bright rise of this building.

A building now doomed.

Violet snatched up two handfuls of loose pages on the floor. This was the code. The blueprint. If she saved this, it meant that in the future—if the human race ever found itself able to handle the Intercept—she could give the gift a second time. Just as Kendall had given it the first time.

What will I tell my father?

Violet had no idea. Maybe she could make him understand. He knew about putting your heart and soul into something, and building it, and wanting to protect it at all costs.

She ran back toward the glass double doors. The countdown ticked away in her head. It was going to be close. No time to dawdle. Down the steps she fled, stuffing the paper into her pocket. In the distance, she saw Kendall's mouth forming the word *Hurry*. She ran toward him.

Violet had just reached the far edge of the plaza, at the outer margin of the safe zone, when Protocol Hall exploded in a monumental geyser of dust and smoke and millions and millions of micro-bits of steel and glass.

She was spun around by the concussive force of the blast. But she was fine; she had caught herself and landed on her hands and knees, her body balanced like a cat's, facing the crater. Kendall wound up a few feet away from her, sprawled on his belly. He grinned at her. His grin was easy to translate: *What a team.*

Violet's ears were ringing. She felt flakes in her hair. She watched the slow twist and turn of ash as it fell to the ground, like thousands of tiny gray dancers performing their delicate pirouettes.

She was dazed and slightly disoriented. Her thinking was temporarily slowed, so at first she wondered what she was looking at, out beyond the drifting gray curtain of debris. The large object was directly in front of her. It was round. It seemed to have some kind of fire embedded inside it. Then she realized that, with the tower now gone, she was seeing what was behind it:

The rising sun.

Acknowledgments

This is a book about the power of emotion. As I was finishing it, I felt that power quite profoundly; one of my best friends, Elaine Phillips, passed away suddenly. In the last conversation I ever had with her, I told her how much her belief in my writing means to me, each time I sit down to make a new world with my stories. And so it does, and will continue to.

I also must thank my wonderful editor, Ali Fisher, whose glorious enthusiasm and luminous imagination helped me see this book in a new light. And I am grateful as well to Dave Seeley, the brilliant artist who designed the cover; copy editor Bethany Reis; and Lisa Gallagher, agent extraordinaire.

I grew up reading and savoring stories about bold quests into the future. As a young girl, my heroes were Ray Bradbury, Eleanor Cameron, Robert Silverberg, Robert A. Heinlein, Arthur C. Clarke, and Madeleine L'Engle. I still revel in such stories, and my hero list has expanded to include Dan Simmons, Alastair Reynolds, Terry Pratchett, Neil Gaiman, Elizabeth Hand, Isaac Asimov, and Octavia E. Butler.

Some of them, like Elaine, have returned to the sky as pure light. But we can still see them. We only have to look.